ELLE GRAY
BLAKE WILDER
FBI MYSTERY THRILLER

NIGHT AT THE ASYLUM

PROLOGUE

Whitehorn Mental Health & Research Foundation; Woodcreek, WA

"YOU SEEM AGITATED TODAY."

Maddy sits in the chair by the window looking out over the rear grounds of the facility, watching as the trees sway in the breeze. The day is sunny, and it looks warm outside, but in the distance, Maddy can see a line of slate gray thunderheads, dark and foreboding, rolling in off Samish Bay. They send a chill through her.

"Maddy?"

She looks up and sees Dr. Langenkamp staring back at her. Maddy doesn't like her very much. The doctor is a tall, thin woman with hair the color of rust, pale skin, and green eyes that seem to penetrate to the very depths of her soul. Dr. Langenkamp unsettled Maddy the first time they met and that hasn't abated in the least.

Maddy doesn't like talking to her and has requested a new therapist several times, but nobody listens to her here.

"I shouldn't even be here," Maddy says.

"Maybe not. But you're here now, so let's make the most of our time together."

"I don't want to. I don't like you," Maddy growls. "I want you to leave me alone."

Langenkamp smiles but it leaves Maddy feeling cold. Makes her feel even more guarded than usual. The doctor leans back in her seat and crosses one leg over the other, settling her notebook down on her leg as those green eyes continue to probe and prod her.

"What has you so agitated this afternoon, Maddy?"

Maddy sighs. She knows that giving Langenkamp what she wants is the fastest way to make this end. She just hates doing it. Especially because she knows that nobody believes her, least of all the good doctor there. But if Maddy doesn't cooperate—or at least give the impression that she's cooperating—this Chinese water torture questioning will go on and on all stinking day.

"Maddy?"

She turns her gaze to the world outside, watching the clouds drawing closer, wishing they would rush in and sweep her away.

"I saw him again," Maddy finally admits.

"Pasha?"

She nods. "He was dressed as one of the orderlies in the day room."

"And what was he doing?"

"Watching me."

Langenkamp nods and jots a couple of things down in her notebook. Probably the word "liar," or maybe "delusional." There were points in time when Maddy wouldn't have disagreed with the assessment. But she's been faithfully taking her meds since they put her in Whitehorn, and she's been perfectly lucid and rational. And she's still seeing him.

Pasha Sobol was her boyfriend. Or something. Maddy never really knew how to define their relationship for the two years they were together. They hung out. Had sex. They did all the things boyfriends and girlfriends do except call themselves that. He was always very caring and sweet. He doted on her, often bringing her little gifts unexpectedly just to make her happy. Maddy cared about him. And she'd killed him.

Now, she's seeing him. At first, Maddy tried to write it off as her having one of her episodes. She tried to ignore him. But having been in this facility for months now and on the proper meds, she feels balanced and normal again. Yet she's still seeing him. The only rational conclusion she can draw is that she's either crazier than she thought, or she's being haunted by the ghost of the man she killed. And she feels more normal than she has in a long, long time.

Langenkamp gives her a sympathetic smile. It's one of the doctor's usual expressions whenever they talk. Maddy thinks it's almost like a crutch to help her avoid saying what she really feels—that Maddy is nuts—and she usually smiles like that right before she says something totally condescending.

"You know," Langenkamp starts. "Guilt can do a lot of terrible things to us. It manifests in a host of different ways. Even delusions. When we—"

"It's not guilt. I don't feel guilty about what I did," Maddy cuts her off. "It's him. He's come back from the grave just to torture me."

"Feeling like you're being tortured is a manifestation of guilt—"

"I told you I don't feel guilty. I did what I did, and I'd do it again in the same situation!" Maddy finally shouted. "If I didn't kill him, he was going to kill me. What are you not understanding about this?"

"All right, I understand that, Maddy," Langenkamp replies evenly. "I'm not interested in the circumstance of how you got here. I'm interested in what's going on now. The fact that you're seeing a dead man is troubling and I want to get to the root of this."

"Isn't it obvious? He's haunting me."

"Okay, let's talk about that then," she says. "Why do you think he's haunting you?"

Maddy rolls her eyes and looks at Langenkamp like she's an idiot and the answer is the most obvious thing in the world.

"Because I killed him. He's haunting me because I killed him," Maddy snaps. "Jesus, you've got that fancy education and all those letters after your name but you're not very bright, are you, Dr. Langenkamp?"

"I know you're upset and lashing out, Maddy. And that's fine. But we need to talk about the underlying issues in play here."

Maddy looks at her bare wrist as if she were looking at her watch then looks up at Dr. Langenkamp. She gives the doctor a vacuous smile. They sit there for a long moment. Maddy doesn't want to talk about this anymore.

"Sorry, we seem to be out of time," the doctor finally relents. "Maybe we can get into that in our next session."

Maddy jumps to her feet and storms out of the office knowing Dr. Langenkamp won't follow her. She doesn't believe in confrontational therapy, which Maddy sometimes uses to her advantage. She knows it's not helping her case in the long run, but every once in a while, she doesn't want to deal with Langenkamp and so, she spikes her sessions. Dr. Langenkamp always lets her go knowing she has no choice but to come back at some point.

It's almost time for lunch anyway, so Maddy makes her way down to the cafeteria. She's fourth in line, so she grabs a tray and shuffles down the line. At the hot station, she receives a plate with a healthy scoop of macaroni and cheese on it. At the next station down the line, she's handed a sandwich made of bologna and a slice of artificial cheese between two pieces of bread slathered with so much mayonnaise, it's soggy. Next, she's handed a small bowl with a salad made of limp lettuce and tomatoes that are more green than red, and a small dish of cherry Jello to round out her meal. It's not much but it'll fill the void.

Maddy grabs a small carton of milk and a bottle of water, then takes her tray over to a table at the far end of the large room, sitting with her back to the corner. The other tables around her are starting to fill up as the other patients come in for lunch. The buzz of conversation is loud, but nobody engages Maddy. That's fine with her. She's not very keen on talking to anybody in this place anyway. She's had a few wobbles in her life, but these people are all nuts, kooks, and sociopaths. She's here because she killed a very bad man who would have killed her. She's not here because she's a psycho.

As Maddy raises her soggy sandwich to take a bite, she freezes. She feels like a fist made of ice is squeezing her heart so hard, it's driving her breath from her lungs. She starts trembling without even realizing it and feels her stomach churning with nausea. Near the doors on the other side of the cafeteria, she sees him: Pasha. He's dressed in an orderly's uniform—dark pants, a white shirt, and a nametag hanging from his breast pocket.

He's lean, fit, athletic, and stands about six-three. Even dead, Pasha is still strikingly handsome. His white-blonde hair is styled in a crew cut and his silver-blue eyes bore into hers, just as intense as she remembers them to be. Pasha's jawline is strong and his cheekbones are high. He's clean-cut and has the sort of cold and distant look as the men you see in commercials for high-end colognes.

The other patients are shuffling by Pasha like they don't even see him. Like he's no more remarkable than any of the pieces of furniture in the cafeteria. He's neither moving nor speaking. All he's doing is standing there and staring at her. The chill gripping Maddy is so strong, she's half-convinced she's going to get a nasty case of frostbite. Maddy swallows hard and licks her lips nervously. She wants to cry out, to alert somebody to the ghost standing on the other side of the room. But when she opens her mouth, nothing but a raspy squeak comes out.

She looks down and takes a breath, trying to steady herself. When she looks up to find one of the other orderlies who might be able to help her, she sees that he's gone. Her body trembling even harder, Maddy looks around but doesn't see Pasha anywhere. He's disappeared into thin air.

"What the hell?" she mutters to herself.

Somehow, the fact that Pasha vanished without a trace is more ominous than having him standing there staring at her.

∽

Maddy wakes with a start, her breath quick and labored, her heart thundering inside her breast. She looks around her room, which is cloaked in thick, inky shadows, with no idea what roused her in the first place. Whatever woke her up has her feeling on edge. Her muscles are tight and she feels on the verge of a panic attack. And she has no idea why.

It's long after the evening meal. Her bedtime meds usually guarantee that she'll sleep through the night, but for whatever reason, they didn't work tonight. She glances at the clock beside her bed. It's just after two in the morning, but she suddenly feels absolutely wired. Maddy feels like she just downed half a dozen quad-espressos. That alone is enough to tell her that something's wrong. She's never felt this scared before.

"Why did you murder me?"

Maddy freezes, every muscle in her body seeming to lock up and refuse to work all at the same time. She's paralyzed with fear, unable to get off her back. She can't do anything but lie there and stare up at the ceiling.

"Wh—who are you?" she squeaks.

"You know who I am."

"I don't."

"You do. You know who I am," he repeats, his deep voice hauntingly familiar. "What I want to know is why you killed me."

"I had no choice. If I didn't, you would have killed me."

"I never would have harmed you. Never, Maddy."

He says it with genuine conviction in his voice and Maddy almost believes him. Almost. The fact that she's able to talk to him helps break the paralysis that's been gripping her. Maddy sits up in bed, and from a particularly thick pool of shadow on the other side of the room, Pasha seems to materialize from the darkness itself. The dim gloom in the room falls half across his face, making him look even more sinister.

"What do you want from me?" she asks, her voice barely more than a whisper.

"Isn't it obvious?" he asks.

Maddy shakes her head. "I don't know."

"First, I want to know why you killed me."

"You know why. You would have killed me, Pasha."

"Never. I never would have hurt you."

He takes another step forward, his icy blue eyes glittering in the gloom. Maddy's heart picks up the pace and her body trembles wildly as he approaches, his presence like a shadow swooping down and smothering her. He stops at the edge of the bed and stands there, and somehow Maddy can't even turn her eyes away. He fills up her entire field of vision.

"I'm sorry, Pasha. I didn't want to—"

"And yet you did."

"I'm sorry."

He shrugs. "Too little, too late I'm afraid. I'm dead."

Though she's no fan of Dr. Langenkamp, she tries to clear her mind like she told Maddy to do when she found herself in a tough situation and sought calm and clarity. Tools she was being taught to dispel whatever was bothering her and bring in a little reality to the situation.

Maddy closes her eyes and focuses on her breathing. And nothing else. After a count to twenty, she opens her eyes again. Pasha is still standing there. He's beside her bed staring down at her and the fear swallows Maddy whole.

"What do you want, Pasha?" she screams.

"I want what you took from me."

Maddy stares in horror as her ex-boyfriend, the man she'd shot and killed, reaches out. She flinches when his hands, icy cold, touch her skin. She doesn't know what to do or say as he wraps his long, delicate fingers around her throat and starts to squeeze.

"Pasha, please," she rasps.

A maniacal light fills Pasha's eyes as he starts to squeeze. Maddy struggles to break his grip, but he answers her defiance with a solid punch to the face. Stars explode behind her eyes and pain radiates from her injured nose, spreading outwardly through her face quickly. His fingers press into her skin as he squeezes even harder. Maddy writhes on the bed and Pasha climbs on top of her, giving himself the leverage he needs to control her.

"P—please," she croaks.

Pasha answers by choking her even harder. Maddy's vision wavers as darkness creeps in at the edges of her sight. She tries to buck him off, squirms beneath him, doing everything she can to break his grip on her, but nothing works. Maddy's eyes are wide, and she feels herself growing weaker. Panicked, Maddy has one last burst of energy, and she thrashes beneath him, trying to break his hold. But Pasha is too strong.

Growing weaker and with her field of vision narrowing, all she can see is the crazed gleam in Pasha's eyes and the cruel smile on his face. She opens her mouth, trying to plead for mercy, but nothing comes out other than a weak, raspy groan.

"Time to die," he says, squeezing with all his might.

Maddy feels herself growing colder. Weaker. She feels her body twitching. And then the darkness claims her.

CHAPTER ONE

Fairbury Harvest Festival; Fairbury, WA

I THROW BACK MY HEAD AND LAUGH WILDLY AS KIT RELATES A story involving a moose, a drunk, and a snow shovel she witnessed in Canada a few weeks back. We're sitting at a small table off the main fairway of the festival as revelers pass us by. Halloween has just about ended so children, many still in costume, run about squealing with delight, their laughter reverberating through the evening air. It's a happy sound on a happy evening.

Kit reached out to me last night to tell me she was swinging through and gave me the directions to Fairbury. It's a small bedroom community outside of Seattle. It's out of the way and not very big, which means that strangers tend to stand out and Kit would be able to spot any tails straight away. She picked tonight, the evening of their annual Harvest Festival, knowing the streets would be crowded and there would be a lot of places to blend into should the need to make a quick getaway arise. I hate that we have to factor these things into our thinking just to have a drink and a talk, but such is life right now.

I take a drink of my hot chocolate and look across the table at my kid sister, grateful and overjoyed to have her back, if only for a short time. And it's always only a short time. Kit is still living her life on the run, to protect her and to protect me. It's how she's lived her entire life, really. I still sometimes think about how she was forced to grow up and it breaks my heart. Raised and trained from an early age to be a spy and an assassin, working for the organization that murdered our parents—I don't know how she managed to hold onto her humanity. Or how she managed to hold on to herself.

If not for my sister, I'd be dead right now. She betrayed the organization, saved my life, and together, we dealt a heavy blow to the Thirteen. But remnants of the organization remain, and so long as they do, she has to stay on the run. She swings back through Washington whenever she can but can never stay more than a couple of days. I can't reach out to her; I always have to wait for her to contact me and I never get more than a twenty-four-hour notice that she's coming. It makes things tricky, but we've always managed to work it out so far.

My sister was gone from my life for eighteen years. I spent practically my entire life thinking she was dead. As frustrating as this arrangement is, if it keeps her safe, then it's all worth it. At some point, we'll find the actual head of the snake, cut it off, and put an end to the Thirteen once and for all. Either that or we'll find a way to make the cost of continuing to pursue us too high for them to want to bother.

One way or the other, there will come a time when Kit and I can be reunited properly. Yeah, I've missed nearly two decades of her life and she's missed the same of mine. But so long as we both come out of this mess alive and not on anybody's radar anymore, we've got the rest of our lives to make up for what we've missed. And that's something I want more than anything.

"So, tell me more about this Charles?" she asks, her tone suggestive.

A small grin touches my lips. The one way we manage to stay in consistent contact is through encrypted email accounts she set up. We don't discuss anything sensitive like travel plans of course, but we do share trivial bits of our lives. It's not much, but it's something. It's a way for me to check up on Kit and make sure she's still out there.

In a recent email, I'd mentioned the fact that I'm dating my neighbor Charles. Sort of. Kind of. I mean, we've gone out a few times for drinks. It's never been anything serious, just a couple of people getting together for a drink and a conversation. I've never been very good at dating, to begin with. But when I learned the Thirteen planted a man in my life and he acted as my boyfriend for a very long time, I've decided that I'm not only not very good at dating, I downright suck at it.

When it comes to my job and dealing with people in my capacity as a federal agent, my instincts are spot on. I'm rarely, if ever, wrong about a person I've dealt with in a criminal investigative capacity. It's like I have this highly tuned BS meter that goes off at the slightest whiff. But when it comes to dealing with people in a personal capacity, my BS meter is about as reliable as an old Ford Pinto. But at the urging of my best friend Astra, I'm rolling the dice and seeing Charles. Albeit cautiously.

I shrug. "Charles is a good guy. A really good guy," I tell her. "He understands my... issues. He's not forcing anything and seems content to take things at my pace."

"I think the fact that he can put up with you at all should put him in the running for sainthood," Kit says with a laugh.

"I hate you so much right now," I say, laughing along with her.

Slowly, our laughter fades and Kit looks at me with a sober expression. "I'm really glad you're putting yourself out there, Blake," she tells me. "I know it can't be easy given all you've gone through but you deserve to be happy. You deserve to have somebody care about you."

A wan smile touches my lips. "Let's not get crazy here. We've gone out for a few drinks. It's not like he's proposing anytime soon."

"No. Maybe not. And maybe not even him. But opening yourself up to the possibility… it's important. Don't discount that," she says.

"When did my little sister get to be so wise?"

She shrugs. "I guess living the life I've lived kind of makes you see things differently."

I nod as a frown touches my lips. "Yeah, I suppose it would have to."

A moment of somber silence passes between us, and the mood seems to be growing grim. But then Kit slaps the table and gives me a smile.

"We're not going to do this," she says.

"Do what?"

"Get all melancholy," she explains. "It's time for a drink. Shots are on me."

"I have like a day left with you. I don't want to waste it by being drunk."

"One shot," she urges. "Just to help shake off the blues."

"All right. One. Just one though."

"One. You got it."

We walk down the crowded street, doing our best to avoid running into any of the other revelers. Not easy to do when there are hordes of children running around. But we manage and make our way down the street with the smell of a hundred different things cooking and the sound of live music somewhere filling the air around us. The atmosphere is chaotic but filled with a happy energy that makes me smile. It seems like it's been a while since I've been out and about in a place buzzing like this. When Charles and I go out, it's usually someplace quiet where we can actually have a conversation.

We step into a pub on the corner of one of the few quiet streets near the center of town. With all the adults running around the festival with their kids, it's pretty empty inside. At least for now. I have no doubt that once the kids start going home, this place will fill up with people who want to keep the party going. For now, though, there's maybe a dozen people in the place, so we make our way over to a booth in the corner.

Kit makes sure to sit with her back in a corner and a view of the entire place. I don't even bother asking if she's strapped because I already know she is. At any point in time, my little sister is a walking armory. I hate that being on such high alert is second nature for her. I hate that although she may look at ease, she's tightly wound and ready to fight at the drop of a hat. More than anything, I wish she knew how to relax and actually be at ease. I wish she had a sense of peace in her life. But Kit's life is a perpetual war. Always has been and will continue to be until we wipe out what's left of her enemies. Our enemies.

The pub is charming, as is most of the town. It's fashioned in the style of a log cabin, with a gas fireplace at the far end of the room. The flames crackle and pop, warming the place nicely. The bar runs along half the wall to the right. It, the walls, and the tables are all made out of a material made to look like distressed, rough-hewn wood. The walls are covered in black and white photos of the town back in the old days as well as who I assume are town notables. Soft country music plays from recessed speakers—definitely not my first choice in tunes—and there are a few TVs showing different ballgames.

A waitress comes by and takes our order, then disappears to grab our drinks. A couple of minutes later, she comes back and drops them off. Kit and I toast each other and take a sip.

"So, what are the odds I get you back for Thanksgiving?" I ask.

Kit frowns. "Probably not good, if I'm being honest."

"Kit—"

"Blake, it's not safe for us to be together," she says. "They're still hunting me and they're simply biding their time with you. They've already taken one shot at you and you're lucky you survived. It's only a matter of time before they try again."

I sigh and nod. The attack on me—in my own apartment no less—served as a stark reminder that I'm most definitely still on their radar. And that I'm not safe. I hate it. I hate living my life worrying that I'll get the phone call that my sister is dead. Or even worse, I never get a phone call or an email from her at all, ever again. I hate everything about this. To finally have my sister back in my life after so many years of thinking she was dead, only to not be able to see her—it's beyond maddening.

"I'd be there if I could, Blake. If it was safe for us both, you know I'd be there," Kit goes on.

I nod, a sad smile touching my lips. "Yeah, I know," I sigh. "We just need to figure out who is leading the Thirteen. We need to find him and put an end to this whole, miserable affair."

"I'm trying," Kit tells me. "I'm trying to figure out who it is."

I reach across the table and take her hand, giving it a gentle squeeze. "I know you are. I just miss you. And I worry about you."

"I miss you too, Sis. And I worry about you too," she says softly. "I think I have it easier because I'm always moving around. You're a stationary target. They can come for you whenever they please."

"That's comforting."

She gives me a gentle smile. "They won't. Not for a while yet," she assures me. "They overplayed their hand with this last attempt. I think they'll go dormant for a while. Try to regroup before they take a run at you again."

"And in the meantime, we can hopefully figure out who these people are so we can end this and bring you home."

She nods. "That'd be really nice."

We both look at each other and I can see that her thoughts mirror my own. Deep down inside each of us is the fear that even if we do identify the head of the snake and take the fight to him— and even if we do beat him—this still might not ever be over. Not really. Deep down inside, part of me worries that we will never be completely safe.

But for now, we're content to pretend like that's not the case. And it works. For now.

CHAPTER TWO

Criminal Data Analysis Unit; Seattle Field Office

"FORGIVE ME FOR BEING SO BLUNT BUT YOU LOOK LIKE hot garbage," Astra notes with a smirk when I step to the front of the room. "Rough night?"

"It was a good night. A really good night. And not in the way you're already thinking," I respond with a laugh. "Kit reached out. She was in town for the night, so we got together."

"Yeah? That's great, Blake."

I nod. "It was good to see her."

"She going to be around for Thanksgiving?"

A frown touches my lips. "Probably not."

"I'm sorry."

I shrug. "That's the way things have to be for now."

"It sucks."

"Yeah."

Clasping my hands behind my back, I pace the front of the room, feeling a little wrung out. Kit left just before first light this morning after we'd stayed up all night talking. I'm getting too old to pull all-nighters anymore, but since I get so little time with my sister and I never know when the next time will be, I wasn't about to waste a minute of it. The door to the shop slides open with a pneumatic hiss and I look up to see Mo and Rick strolling in.

"Good morning," I say.

"Mornin'," they both mutter in unison as they trudge to their stations.

I walk over to the coffee station and fix myself a fresh mug, giving them a moment to get themselves settled in. I take a sip, then add another sugar to the mug and taste it again. Just right. By the time I turn back to Mo and Rick, they're already set up. They both give me a nod, ready to get started on another day.

I stop pacing and turn to take in my team. "All right," I start. "What do we have?"

"I've been tracking a rip crew that has so far hit a check cashing place, a gaming house, and a strip club," Mo announces.

"So, all businesses that deal in large amounts of cash," I nod. "But how do we know it's the same crew?"

"Witnesses say it's three men with ARs wearing luchador masks," Mo replies.

"Could be guys with ties to a Mexican street gang," Astra offers. "Or even worse, maybe even a cartel."

"Or somebody who wants us to think that," I counter, then turn to Mo. "Do we have any surveillance footage?"

"Not much. One of their first plays is to take out the cameras," she says. "But we do have a couple of stills. On screen now."

I step to the side and turn around. On the wall-mounted screens, grainy black and white photos pop up showing three men dressed in black from head to toe. They're all wearing gloves and luchador masks, as Mo mentioned. They're so covered up, there's no way of telling if they're black, white, Hispanic, or Asian. It's going to be a hard case to make but we've started with less.

"All right," I say. "Mo, gather up all the intel you can. Police reports, witness statements, whatever you can get. We'll start taking a closer look."

"Copy that, boss."

"What else is on our radar?" I ask.

"We have a potential serial arsonist," Astra pipes up. "We had two buildings go up in flames under suspicious circumstances."

"Fatalities?"

Astra shakes her head. "Fortunately, no. Both buildings were abandoned and empty," she tells me. "But you know how quickly these things escalate."

"These guys have to up the thrill factor," Mo comments.

"Exactly right," Astra confirms. "And to these freaks, there's nothing more exciting than burning up an apartment full of people."

"Anything linking one fire to the other?" I ask.

"Other than the location and a gut feeling, no. We've got no physical evidence," she replies. "Because of the area the fires were started in, there's no surveillance footage, no eyewitnesses. But two fires in the same geographic location a week apart seems too coincidental."

"I agree. Let's keep an eye on that and see if we can dredge up any physical evidence to go along with the gut feeling," I tell her. "For now, let's focus on the rip crew. We seem to have—"

The telltale hiss of the door opening distracts me. I turn to see our boss, Special Agent in Charge Rosalinda Espinoza, strolling in. When I see the red folder under her arm, I know we're going to have to put our plans to chase this rip crew on hold. The red folders indicate a hot case that's been assigned to a specific unit by the Director of the FBI himself. And given that she's in my shop, it's obviously been assigned to us.

"Good morning," Rosie says in her crisp, all-business tone.

"Mornin', boss," I reply. "That red folder tells me you have a job for us."

"Nothing gets by you, Wilder. That must be what makes you such a good investigator," she replies. "The Director feels your team is best suited for this case."

"Looks like we're moving up in the world," Astra comments.

"Must be," I reply with a laugh. "So, what glad tidings are you and the Director bringing us this morning?"

"I bring you a locked room mystery," she says and hands me the folder.

"The Whitehorn Mental Health and Research Foundation," I read from the top page of the incident report. "Intriguing."

"In addition to being a mental health hospital, Whitehorn is an innovator in the research and manufacturing of drugs designed to combat various mental health issues," she tells us. "And because the foundation sits on land they lease from the federal government, and they have a few federal contracts to boot, some folks in DC are apparently feeling a little antsy about a mysterious murder on their grounds."

"Which seems a little hypocritical since they're apparently all right with the experimentation they do on their patients," Astra notes.

Rosie rolls her eyes. "Let's not be overly dramatic, Agent Russo. Any experimentation they're doing has been approved by the appropriate agencies," she tells us. "It's not like they're cutting people open just to pick through their insides."

"Are we sure about that? Because I have to be honest here, I don't really fancy the thought of busting into a room and finding somebody cobbled together from the parts of a lot of other people," Astra cracks with a grin.

Rosie shakes her head and looks at me. "Is she always this dramatic?"

I nod. "Yeah, pretty much."

"Definitely," Mo adds.

"She's always in the running for an Oscar," Rick chimes in. "At least in her own mind anyway."

"Thanks for having my back, guys. I really feel the love here," Astra groans, putting on a mock wounded face.

Rosie grins. "Get on this one. And I don't think I need to tell you there will be a lot of eyes on this case, so no funny business."

"Funny business? You know us better than that," I raise an eyebrow.

She chuckles. "I do know you. Hence the reason I needed to remind you—yet again—to do things by the numbers," she insists. "If you need anything let me know. And be sure to check in with me. I want to know the status of your investigation."

I snap her a salute. "Yes ma'am."

Rosie nods and walks out of the shop, and I take a moment to flip through the file. It's not very thick so it doesn't take long. There are a lot of gaps that need to be filled in.

"All right, so it looks like our vic, one Madeline Donaldson, age twenty-eight, was allegedly strangled in her room at Whitehorn," I read out. "Nobody on camera going in or out of her room around the time she was murdered, and her door was locked. Doors in the wards use computerized keypads that are logged electronically, and the logs show that her room wasn't accessed either."

Astra whistles low. "So, Rosie wasn't lying. It really is a locked room mystery."

"Looks that way."

"This sounds fun," Mo says. "I always love a good mystery."

"I'm assuming you're going to need me to analyze the surveillance video and computer keystroke logs," Rick offers.

"You are a mind reader, my friend," I smile. "I need to know if they're legit or whether they've been tampered with."

"I'm on it," he replies.

"What do you want me to do, boss?" Mo asks.

"I'm not sure yet. Astra and I are going to head up to Woodcreek and we'll know more once we get there," I tell her. "Until then, stay on the rip crew. As soon as we're done with this case, we're going to pivot and go after those guys."

"Copy that."

I turn to Astra. "All right, it's a few hours' drive, so we'll likely stay over," I tell her. "Get home and pack a bag. Assume we're going to be up there a few days… assuming Benjamin will be cool with you going?"

She waves me off. "Benjamin accepts that this is part of my job. He's fine with it. Don't even sweat it."

"Good," I nod. "Then I'll swing by and pick you up in an hour?"

She glances at her watch. "Benjamin should still be at the house. He's not going in until later," she says. "Make it two."

I give her a grin. "Fine. I'll see you then."

CHAPTER THREE

Bayview Motor Lodge; Woodcreek, WA

"RUSTIC," Astra notes. "Quaint. Charming, really."

"How many other adjectives can you use to describe the place?"

Astra grins at me. "Cute? Vintage? Timeless? As many as it takes to get me comfortable staying in a place that looks like a serial killer's playground."

"Yeah well, it's not like Woodcreek's got many five-star properties to choose from," I reply. "It was either this or a place that looks like this, only dirtier. There might actually still be bloodstains on the sheets at that place."

"Are you sure there aren't bloodstains on the sheets here? I mean, it's not like we've checked the rooms yet."

I give her a shrug and a grin. "Let's just cross our fingers and hope for the best."

"Wonderful."

The Whitehorn Mental Health and Research Foundation was originally built at the turn of the twentieth century as an asylum for the criminally insane. Woodcreek was little more than a village back then. Some say the isolation was the very reason for building the asylum out in the sticks—little oversight. The stories say the doctors conducted inhumane experiments on the patients they housed. Legends say more than two hundred people lost their lives there, but there is nothing official to back that up.

Eventually, the asylum was forced to shutter its operation. At some point in the late sixties, the military took over and converted all the buildings to use for their purposes. Some say the military picked up right where the old asylum hacks left off and restarted the human experiments—this time, with an official US government stamp of approval backing them up. The tales of torture and death the asylum was famous for started all over again for a new generation of ghost stories.

Personally, that stuff makes me sick to my stomach. Knowing what I know about the Thirteen, and all their sick, twisted fingers into every avenue of human suffering, I have no doubt that horrific, monstrous experiments have been carried out there in the past. And I can only hope that they haven't continued to the modern day.

The town around it is nice, though, if a little—quaint, as Astra described. Woodcreek isn't a town that was built with tourism in mind. Originally, it was a town that sprung up around a military base, research facility, and VA hospital. The story is, the base was a cover for the research facility—a facility that specialized in biological weapons. No government official is on record confirming that of course, but that's the scuttlebutt about the place. When the military pulled out and decommissioned their Woodcreek facility, the town began to flounder, but then the Whitehorn Corporation secured a lease for the land and things changed.

Using the buildings the military left behind, Whitehorn set

up shop. They spent several million dollars refurbishing the interior of the buildings to suit their purposes. Though the town has flourished with the influx of money the reopening of the facility has brought. Thousands of people associated with the facility have moved to Woodcreek and pumped a lot of money into the town. It's grown and has become, if not an affluent community, then one that's solidly middle class.

Even still though, tensions between the original residents and all the newcomers. While they presumably had no trouble with the military facility looming over their town, they don't have those same sentiments for Whitehorn and its facility. From what I've read when I was doing my research on the place, tensions exist between the Woodcreek townies and the Whitehorn people. My understanding is that the townies don't take kindly to outsiders for one thing, but they also apparently don't appreciate the work they're doing up at the facility. They don't like having a mental health hospital in town.

They say it brings back the stories of the experiments, the atrocities that were committed here long ago. I don't know for sure, but after everything I've seen, I can't blame the community for being distrustful.

"Well, shall we check out our luxury digs? We should probably get acquainted with our home away from home for the next few days," I say.

"Yeah, probably."

"Meet back out here in half an hour," I tell her. "We'll go grab something to eat."

"Deal."

Astra frowns as she plucks her key from my hand and heads off to her room. I'm not a princess or anything, but the Bayview is definitely one of the more rural and rustic places we've ever stayed while on a case. Ringed by massive pine trees, the motor lodge is set on a bluff that overlooks Samish Bay, giving it that ever-so-original name. It's made up of about a dozen small cabins and an area off to the right for RVs to park and stay. All the cabins are brown clap-board with green shingle roofing and give off an ominous "cabin in the woods" kind of feeling.

I walk over to my room, unlock the door, and it lets out an eerie creak and groan as it swings inward. Reaching my hand around the doorway, I fumble around until I find the light switch and flip it on. The sudden flare of light dispels all the shadows and reveals a room that's just as rustic on the inside as it is on the outside. The dark green carpet reminds me more of Astroturf than actual carpet. All the furniture is made of rough-hewn wood, though I don't think it's a stylistic choice. The bedspread is dark and aggressively patterned, probably hiding all the stains I'm sure it's dotted with.

"Lovely," I mutter.

I pull back the bedspread to find that the sheets are actually crisp and white. They look clean and fresh. To say I'm surprised would be something of an understatement. Part of me actually did expect to pull back the comforter and find bloodstains on the sheets. I set my bags down on the chair and check out the rest of the room, making sure there are no hidden peepholes or secret entrances. Yeah, maybe I've seen too many movies.

Grabbing my shower kit, I walk into the bathroom and turn on the shower. Steam billows from the shower in no time flat and there's decent water pressure.

"Another unexpected bonus," I note to myself.

After brushing my teeth, I get undressed and take a shower, luxuriating in the heat of the water for a long moment. When I'm done, I towel off, then throw on a pair of blue jeans, a black turtle-neck, white sneakers, and pull my coat out of my bag. Once I'm ready, I take my laptop bag and stick my valuables into it, then sling it over my shoulder. Force of habit. I never leave anything valuable in my hotel room, whether it's five-star accommodations or a place like this. Crime is crime. It doesn't discriminate based on whatever zip code you're in.

I back out of my room and lock the door behind me. Astra is already at the car waiting in a green sweater, black jeans, and black Doc Martens. The dirt and gravel crunch beneath my shoes as I cross the lot.

I'm almost to the car when the hair on the back of my neck stands on end. I suddenly can't shake the unsettling feeling that we're being watched. I casually glance around, trying to see if I can pick up our unseen admirer. No such luck. There are no faces pressed to the windows in the cabins or the manager's office, nor do I see anybody lurking in the deep pockets of shadow in the forest that surrounds the place. And yet, the feeling persists.

"So? How's your room?" I ask, trying to sound casual.

"Yeah, if I were ever going to torture and murder somebody, I'd probably do it here," she replies. "I swear, it's like we stepped into the *Hills Have Eyes* universe or something."

I laugh. "Let's go eat. I'm starving."

"Ditto," she nods. "But what do you think the chances are we're able to get something that isn't deep-fried?"

"Keep an open mind. This place can be surprising," I tell her. "I mean, I got clean, crisp sheets on my bed."

"Yeah, bloodstains are notoriously hard to get out. Probably had no choice but to get new ones," she cracks with a grin.

I laugh. "Get in the car."

We pull out of the lot and onto the main highway that will lead us back to the heart of town. I consider asking Astra if she felt the same feeling, but opt against it. The last thing I want to do is make her more paranoid about staying at that place. It isn't like we have much of a choice though. Unless we want to stay in a bigger city and take the daily hour-long commute into Woodcreek—which I don't—the Bayview is the best of the options we had.

It takes us about five minutes to get to Hamilton Avenue, which is the main drag through Woodcreek. It's a lot like most other small towns in that the main street is lined with small businesses.

Mom-and-Pop shops over the big box stores. The town is clean and well-kept. All of the storefronts seem to be freshly painted and orderly. And as we cruise down Hamilton, I see people stopping each other just to talk.

I make a lot of jokes about small towns like Woodcreek but there is an absolute charm to the place. There's a sense of community I find entirely appealing. In a place like Seattle, you'll never see people stopping others on the street just to have a conversation like you do here. In a big city, people seem to take pains to avoid eye contact with strangers. And you can forget about conversation. People in bigger cities seem to keep themselves insulated in plastic bubbles, only allowing those members of their tribe inside.

Woodcreek, I guess, makes me remember Cockeysville, Maryland, where I spent the first twelve years of my life. It conjures up a lot of warm feelings. Cockeysville is a place where people are friendly and welcoming. They would absolutely stop each other on the street to talk about their families, or just to check in on each other. And I like that. I like that a lot, actually. Seattle, like a lot of big cities, I imagine, can be cold and superficial. It can be a place where it's hard to get to know people. Where it's hard to fit in. I'm lucky, I had people. But for someone who doesn't, I'd imagine it can be difficult in a place where nobody stops to check on you or engage you in friendly conversation just because.

Truth is, when I retire—many years from now, of course—I want to end up in a place like Cockeysville, or even Woodcreek. A place that's got a real feeling of community about it, rather than a big city that's cold, sterile, and unwelcoming. It could be the nostalgia I'm feeling for a childhood that was cut short in a place I regarded back then as a slice of heaven on Earth. But it's a feeling that's deep within me and strong enough that it's nearly overwhelming.

"How about that place?" Astra asks.

I look over and see she's pointing at a small restaurant called the Laughing Salmon. I'm sufficiently intrigued by the name—which sounds like the name of an old Medieval tavern rather than a modern restaurant—to give her a shrug and pull into the lot. The building is painted salmon pink and has caricatures of the fish all over the wall in the parking lot. The front is tastefully landscaped and two large panes of glass that give a view of Hamilton flank the doorway. Astra holds it open for me as we step inside and are immediately inundated with a thousand different aromas, all of them heavenly.

At the same time I'm noticing the plethora of amazing smells, I become aware of just how quiet the place falls the second we enter. It's as if a conductor in an orchestra motioned to cut everyone off simultaneously. All the eyes on the two of us feel like a physical weight pressing down on me. Seeing everybody turning to stare at Astra and me reminds me of the downside of small-town living—the automatic distrust and dislike of strangers. That nostalgia that swept through me earlier blinded me, albeit temporarily, to the fact that small communities can be totally insular. The original residents form one tribe, and anybody not part of that group is suspect from the jump.

It often takes years, sometimes a generation or two, before you're truly considered to be a resident. Until then, you're going to be regarded with suspicion. You're thought of as an alien from another planet who decided to set up shop in a place like Woodcreek and launch your plan to take over the world from there. It's a good reminder for me to look past the nostalgia and remember that no place is perfect. Every place will have its flaws and drawbacks. That innate distrust of those you consider outsiders is a checkmark in the negative column when considering my retirement options.

"Hi, go ahead and sit anywhere you want, ladies," says a waitress who passes by carrying a tray loaded with food. "We don't stand on ceremony here."

Astra leads me through the restaurant, and I can't help but feel the eyes following us. Astra, though, raises her chin and regards those people we pass icily. I do my best to ignore them and focus on my surroundings. The Laughing Salmon is done in earthy tones of green and brown. The lighting is dim, and every table has a candle in a glass holder, telling me this is Woodcreek's romance restaurant. That assessment is confirmed as I look around and see nothing but couples. No children, no families, just couples.

We take a seat at a table near the back corner of the place. It's strange to me to see Astra employing the same tactics as my sister—sit with her back to the wall while giving herself a clear view of the entire restaurant. They're both far more vigilant than I am, which I think is a problem considering the fact that I actually do have people hunting for me.

"I'm feeling a lot like a zoo exhibit," Astra says.

"No joke."

I look around and most of the people have the good grace to look away and stare at us with a little more subtlety. But a few folks continue to gawk at us openly. It seems pretty clear from the looks on their faces they're not all that impressed with what they see. The waitress comes by and takes our drink order and hands us a pair of menus. Astra and I flip through them, and I have to admit, I'm impressed with the selection.

The waitress comes back a couple of minutes later to drop off our drinks and take our order. She's brisk and efficient, though not overly warm. She's not nearly as openly hostile as some of the other people look, but she's not overflowing with friendliness either.

"You think you could live in a town like this?" Astra asks lowly, to escape from prying ears. "Where you're regarded as an outsider, and you get people looking at you like this wherever you go?"

I nod. "I do. There's just something about the charm of a small town that appeals to me."

She laughs. "You and Benjamin both. He says he wants to get out of the big city and raise a family in a small town like this."

"Are you guys talking about having a family?"

She shrugs. "Not officially or anything. I mean, he hasn't even proposed—"

"But you think he's going to?"

She bites her bottom lip, trying to keep the smile from spreading across her lips. She's only partially successful. Astra looks at me and nods.

"Yeah," she says. "I think he's going to."

"Wow. Wow, Astra... I don't even know what to say."

And I don't. Astra was always a good time girl when we were younger. She eschewed things like marriage and raising a family, saying she wanted to enjoy her life and not be tied down. Some of the stories I've heard about her wild days would make a hooker blush. But then she met Benjamin and her entire life's trajectory changed. To hear her talking about marriage and possibly raising a family is shocking. I reach across the table and give her hand a firm squeeze.

"You seem happy, Astra. I'm really happy for you," I say, then frown as a thought occurs to me. "But if you start a family—"

"I don't think we're talking about anytime soon. Definitely not right away," she cuts me off. "It's going to be a while yet."

I nod but still can't keep the thoughts from running around in my head. The idea of not having Astra on my team anymore isn't one I'm real thrilled with. Astra always being here is something I guess I've taken for granted. She's always been married to this job as much as I have. So, although I'm thrilled for her, I'm also kind of torn on the issue. She's been my right hand forever, and the idea of her not being there is a kick in the gut.

More than anything though, I want Astra to be happy. I want her to be content and fulfilled in her life. And if this is the path that will take her to that joy, then far be it from me to stand in her way.

"Don't worry," she says as she grips my hand reassuringly. "We're talking about years from now. You're going to have me in your hair for a good, long while to come."

I give her a smile. "I'm glad to hear that."

I'm not one who embraces change the way some people do. I tend to get into a set routine and stick with it. It's something both Astra and Kit have gotten on me about over the years. Having your parents murdered, your sister abducted, then being sent across the country to live with an aunt and cousin you barely know does that, I suppose. The mere idea of Astra leaving would represent one of the biggest changes in my life. And though I'm happy for her, I'm not really embracing that possible change.

How can I? And how can I not worry about it?

CHAPTER FOUR

Woodcreek Sheriff's Station; Woodcreek, WA

"**N**ICE TO SEE YOU WEREN'T MURDERED IN YOUR SLEEP," Astra greets me as I walk to the car.

"Right?" I respond. "There were a couple of moments I wasn't so sure though."

We laugh as we climb into the car. The sun is barely over the horizon and the clouds that streak the sky are cast in hues of red and orange. After a good meal at the Laughing Salmon and a good night's rest, we thought it best to get an early start. We pull out and drive back to town, stopping by the local coffee shop for a couple cups of a dark, rich brew that smells fantastic. After picking up our go-juice, we headed for the sheriff's station.

We need to be doing this all by the numbers, so I need to stop by and announce our presence to local law enforcement. These things can get touchy, so I remind myself to use the velvet glove.

The last thing I want to do is alienate the local LEOs. But I know going in that a lot of these guys, especially some of the small-town sheriffs I've dealt with before, hate us from the start. They hate feds to start with, but a lot of these guys seem to hate female feds even more. There are still a lot of men who think women shouldn't be part of law enforcement. It's sad to think that in 2021, that's still a thing. But here we are.

We pull into the lot that serves the sheriff's station and climb out. There are half a dozen Ford Broncos in the lot painted with the green and gold scheme of the department. I see a couple of deputies huddled together and talking on the far side of one of the vehicles, and when they glance at us, I see the curiosity on their faces. They both give us a wide, smarmy smile. Astra turns to me so they can't see and rolls her eyes. I laugh as we walk away from them and head into the station.

It's a one-story building made of red brick. The windows are small and even the front door is made of two panes of glass with steel bars in between them. It seems more like a fortified bunker than an office and seems a bit much for a small sheriff's department in a small town. I don't know how many deputies there are, but I can't imagine there are that many—and yet the building seems like it's built to withstand an attack.

"They afraid of being invaded by a hostile foreign army?" I raise an eyebrow.

"Might be. I read that this place can get pretty wild during salmon season," Astra cracks.

"That must be it."

I pull the door open, and she steps through. I follow her in and let the door close behind me, surveying the lobby in front of me. Half a dozen hard plastic chairs line either side of the lobby and standing before about twenty feet before us is a counter that's about chest-high. To the right of the counter is a swinging gate that's about waist-high, which is obviously the only way you're getting into the bullpen behind that. Standing behind the counter is a tall, stout woman. She's got iron-gray hair that falls to her chin and is so straight, I almost think she ironed it. She's got dark eyes, pale skin, and frown lines etched deep into her face.

She's eyeballing us from across the room, her lips pursed and an expression of annoyance on her face. I don't know if that's her default look, though, so I'm trying not to take it personally. She's dressed in the same dark brown pants and khaki-colored shirt as the rest of the deputies and is sporting sergeant's stripes on her sleeves. We step to the counter and flash her our badges.

"Good morning," I say. "SSA Wilder and Special Agent Russo. We're here to see Sheriff Harold Block."

"Do you have an appointment?" she replies, no more impressed with us than the people who were staring at us in the restaurant last night.

"No, we don't," I reply. "We're here to make a courtesy call."

The woman arches an eyebrow and clucks her tongue. "I'll see if Sheriff Block has time to see you."

Astra laughs softly. "No offense, but we've been around town and there isn't a whole lot going on," she says. "I certainly hope he can fit us into his busy schedule."

The woman scowls at Astra, then turns away and walks deeper into their shop. I watch as she heads for an office set behind the bullpen and steps through the door, closing it behind her. There are blinds on the window in the door as well as the large plate glass window that looks out into the bullpen and they're all closed.

"How long you think they'll make us wait?" Astra asks.

"After your comment? Ten minutes minimum," I reply.

We share a laugh then walk over to the chairs and take a seat. Astra and I make small talk as we wait and sure enough, about fifteen minutes later, the desk sergeant comes back and retakes her post. We have to sit there another few minutes as she checks her computer, makes a quick phone call, then apparently straightens up a few things on her desk. It's all I can do to keep from rolling my eyes.

"Oh, I'm sorry. Sheriff Block will see you now," she comments, as if she'd forgotten we were sitting there. "Just go on through to the back."

"Great, thank you," I say as we get to our feet.

We step over to the gate and there's a loud buzz as the gate is unlocked for us. I push it open then follow Astra through. I give the woman a saccharine sweet smile, which makes her shake her head and turn back to her game of Solitaire or whatever she was doing when we walked in. I mean, Astra's not wrong. Woodcreek doesn't strike me as a high-crime area, so it's not like the sheriff has the busiest schedule around. The slow-walk they just did was pure theater. A message meant to convey their displeasure with our presence.

We pass through the bullpen, the deputies on duty all openly staring at us, none of them offering the slightest smile. There are a dozen desks in all and only four of them are currently being used. There is an aisle down the middle with two rows of three on either side. The rows are all military-precise and all the desks are clean, organized, and tidy.

I see it as a reflection of the man at the top of the food chain, which makes sense since he's a man with a military background. According to his file, Sheriff Block, a native of Woodcreek, served in the Army for twelve years before coming home and joining the sheriff's department. He was elected sheriff at age forty, and at fifty-three has just won his fourth four-year term as the head of the county's law enforcement.

All of that is useful information to have, but none of it tells me the first thing about him as a person. Having served the military, I want to imagine he's a man of character and integrity. A no-nonsense sort of man. But the slow-walk he pulled on our arrival tells me something different. It tells me he's a man not above playing political games. That he's a man easily threatened by other law enforcement types who aren't his direct subordinates. And that he can apparently be petty and vindictive. None of which is a good look, in my opinion.

I knock on the half-open door, and he gives it a couple of beats, drawing out the slow-walk to the nth degree, before answering.

"Come," he calls.

Irritation is flowing through me freely as I step through the door, and I can feel Astra bristling just as hard beside me. For being fifty-three years old, Sheriff Block is in great shape. He looks like he could be ten years younger. I'd put him at about six-two—I can't say for sure though, since he doesn't stand up to greet us or offer to shake our hands. He's got dark hair with flecks of gray cut in a flat top and a thick goatee that matches. His eyes are dark and flinty, he's broad through the shoulders with a barrel chest, and he has a square jawline. He's a ruggedly handsome man, there's no question about it.

He's sitting at his desk, a pair of round spectacles on the end of a long, patrician nose. There's an open folder in front of him and a pen in his hand. I look closely at his paperwork and think it's all window dressing. He's making it appear as if he's busy and that by meeting with us, that we're taking valuable time out of his day. Just more petty games.

"What can I do for you, ladies?" he asks.

Not offering a friendly handshake is a slight I can overlook. But the pointed refusal to use our proper ranks and simply addressing us as "ladies," really strikes a nerve with me. Rosie is always getting on me about picking my battles and she'd probably tell me that this isn't a hill I want to die on. And maybe she'd be right. But the fact that he refuses to address us appropriately shows me the absolute lack of respect he has for us.

A stupid, petty game like slow-walking the meeting with us is one thing. But to be so blatantly disrespectful lights a fire under my butt. And one thing I've learned is that nobody is going to give you respect. Especially not in the old boy's club of law enforcement. Not until you demand it. Not until you force them to sit up and take notice of you. Until you force them to give you the respect you've rightly earned. And at this point in our careers, I think Astra and I have absolutely earned it.

I push the anger boiling inside me down as best as I can. But I know if I'm this irritated, Astra is probably ready to blow. I cut a glance at her to see that she's got that look on her face that tells me I'm right. I give her a subtle shake of the head, letting her know I've got this. I turn back to the sheriff and give him the same saccharine sweet smile I offered his sergeant.

"Well, Harry, we thought it would only be proper for us to stop by and let you know we were in town," I say.

He visibly bristles and frowns at me. "That's Sheriff Block."

"Oh, is it? And here I thought we were familiar enough with each other to dispense with trivial things like proper rank," I shoot back.

He frowns and looks at me over his glasses but in his eyes, I see the tiniest modicum of respect. He seems to respect somebody who doesn't simply roll over when challenged. And Block now knows I'm not a woman who is going to back down. Nor will I put up with the casual sexism displayed by some members of the law enforcement community. He sits up in his chair and drops his pen onto the folder open in front of him then gestures to the pair of chairs in front of his desk. Astra and I both sit down, and a tense moment of silence ensues as we all sit there assessing each other.

Block's office is as neat and orderly as the bullpen outside. As I said, I've always thought the room outside reflects the man in the big chair. The wall to the right is one big bookcase filled with binders and manuals on the lower shelves. The top two shelves are reserved for personal knick-knacks—shadow boxes with medals earned while serving, and some kitschy mementos that are obviously sentimental. The wall to the left is filled with picture frames—all meticulously even and orderly that show his time overseas, shots of his unit, and other candid, personal photos.

"So, what is it I can do for you, Agents Wilder and Russo?" he finally asks, his voice a deep baritone rumble.

"We're just here as a courtesy visit, Sheriff Block," I tell him. "We wanted to let you know we were in town and are investigating a death up at the Whitehorn Foundation."

"Ah yeah, that whole mess. Well, good luck with that."

"What do you mean?" Astra asks.

"What I mean is them Whitehorn folk are absolutely secretive. More than that, they're highly connected," he tells us. "If one of their interns hadn't given us a call to let us know somebody died up there, we probably never would've known."

Astra and I glance at each other then I turn back to Block. "And so, I'm assuming you went up there and investigated?"

"'Course I did," he bristles, sounding slightly offended.

"I apologize. I didn't mean that to sound the way it came out," I reply. "I just meant, what did you find? And what makes you say they're highly connected."

My apology seems to mollify him because the scowl leaves his face. He sits back in his chair though and I can see the irritation that's flowing through him. It's not because of us, though—at least, most of it isn't because of us. I can tell that whatever happened up at the Foundation and with his investigation is troubling him. I can see he takes his job seriously. His agitation, at least most of it, is because he cares. And I can respect that.

He runs a hand across his face. "They stonewalled us at every turn. Made investigating it impossible," he admits. "Then, when I spoke with the US Attorney, a fella named Craig—James Craig—he told me we got nothin' and to drop the investigation."

"He told you to drop it?" I raise an eyebrow.

Block nods. "Yep. Sure did. Said he'd spoken with the Foundation's administrator, Franz Stein, who assured him it wasn't a murder. Said it was a suicide and that he'd seen the reports and was satisfied with Stein's conclusions."

"A suicide," I note. "That's not what was presented to us."

He shrugs his broad shoulders. "Me either," he replies. "But that's what this guy Craig says happened. Said there's no case to be had and to leave off."

It's surprising to me that a US Attorney would accept the information provided by a man whose organization is the one under investigation, all the while telling a local cop to stop investigating. I've personally never seen anything like it before. But I also know I'm only hearing one side of the story. Block has a vested interest in casting his department in the best light possible. I understand that.

I'm not saying Block is lying. I'm just saying that perhaps certain things were lost in translation. It's possible he misunderstood what this US Attorney Craig was telling him. It's equally plausible that this guy Craig simply didn't explain himself very well. In my experience, attorneys are sometimes so in love with the sound of their own voices, they talk in circles and can lose the thread of what they were talking about in the first place. There's no telling which this is a case of until we start digging into it.

"What's the Bureau's interest in this?" Block asks.

"Federal land, federal grants," I tell him. "They just want to make sure everything's above board and that the information they're getting is kosher."

"So maybe Craig did follow up on it after all," Block noted.

"Yeah, maybe. I don't know where this case file originated, but it could have been him."

He sighs again. "All right, so what do you need from me?"

"Nothing. We just wanted to give you a courtesy call to let you know we were in town," I tell him. "Believe it or not, we're not trying to step on your toes, Sheriff."

He stares at us for a moment and frowns. "Guess we'll see about that," he says. "Anyway, good luck. Hope it works out for you better than it did for me."

Astra and I get to our feet. "Thank you, Sheriff."

CHAPTER
FIVE

Whitehorn Mental Health & Research Foundation; Woodcreek, WA

THE FOUNDATION SITS ON THE OUTSKIRTS OF TOWN AND the only way to access it is by a long, winding road that cuts through a thick knot of forest. The hospital and its grounds sit atop a hill that overlooks the town below. With tall spires, steep slate roofs, and arched windows and doorways, the buildings all look to have been inspired by Central European gothic architecture. The bricks are all aged, the red no longer vibrant but dull and dingy, giving the building an eerie feel. It's a large, imposing place.

The property is surrounded by a high brick wall that has guard stations at the four corners. They're no doubt leftover from the days when this was a military facility, but as we stop at the gate, I see that the outposts are manned and I'm not sure if it's to keep the patients in or keep the lookee-loos out. A heavy man steps out of the booth, and I hit the button, sliding my window down. He leans down and looks into the car as Astra and I badge him.

"Feds," he says. "What can I do for y'all?"

"We're here to speak with Dr. Franz Stein," I reply.

"He know you're comin'?"

"I imagine he will when you call to tell him we're here."

The man chuckles. "I suppose he will."

He steps back into his booth and picks up the phone. Through the windows, I can see him talking, and judging by the look on his face, it seems like he's getting reamed. But then he hangs up and comes back to my window, his smile shaky and not reaching his eyes.

"Yeah, you can proceed," he tells me. "Just follow the road and take a right at the first fork. After that, follow it to the lot in front of the Admin building. Dr. Stein will meet you there."

"Terrific. Thank you," I say.

He gives us a tight smile and steps back into his booth. A moment later, the tall wrought iron gates swing inward, admitting us to the facility grounds. There is a lot of green between the walls and the buildings. It's lush and beautifully landscaped. It looks almost more like the grounds on a country club rather than a mental health facility. The place has a calming, soothing atmosphere, which I imagine is helpful. We pull into the lot the guard had directed us to and slip into a space. I shut the car off and we get out.

"This place is beautiful… but creepy. It's totally the kind of place I'd expect to find somebody running horrible human experiments," Astra comments, then casts me a wicked grin. "Especially somebody named Franz Stein. I mean, it's kind of on the nose, isn't it?"

I cock my head. "What does his name have to do with anything?"

"Come on. Dr. Franz Stein? Seriously?" she says, sounding exasperated.

"What?"

She laughs. "Doesn't it sound strangely like Dr. Frankenstein to you?"

I cock my head and laugh softly. "You know what? You're right. It kind of does."

Astra rolls her eyes and shakes her head. "You are hopeless, my friend. Absolutely, positively, and without a doubt, hopeless."

I nod. "I can't argue with that."

She laughs as we walk across the parking lot, and as we go, I see a man standing at the top of the stairs waiting for us. I have to assume that's Whitehorn's Chief Science Officer, Dr. Franz Stein. He looks neither warm nor welcoming as we mount the steps and walk to where he's standing. Nor does he invite us into the facility, physically placing himself between us and the doors. It's not accidental, or an oversight either. It's a subtle, perhaps subconscious gesture that says he's not going to allow us into the Foundation, which I sense he views as his own personal fiefdom. It tells me how this is probably going to go.

I give him a smile that's cold and official. "Dr. Stein, I presume?"

"You presume correctly," he replies curtly, his voice tinged with what sounds like a German accent. "I mean no offense, but may I see your credentials please?"

"Of course."

We hold our creds up for him to see and a shadow passes across his face, his features tightening. It's not an unusual reaction to having a couple of feds show up on your doorstep. It's something I've seen more times than I can count. But that shadow is gone in the blink of an eye, his features smooth and expressionless once more. Stein is obviously a man well-schooled in controlling his emotions as well as the outward physical manifestations of them.

He's not a large man, standing no more than five-six I'd say, with a thin, wiry build. His thinning dirty blonde hair is wild and unkempt, and his mustache is comically bushy. It's as if he's shooting for the Einstein aesthetic. Stein's got a long face with a prominent chin, and deep blue eyes hidden behind thick, dark-rimmed glasses.

There's something about him that sets the red flags waving in my head. I can't say what it is specifically, but he seems nervous. And not simply because we're FBI. There's something more that I can't put my finger on. But he's shifty. Squirrely. The fact that he won't quite look either of us in the eye. When he turns his attention back to us, he appears like he's making eye contact, but I can tell he's looking past us. At some point on the grounds behind us. It's subtle—he's definitely mastered the art of appearing engaged without actually being engaged, but I can see the difference clear as day.

"Agent Wilder. Agent Russo. Thank you," he greets us. "Well, what can I do for you today?"

"As you were notified by our field office, we've been tasked by the Director of the FBI to look into the death of one of your patients," I nod. "Madeline Donaldson."

Stein clears his throat. "Yes, well, as I told Sheriff Block and Mr. Craig, the US Attorney for this district already, Ms. Donaldson's death was an unfortunate suicide," he tells us. "I've already given over all the documentation to Mr. Craig, and he's signed off on it."

"We understand that, Dr. Stein," Astra says. "There were some… irregularities… that the Director has asked us to resolve."

"I don't understand—"

"It's all very routine, Dr. Stein," I interrupt, hoping to cut in before he can start defending himself too much. "You know how the bean counters and paper pushers back in DC are. They just want to be sure of the facts before any decisions on your foundation's lease or grants and contracts are made."

A stricken expression crosses his face. "What do you mean?"

"We mean that unless we can conclusively put this matter to bed to the satisfaction of the folks in DC, there is a possibility that it could impact your lease here, as well as the grants and contracts Whitehorn currently enjoys," Astra explains.

"This is absurd. That young lady was troubled, and she took her own life," he stammers. "It's terrible and unfortunate that we were not able to help her in time, but it was a suicide. There is nothing illicit going on here."

"And we're not saying there is," I say evenly. "But you know how DC is. They want to avoid even the merest hint of a scandal or whiff of impropriety."

"So, if you'd just let us do our jobs and get those I's dotted and T's crossed, we'll be out of your hair in no time," Astra adds.

Stein is growing more agitated by the second. It's more than obvious he doesn't like having us here. For a second, nervousness radiates off him in waves so thick I can practically smell them. But he quickly recovers and gives us a calm, controlled expression with even the hint of a smile curling the corners of his mouth upward, making his bushy mustache twitch.

"I'm afraid this is an inconvenient time," he says. "We're in the middle of a clinical trial and I can't—"

"I'm afraid you don't have a choice in the matter, Dr. Stein," I insist. "When you take government money, the government has a say in how you conduct your business. That includes allowing us access when an investigation is warranted."

"This was a suicide, there is no need for an investigation—"

"That's for us to decide, Doctor," Astra says coldly.

"Now, you can let the two of us in to do what we need to do to satisfy our bosses that everything is kosher. Or we can shut you down and have an entire team come in to take this place apart, brick by brick, until Agent Russo and I are satisfied that everything is kosher," I press. "The choice is yours."

He sighs. "Agents, I assure you that Whitehorn Biomedical holds itself to the highest of standards and if anything untoward—"

"And while I have no doubt that you do, Doctor, I'm afraid the US Government isn't satisfied with merely taking your word for it," I reply.

"This is such an inconvenient time," he huffs.

"I'm so sorry that you find a young woman's death so inconvenient, Dr. Stein," I say, my alarm bells already ringing at how obstinate he's being. "I would imagine if she were here, she would be so terribly sorry to disrupt the valuable work you are doing here."

"But she's not," Astra says. "And we are."

"I'm going to call Mr. Craig—"

"You're welcome to do that, but I think you'll find that as well-connected as you are, we're better connected," I shrug. "If I call the Director, he's going to call the Attorney General of the United States, who will then call Mr. Craig, who will then call you to tell you that he can't help you. And we will still be here."

"Wouldn't you rather avoid that hassle and running around just to end up at the exact same point we're at now?" Astra offers. I don't even have to look at her to know that she's already picking up the same signals as I am. I expected some pushback to be sure, but this is practically turning into a standoff at high noon.

He frowns and looks away, the frustration on his face more than clear.

"So, which will it be, Dr. Stein? Will you give us access to conduct our investigation?" I ask. "Or would you prefer we shut down your facility and call for our team to get here?"

I pull out my phone to emphasize my point. It's a bit of an overly dramatic gesture since I don't actually have the Director on speed dial—I'd have to call Rosie who'd make the call for me. But Stein doesn't know that, and it provides a theatrical visual for him to consider. He finally turns back to us, not bothering to hide the displeasure and annoyance on his face.

"Fine," he snaps. "Do what you need to do and do it quickly. As I said, we are in the middle of an important clinical trial at the moment."

"It's going to take as long as it takes, Dr. Stein," I warn him. "We intend to conduct a very thorough and vigorous investigation."

"To that end, we expect that you will make available all records we request and produce all personnel we need to speak with," Astra offers.

He shakes his head. "Out of the question. We do proprietary work here and—"

"Dr. Stein, if we were interested in corporate sabotage or in stealing your recipe for your newest and latest drug, we'd simply go to the appropriate agencies in DC and acquire it there, since you are required by law to provide them with all necessary information as it pertains to your work," I tell him. "You do understand that by the terms of your contract with the government, the decision-makers at Whitehorn Biomedical have agreed to a lengthy set of rules that you, as the CSO, are bound to. By law. And one of those rules is that you are required to cooperate with any investigations that arise due to the nature of your work. If you like, I can provide you with the exact citation in the contract—"

"I'm aware of this. I do not need you to read it for me," he growls. "But this was a suicide. It has nothing to do with our work."

"That is for us to determine," Astra says. "As the Director himself tasked us with doing."

"You can keep standing here arguing with us, Doctor. But it will get you nowhere," I say. "If you refuse us entry or refuse to provide material cooperation, the FBI and a host of other alphabet agencies will descend upon this place and strip it of everything."

"You'll be lucky to walk out with that spiffy lab coat," Astra adds.

He sighs dramatically and looks away. I can practically hear his thoughts, cursing Madeline Donaldson for having the temerity to up and die the way she did. Blame the victim, not the perpetrator, must be his mindset. The man seems so used to having power and not being put in check by anybody, so used to doing what he wants, when he wants, and how he wants, that he's obviously been knocked off balance by Astra and I showing up. He doesn't like being held accountable, nor does he seem to be used to—or comfortable with—being challenged. I'm sure everybody in his world is nothing but deferential to him.

Yeah, well, that's about to change. I don't know if Madeline Donaldson is a murder victim or a suicide yet. And I don't know what Dr. Stein's story is. All I do know is that he's hiding something from me. Maybe it has to do with Madeline's death and maybe it doesn't. But he's clearly not happy with us being here and poking around into his business. There is definitely something here he doesn't want us to see.

I don't know what it is but we're going to find out.

CHAPTER SIX

Office of Dr. Helen Langenkamp, Whitehorn Foundation; Woodcreek, WA

"So, you were Madeline's primary therapist?" I ask. We're sitting in the spot in her office where she meets with her patients. It's next to a large window that overlooks the lush gardens on the rear grounds of the facility. Langenkamp is an older woman with perfect posture and a very precise, professional demeanor. She's sitting in a plush leather wingback that makes me think of stodgy old academics. All she needs is a pipe and a glass of scotch to complete that image for me.

She sits across from us with her back straight, her legs crossed, her hands in her lap. We're all seated in deep, plush, very comfortable chairs that sit atop an elegant Persian rug. There are several plants on stands surrounding the small area, partially screening it from the rest of the office, obviously meant to provide a calm, soothing environment. The office as a whole is clean and organized but lacks any personal amenities that I can see. There are no pictures of Dr. Langenkamp and friends, no personal knick-knacks, and nothing that gives any sort of indication about who she is. Other than the office's ruthless organization and efficiency.

"Yes, I was assigned to work with Maddy," she says, her voice thick with emotion.

"And what was your initial diagnosis?" I ask.

"Maddy had a mild case of schizophrenia. When she was medicated Maddy had full control of all her faculties," she explains.

"And did you have any sign that she was suicidal?" Astra asks.

Langenkamp frowns and looks down at her hands, remaining silent for a long moment. There's a strange look on her face I can't quite interpret. There is a lot of emotion in her eyes though. It seems that she's taking Madeline's death to heart.

"No," she says softly. "I had no idea she was suicidal."

I cock my head and look at her for a long moment. She's looking down at her hands again, unable to maintain eye contact with us. Whether it's grief or guilt for not being able to help Madeline, I'm not sure. But there is definitely something there beneath the surface.

"Can you tell us what she talked about in her sessions?" Astra asks.

Langenkamp shakes her head. "No, I'm sorry. Doctor and patient confidentiality doesn't allow me to relate any information. Technically speaking, I shouldn't have even told you my initial diagnosis."

"Dr. Langenkamp, I can tell Madeline's death has hit you hard. I can see you care," I tell her. "We're trying to determine whether this is suicide or not."

"Why would you think it wasn't?" Langenkamp asks.

"We spoke to Sheriff Block," Astra says. "He tells us he received a call from an intern that suggested Madeline was murdered."

"Ah, that. Our intern misinterpreted what happened. She had

never seen a body before and had a bit of a freak-out," she explains. "She never should have called the sheriff. We prefer to keep those things in-house. There's already enough tension with the residents of the town as it is without adding to these conspiracy theories."

"Be that as it may, it's our job to follow up and get to the bottom of it all," I point out.

"There is nothing to get to the bottom of, Agent Wilder," she says. "Madeline killed herself. She…" At this point she sighs, as if still not wanting to believe it really happened. "She fashioned a noose out of a bedsheet, tied it off to the door handle, and sat down, cutting off her air, which eventually killed her."

"And I understand that's the Foundation's position, but as I explained to Dr. Stein, we have been tasked by the Director of the FBI to run a thorough and vigorous investigation surrounding the circumstances of Madeline's death," I tell her. "And due to the Foundation's ties to the federal government, your cooperation, along with everybody else who works here, is required. It's not optional."

She purses her lips, and her expression darkens. Langenkamp is suddenly the living embodiment of the word "peevishness." She looks at us sourly.

"Well, that may be your mandate, but even that cannot compel me to break doctor and patient confidentiality," she says. "As I'm sure you know, confidentiality even survives death."

"I'm aware. And I will be speaking with Madeline's family about waiving confidentiality," I tell her.

"That is your prerogative," Langenkamp replies curtly. "But until such a time as it is waived, I am unfortunately unable to reveal the details of our sessions."

"Can you tell us what medications you had her on?" Astra asks.

She shakes her head. "I'm sorry. But that, too, falls under the confidentiality rule."

"I'd think that if you cared about Madeline as much as you seem to, that you would want to help us, Dr. Langenkamp," Astra presses.

"It's not that I don't want to help. I am bound by privilege rules, Agent Russo," she replies. "Also, there is no reason for this investigation. Maddy killed herself. There's no mystery to solve here."

"And that may be," I say. "But there are enough questions in our mind that it warrants our presence and a thorough investigation."

She shrugs. "If you say so."

We're not getting anywhere with Dr. Langenkamp. It's like Sheriff Block said, between Dr. Stein and now Dr. Langenkamp, it does seem like they're stonewalling and throwing up roadblocks. Unlike her boss, though, I don't think she's doing it out of a sense of maliciousness or that she's trying to conceal something. My gut tells me she's simply a straight arrow. She's somebody who follows the rules and isn't part of some conspiracy. That opinion could change, of course. But that's my initial read on her, for whatever it's worth.

"I'd like to see her room," I say as I get to my feet.

She opens her mouth and looks like she's going to object but Astra cuts her off. "I'm fairly certain that her room doesn't fall under doctor/patient privilege."

Langenkamp frowns again but gets to her feet. "I'll have an orderly escort you," she says. "But I don't know what you hope to learn, since the room has already been cleaned and prepared for the next patient."

I shrug. "We'd still like to see it."

She stares at us for a long moment with an inscrutable expression on her face. "Very well. Let me call somebody to take you."

~

"I can see what Block was talking about," Astra remarks once the orderly leaves the room.

I shut the door behind him. After being informed that security regulations, as well as insurance concerns, didn't permit us to roam the facility by ourselves, an orderly was assigned to shadow us wherever we went. Jonathan is his name, and he's half man, half mountain—which, judging by the orderlies we've seen, seems to be a job requirement here. Given the fact that they've got some patients with violent backgrounds, it's probably smart to have orderlies who can handle themselves if things go sideways.

Jonathan seems to have somewhat recently shaved his head, as it's dotted with stubble. He's otherwise clean-cut and strangely enough for somebody so large and imposing, has a soft, baby face. He's got blue eyes and his scrubs seem near to bursting as they struggle to contain his bulky physique. I've been trying to get him talking since he started to shadow us but so far, he's been about as chatty as the Sphinx.

"Langenkamp wasn't kidding. They cleaned this place top to bottom," Astra notes.

I nod. "I can still smell the bleach."

We poke around the room, looking in the dresser and desk drawers and the standing closet but find nothing. I even lift up the mattress just in case, but find nothing there either. It looks like they went over this place with a fine-toothed comb. There's absolutely nothing to see here. Not that I expected there would be. Their efficiency in turning this room over is remarkable. But is it sinister and proof they're covering something up? I don't know yet.

The door opens and Dr. Stein steps in. He slips his hands into the pockets of his lab coat and looks at us with a smug look on his face, which I'm beginning to notice is just his default expression. This is not a man I'd enjoy being around in a social setting since.

"As I said, there's nothing to see here," he tells us.

"And as I said, it's our job to follow up on this case."

"There is no case, Agents."

"That's for us to determine. You just do your job and let us worry about the scope and nature of our job," Astra growls.

A small frown pulls the corners of his mouth down. "And I promised to stay out of your way. Which I will. But I am telling you, this is all a monumental waste of time. That poor girl killed herself. That's just all there is to it."

"And if that's true, we'll be out of your hair sooner, rather than later," I tell him. "But until such a time as I'm comfortable ruling it that way, trying to downplay the event or coerce us into leaving prematurely is only going to make us dig our heels in harder."

"Your insistence that we leave isn't a good look, Dr. Stein," Astra adds. "If I were the cynical sort, I'd say it shows you're hiding something."

His face pinched, he sighs again as if pained by what he obviously sees as a tedious conversation. His arrogance is starting to really wear on me.

"Do what you must, Agents. As you'll find, I am hiding nothing," he says.

"That's good, Dr. Stein. It'll make things easier for us," Astra says.

"I will want to have Madeline's body transferred to our medical examiner—"

"I'm afraid that won't be possible. We've already sent Madeline's body home to her parents for burial," Stein says.

"Are you kidding me right now?" I ask.

He shakes his head. "No, I—"

"Why would you do that when an investigation hasn't been concluded?" Astra asks.

The muscles in his jaw flex as he grits his teeth while staring hard at us. Stein is obviously not a man who likes being challenged.

"As I told you before, US Attorney Craig closed the case. There was no further need for us to keep Madeline's remains here," he snaps.

"And as you were informed by SAC Espinoza, we were coming up to conduct an investigation into her death," I growl. "You were obligated at that point to preserve the evidence pertaining to this investigation."

"And yet, you've bleached this room and sent her body off,"

Astra points out. "Like I said before, this isn't a real good look for you, Dr. Stein."

He shakes his head, the annoyance on his face more than clear. "Mr. Craig assured me—"

"Mr. Craig doesn't hold jurisdiction over Bureau investigations."

Stein blows out a long breath and when he looks up, tries to strike a more conciliatory expression on his face and tone when he speaks.

"This is all a misunderstanding," he says. "It seems as if our wires were all crossed. I believed Mr. Craig's directive was what I needed to be following."

I run a hand over my face then stare at Stein, doing my best to keep my temper in check. On the one hand, I can understand why from Stein's point of view, following the advice from a US Attorney seems legit. But the fact that Craig would accept the results of an investigation—from the very people who we targeted for investigation—is a mind-boggling case of either stupidity or professional malfeasance. That's a conversation I'm going to need to have with US Attorney Craig—and possibly his superiors.

"I'm going to need the information for Madeline's family," I grumble, shaking my head.

"Of course," Stein replies.

"This investigation is far from over, Dr. Stein, so you may want to have security badges made for us since we're likely going to be in and out," I tell him.

"For how long?" he asks.

"Until I'm satisfied," I snap.

He grits his teeth again and his face flushes, a look of absolute displeasure etched into his features. I'm sure his hands, which are still in his pockets, are balled into fists. We stare at each other for a long moment, the room around us crackling with silent tension. He finally looks away and nods.

"Of course. Whatever you need," he finally says.

CHAPTER SEVEN

Donaldson Residence; Pocatello, ID

"**T**HANK YOU FOR SEEING US, MR. AND MRS. DONALDSON," I say.

"Of course," Mrs. Donaldson says, wiping a tear from her cheek.

Astra and I sit across the dining room table from Madeline's parents, Joe and Shelly. Being the ever-gracious host, Shelly had brought out coffee for us, so we all take a minute to dress our cups and compose ourselves, readying for the conversation we have to have with them. I take the brief silence we share as we sip our coffee to study the parents closely.

Joe is nearing fifty with eyes the same shade of green as Madeline's. His hair is as dark, though his streaked with gray. He's tall and thin with a prominent Adam's apple and a quiet demeanor about him. Shelly is a couple years younger and has light brown hair and brown eyes. She's half a foot shorter than her husband, is as beautiful as her daughter, and has what my Aunt Annie would call "birthing hips."

They seem like real salt of the earth kind of people. Maybe it's a stereotype, but they're the sort of folks I'd expect to find in Idaho. She's a kindergarten teacher, he's a manager at the local bank, and they were both born and raised in Pocatello. They're also completely shattered about the death of their daughter. I can't imagine the pain they must be going through right now and I hate that I'm going to cause them even more distress. But this is the job. An incredibly tough part of what we do, but something the job requires.

After the scene at the Foundation yesterday, I filled Rosie in on what happened. She's just as outraged as we are and got the green light for us to take a flight to Idaho to sit down with Madeline's parents.

"Again, we are terribly sorry for your loss," I say.

Shelly is holding a framed picture of Madeline when she was younger—sixteen or seventeen maybe—and gives me a tight smile. She's holding it tightly to her chest as the tears spill from the corners of her eyes. Joe is sitting in his chair, slightly slumped, but remaining stoic about it all. His jaw is clenched tight, his eyes narrowed to slits. I can see he's holding back his emotions, obviously being the rock he thinks his wife needs right now.

"I—I'm sorry, but what's the FBI's interest in our daughter?" Joe finally breaks his silence.

"We're investigating the circumstances surrounding Madeline's unfortunate death," Astra tells them.

"But that Dr. Stein fella said it was a suicide," Joe frowns.

I nod. "I understand that. But there are some things we want to look at before we're satisfied ruling it as such."

Joe and Shelly exchange a look and I can see the confusion passing across their faces. I feel for them and can only imagine how difficult this has to be. He finally turns back to me and I see the first cracks in that stony façade of his.

"What do you mean before you're satisfied? I don't know what this is all about," he says.

"Dr. Stein told us everything that happened. Said she... said she took her own life," Shelly adds, her voice cracking.

"There have apparently been some miscues," Astra says gently. "The case shouldn't have been closed just yet, since we're only now getting on the scene to investigate. Dr. Stein never should have given you the information he did."

"We're very sorry, Mr. and Mrs. Donaldson," I tell them. "I know this is hard to understand, especially at a time like this, but as Agent Russo said, we're only just now getting into the investigation."

Joe shakes his head. "But Dr. Stein said Maddy hu...," he sniffs loudly and takes a beat to compose himself before continuing. "Dr. Stein said she hung herself with a bedsheet."

I look down at the cup of coffee I've got clasped in my hands and try to formulate the best, most gentle response I can while at the same time, trying to steer the conversation toward what we need.

"And we understand that's Dr. Stein's position," I say gently. "But we have to investigate properly before an official determination can be made. And we have not yet run a proper investigation. There are some questions we need you to answer, Mr. and Mrs. Donaldson."

Joe shakes his head. "What questions?"

Astra and I exchange a glance. I was kind of hoping she'd jump in right there but the look on her face tells me she's letting me take the lead on this one. I clear my throat and turn back to the Donaldsons.

"I want to be fully transparent with you, but I feel it's only fair to warn you that this may be very upsetting to hear," I tell them.

Their faces are twisted with emotional agony and trepidation, but Mr. Donaldson gives us a nod. His wife's nod is weaker, and she looks down at her hands, which she's folded on the table in front of her. I don't want to tell them this, but I fear it's the only way we're going to get their cooperation.

"All right," Joe says. "We've been warned."

"And we appreciate you wanting to be transparent with us," Shelly adds, to which her husband nods.

"Well, to be honest, this case was presented to us as a homicide. That's a claim that was backed up by the local sheriff in Woodcreek, who then said he was stonewalled from investigating Madeline's death," I tell them. "Then, we get to the Foundation and the story has suddenly become that your daughter took her own life."

"The discrepancy in the stories warrant further investigation," Astra says.

The Donaldsons both sit back in their chairs, stunned expressions on both their faces. This is obviously the first they're hearing of this. I know I probably shouldn't be telling them this much, but it's not like I'm divulging intimate details of the case. I was sincere when I told them I want to be transparent with them. As Madeline's parents, they deserve to know the truth about what happened to their daughter, no matter how upsetting it might be.

Mr. Donaldson reaches over and takes his wife's hand, giving it a firm squeeze. I can see his eyes are red and watery and he seems to be fighting like hell to keep his emotions in check. Mrs. Donaldson gave up that fight already and has her head down, her body trembling as she quietly sobs.

"Murdered," Mr. Donaldson gasps softly. "That doesn't make sense. Who would want to hurt our little girl?"

He shakes his head and the grief in his face starts to ebb and is replaced by a flow of dark anger. His eyes narrow, his jaw clenches, and I know I need to stem this tide before it gets out of hand and leads him somewhere he shouldn't be going.

"We're not saying that's exactly what happened. The truth is, we don't know yet," I explain to them. "That's why we need to investigate this. We want to find out what happened to your daughter, and maybe, bring you a little closure."

I hate saying that simply because I know firsthand that closure is a myth. When somebody you love is snatched away from you violently, there is no closure. You'll never find peace. And you'll never be completely okay with it. Ever. About the best you can hope for is that you get to a place where you find acceptance. You accept what happened but know it will forever remain a wound that will never fully heal. And once you get to that place, where you can accept it, maybe then you can find a way forward for yourself. You can learn to move on.

"What is it you need from us, Agent Wilder?" Mr. Donaldson asks.

I draw in a breath and slowly count to five. This is the part where we ask them to make one of the most difficult decisions they'll ever have to make. It's delicate and it's sensitive. But it's necessary. If we ever want to find out the truth about Madeline's death, it's vital.

"What I have to ask of you is incredibly difficult, but I can't stress enough just how critical it is to our investigation," I start.

"I don't mean to be blunt, but don't sugarcoat it, Agent Wilder," Mr. Donaldson says. "Just spit it out."

"All right. I'd like to have your permission to have Madeline exhumed," I tell them. "I'd like for our medical examiner to conduct an autopsy—"

Mrs. Donaldson looks up, a horrified expression on her face. Mr. Donaldson blanches and he looks away but not before I see his stricken countenance.

"I know what I'm asking is terribly difficult to even consider," I continue. "And I wouldn't be asking if it weren't absolutely necessary—"

"You want to dig up our little girl? After we already laid her to rest?" Mrs. Donaldson gasps, her voice thick with horror.

"We want to find out what happened to your daughter, Mrs. Donaldson. And if it's not exactly as Dr. Stein told you, we want to find out who's responsible," I press.

"I don't know," Mr. Donaldson mutters, looking as if he's aged ten years in the past ten minutes. "That... it's monstrous. What you're askin' is monstrous."

"I know it is, and I am so terribly sorry that I have to ask it of you. But it's unfortunately necessary if we want to find out what really happened to Madeline," I tell them.

"Isn't there any other way?" Mrs. Donaldson asks.

I shake my head. "Unfortunately, there isn't. We need to physically examine Madeline's body and take note of the injuries sustained," I respond. "And I can assure you that we will handle Madeline with the utmost respect. You have my word."

Mrs. Donaldson shakes her head as she stands up and walks out of the dining room. I hear her feet on the stairs and the sound of her sobbing echoing throughout the house, followed by the slamming of what I assume is her bedroom door. Not even that can completely muffle the sound of a mother's agony, though. Right now, I feel like the world's biggest piece of crap. It makes me feel like a ghoul.

I exchange a glance with Astra, who frowns before turning my attention back to Mr. Donaldson. He won't meet my eyes for a long moment as he struggles to control himself, to keep his emotions in check, and to remain as composed as he can. He finally raises his eyes to mine though, and in them, I can see his grief, but it's colored with resolve.

"Do you really believe there was a chance my little girl was murdered?" he asks.

"I do, Mr. Donaldson. I believe there's a chance," I say softly.

"And there's no other way you can prove it?"

I shake my head. "Unfortunately, no. I know how terrible it sounds, but we need to examine her body, Mr. Donaldson."

He sighs and runs a hand over his face. The weight of his daughter's death is pressing down on him, bowing his shoulders, threatening to crush him. But he shakes his head and looks at me, his eyes locking onto mine.

"I want you to keep me in the loop every step of the way, Agent Wilder," he says firmly.

I pull a pen and a card out of my pocket and jot my cell phone number down on it, then slide it across the table to him.

"You have my word, sir," I tell him. "And that is my personal cell. You can call me anytime for an update. I will keep you in the loop."

He takes my card and looks at it for a long moment, his eyes welling with tears. This time, though, he doesn't turn away, nor does he try to brush them off. He looks up at me again, his face etched with his pain. Mr. Donaldson sniffs loudly as the tears roll down his cheeks.

"Promise me one more thing," he says.

"Name it."

"That if you're right, and somebody did murder my baby girl, that you'll find them," he says lowly. "You'll find them and put them in a cage for the rest of their miserable life."

Making promises is stupid. It's something I avoid doing like it's the plague. There are so many different variables that come into play, things I can't control, that making a promise to a grieving parent is a recipe for disaster. And more heartache for them. But something in the man's eyes stirs me. It moves me. It makes me more determined than ever to find out what happened to Madeline Donaldson and bring her parents, if not closure, then some sort of acceptance and peace. They deserve that. Madeline deserves that.

"I swear to you that I will do my very best, sir," I tell him. "I will not stop until I close this case one way or the other."

I know it's less than he wanted but it's the best I can do. The last thing I want to do is give him false hopes or make commitments I can't keep. He seems to realize and understand that because he gives me a firm nod.

"I guess that'll have to do," he says, his voice barely more than a whisper.

CHAPTER EIGHT

The Hungry Bear Café; Woodcreek, WA

IT TOOK US ANOTHER DAY AND A HALF TO GET MADELINE'S BODY exhumed and in a van for transport down to Dr. Rebekah Shafer at the King County Medical Examiner's office. I wanted somebody I trusted to do the examination on Madeline's remains and she's the best I know. Beks is an old friend from college and I trust her implicitly. If there's anything to be found, she'll find it.

Astra and I flew out of Pocatello at the crack of dawn this morning and by the time we made it back to Woodcreek, we were both starving. We stopped at the first place we saw, which was the Hungry Bear. It's not a fancy place by any means. The booths are all made of red vinyl, the floor is covered in linoleum that looks like it's been on the ground for a generation, and the plastic plants are all covered in a thin layer of dust. In truth, reminds me a lot of a Denny's—but with food that actually looks and smells appetizing.

We thankfully missed the breakfast rush, so the place is only about a quarter full. It's mostly old-timers sitting at the u-shaped counter drinking coffee, telling stories they've told each other a hundred times already and razzing each other about it. But they're all laughing and having a good time with each other, which makes me smile. The restaurant may be drab, but the old guys make it lively and vibrant.

We're sitting in a booth near the back, silently huddled over our mugs of coffee as we wait for our meals to come out. I look at the old men again as they erupt into loud guffaws of laughter, this time drawing in the waitress as she refills their coffee. It's obvious they're regulars and have an easy rapport with her.

"That's going to be us one day," Astra says. "Old, fat, sitting around in our muumuus telling each other the exact same stories a thousand times over."

"And happy," I add. "They all look happy."

"And happy," Astra grins. "Of course, we'll be happy."

I sit back in the booth and watch the men again, still laughing and slapping each other on the back. I can't remember the last time I laughed as hard as that. I can't remember the last time I laughed until my belly hurt. Even on those rare occasions I'm with Kit, I can't ever let myself truly be free since I'm always aware that somebody is hunting us, and that my time with her is limited. I long to be genuinely happy. To be able to laugh as freely and unabashedly as those guys at the counter. I just don't know that I ever will be.

"You think we can ever be happy like that, Astra?"

"What? Of course, we can."

I turn and meet her eyes. "You think so?" I ask. "Seeing what we do day after day, seeing the depths of human depravity, do you really think we can ever genuinely be happy?"

"Yes, we absolutely can. But we need to have something in our lives other than work. If all you do is work—and think about work when you're not working—you don't leave room for happiness,

Blake," she tells me, for what's probably the millionth time. "If you marinate in that depravity and misery twenty-four/seven, that's all you're going to feel twenty-four/seven. But if you have something else, a safe harbor where you feel nothing but joy, you can pull yourself out of the muck and make room for something better. Something good. Something that genuinely makes you happy."

"Benjamin," I say.

She nods. "Benjamin. He's my safe harbor. When I'm with him, I can shut out all the horrible stuff we see every day," she tells me. "That's why I'm always harping on you about finding somebody. You need that safe place, Blake. You need somebody you can be with who will help you turn off everything we deal with. Somebody who can just let you be yourself and take some of those burdens you carry off your shoulders."

I take a sip of my coffee then stare down into the dark brew, letting Astra's words echo around in my head. Intellectually, I know it's good advice. Emotionally, I'm not there yet. It pains me to admit, but Mark Walton did a number on me. I obviously can't trust my judgment when it comes to men. How can I when I obviously can't spot somebody planted in my life to watch me—and kill me if necessary?

"I know it's difficult and maybe seems impossible, but you need to find a way to let go of the whole Mark situation," Astra says as if reading my mind. "That was a bad situation, no doubt, but I know it's not one that's going to happen again."

"How do you know? I don't know that."

"Because I trust your instincts," she says. "You got burned once. I get it. But I have a feeling you know what to look for now, even if it's on a subconscious level. I really don't see something like that happening again."

"I wish I could be that sure."

"Trust yourself, Blake."

"It's not that easy. Mark blew a massive hole in me. In my ability to trust myself," I admit. "How do I know I won't let my emotions screw up my instincts again?"

Astra grins at me. "Well, for one thing, I really don't see the Thirteen playing that card again. Not so soon anyway. They'll know you're going to be on guard," she says. "And second, you are the kind of person who learns from your mistakes. There is absolutely no way you wouldn't be able to pick up on those subtle clues and tells if somebody wasn't being straight with you. I mean, you told me in hindsight about all the clues you either missed or pushed aside with Mark. I know you won't let that happen again. If for no other reason than you're too anal-retentive to make the same mistake twice."

We share a quiet laugh together and I nod. She's not entirely wrong. Repeatedly making the same mistake is something I strive to avoid. But opening myself up to somebody again just feels like I'm setting myself up to do just that. I know it's my hang-up. It's something I've spoken with my therapist, Dr. Reinhart, about more than a few times. And her advice is always a lot like Astra's, which is essentially for me to get back on that horse.

Easier said than done, though. When you've had your confidence shaken and lost your ability to trust your own judgment to the extent I have, it's not simply a matter of picking yourself up, dusting yourself off, and carrying on. It's a process and it's going to take some time. I would love nothing more than to have that safe harbor Astra's talking about in my life. It would fill me with the purest joy to be able to go home to somebody who can help me forget about all the terrible things I saw that day. But my trust and my belief in myself isn't just a switch I can flip on when I want to.

"I want to see you happy, Blake. I want to see you in love. But when I push you toward somebody it's mostly because I want to see you have that safe place I talked about. I want to see you with that person who just gets you," she presses. "And it's because I really believe with all my heart that you need some balance in your life. You need some joy to even out the misery we deal with every day.

I'm afraid if you don't find that balance you're going to burn out. I'm afraid if you don't learn to trust yourself again, you're going to end up all—Annie."

A rueful smile curls a corner of my mouth upward. "Even my aunt has somebody these days," I tell her. "A man named Marlon she met through her book club."

"You're kidding me," she gapes.

I shake my head. "Nope. My aunt is officially off the market."

Astra shakes her head, a dumbstruck look on her face. For a really long time, my Aunt Annie, the woman who took me in and raised me after my parents were killed, lived the life of a cloistered spinster. She was angry. Distrustful of men. She locked herself away from the world and even worse, her own issues were rubbing off on my cousin, Maisey. I doubt it was Annie's intent, but her bitterness and anger were turning my cousin into a carbon copy of her.

That's all changed now. Maisey is living with a man who treats her like a queen and is happier than I've ever seen her in my life. And while it's still early between Annie and Marlon, she's already seemed to become a different person. Somebody I don't even know anymore. She's happy. Smiles all the time and seems to be in good spirits whenever we talk. She's no longer obsessing over Maisey's life—or mine for that matter—and is enjoying herself and this new-found joy in her world. It's honestly good to see. Unexpected, but good to see.

"I don't even know how to respond to that," Astra chuckles. "I did not see that one coming."

"That makes two of us," I tell her with a grin. "But still, it's a good thing. Annie deserves to be happy and have somebody who loves her."

"As do you."

"So you keep saying," I reply.

"Charles is a really good man," Astra points out. "And it's more than obvious that he is absolutely hooked on you."

"Yeah, I know he's a good guy."

"He worships you, Blake."

I look away and listen in to the men still talking and laughing with one another, feeling that desire to be connected to somebody, to be happy and free, welling up within me again. But so too does my fear. I stuff it all down ruthlessly though and turn back to Astra.

"Let's talk about something else," I say.

She laughs but nods and holds her hands up in mock surrender. "All right. I'll let it go," she says. "For now, anyway. Expect me to keep hounding you. This is important, even though you might not think so."

"You wouldn't be you if you didn't hound me."

We share a quiet laugh as the waitress brings our food over to the table. A chicken fried steak with hash browns and a two-stack of pancakes for me, a full stack of blueberry pancakes and a side of sausage for Astra. The aroma is heavenly as I breathe it in. My stomach rumbles in agreement and encourages me to dig in. Which I do.

"Hey, since Kit's not going to be around for Thanksgiving, why don't you come over and stuff your face with us?" Astra offers.

I nod as I chew the food I'd just crammed in my face. "I'll do that."

"Bring Charles."

My mouth is still full of food, and I nearly choke as I laugh. I take a minute to swallow the bit of steak then wash it down with a mouthful of coffee. No, Astra wouldn't be Astra if she didn't keep hounding me. And I love her for it.

CHAPTER NINE

King County Medical Examiner's Office; Seattle, WA

WE'D BEEN IN A HOLDING PATTERN FOR THE PAST COUPLE of days, waiting for Rebekah to finish up her examination of Madeline's remains. So, rather than stick around Woodcreek, we came back to Seattle to wait it out. Astra was glad to be able to spend a little time with Benjamin and I worked on some cases, glad to have something to do to keep me busy.

Kicking around Woodcreek with nothing to do wasn't going to hold my attention and would probably only serve to irritate me. I don't like being idle. But until we got word from Rebekah, there was no use in doing anything. Until we have a definitive ruling, be it suicide or homicide, we won't even know if there even is a case here. Until we know what the shape of our investigation is going to look like, I don't want to do anything else.

"So, what do you have for us?" I ask.

Rebekah is in a pair of mint green scrubs and is standing across the stainless-steel procedure table from us. And on top of the table are Madeline Donaldson's remains. I look at the discoloration around her neck and frown. The area of discoloration is mottled, but it's thick like she had indeed wrapped a sheet around her neck.

"I've finished with her examination obviously, and I'm comfortable ruling this a homicide," Rebekah tells me.

I nod, part of me expecting to hear the word suicide the moment I saw the thick band of discoloration around her neck. But then it hits me, and I freeze. It takes a couple of moments to register the fact that Rebekah hadn't said suicide. She'd said homicide. I look up at her, a thousand questions scrolling through my mind simultaneously. I look over at Astra and she seems every bit as shocked as I am. We turn to Rebekah in unison, looking for an explanation. Rebekah, probably seeing the confusion on our faces, laughs softly.

"You were expecting me to rule this a suicide," she says.

I nod. "Well, yeah. Seeing her body and that ring around her neck, I honestly thought you'd rule it a suicide."

"If I weren't paying attention, I would have," she replies. "Good thing for you that I know how important it is to get this one right, so I made sure to look close."

"You look closely at all your cases," I counter. "Who are you trying to fool?"

Rebekah shrugs. "Yeah, but it sounded good."

We all share a laugh that quickly tapers off. It's as if being in Madeline's presence, even though she's nothing more than an empty shell, somehow dampens and sours the mood. There's a hushed reverence for her that fills the room despite the fact that none of us knew her. I guess it's just being around death that naturally tempers our moods. Rebekah clears her throat and points to Madeline's neck.

"I don't know what this Dr. Stein was thinking or seeing," she says. "I assume he's not a practicing medical doctor?"

I shake my head. "Degrees out the wazoo in psychiatry,

pharmacology, and a couple of other associated fields, but to the best of my knowledge, he's not an internist or anything. Nor has he ever worked in an ER or performed a single surgery that I could find."

"So, unless it deals with the medicines he's manufacturing up there, his main function is psychiatry," Rebekah says.

"Psychiatry and medicinal research. His main function seems to be determining the effects of his meds on his psychiatric patients," Astra notes. "He doesn't really seem interested in the people at all, to be honest."

I nod. "Yeah, I have to agree. I could be wrong, but I don't believe he even offers psychiatric counseling to the patients there," I tell her. "He seems all-in on manufacturing the meds that he feeds them."

"That makes sense. If he's not familiar with the human body other than what his medicines do to it, it makes sense that he'd miss these things in his examination," she says. "But he signed off on all the paperwork labeling this a suicide anyway and that's a problem."

"If we try to hit him with that, he'll probably just tell us it's a matter of perspective and professional disagreement," I say. "He's slippery."

"Oh, I don't doubt that. And I'm not telling you all of this so you can go confront him about it," Rebekah says. "This is all more for your edification. It's to help you with your investigation into this girl's death."

I nod. "I appreciate that."

"And judging by the way you said all that he missed some things," Astra says.

Rebekah nods. "Yeah, he did. I mean, it looks like all they did was a perfunctory postmortem exam," she tells us. "A sloppy one at that. The hyoid bone was broken, for one."

"Couldn't that have been broken when Madeline hung herself?" Astra asks.

"It's possible. But it usually takes violent force to break the hyoid," she says. "In the notes, Madeline was said to have wrapped a sheet around her neck and hung herself by a door handle by sitting down."

"Like Robin Williams," Astra notes.

"And like Chester Bennington and Chris Cornell as well. The act is a slow asphyxiation that, for lack of a better word, is gentler. It's still possible but less likely to break the hyoid bone," she says. "But with violent strangulation, you're just about guaranteed to break it. As is the case with Madeline."

Astra and I both nod as we take in the information. The question of whether Dr. Stein is a suspect or just an incompetent administrator rises in my mind once more.

"I can't believe this man signed off on this as a suicide," Rebekah mutters. "It's one of the shoddiest examinations I've ever seen."

"Yeah well, Dr. Stein didn't really seem all that shaken by the fact that she was dead," I say. "I'm not surprised his exam was cursory. If there was one done at all."

"Like we said, he's not interested in the living people in his facility," Astra says. "All he seems interested in are making the meds that will make him the money."

I nod. "He was very perturbed by the idea of our investigation getting in the way of a clinical trial he's running."

"That could definitely account for the shoddy work," Rebekah acknowledges.

There's something in her voice though that hints at something more. I can tell she's reluctant to say more, perhaps not wanting to open a can of worms that might lead us in the opposite direction of the truth. But at the beginning of any investigation, I like having all the different theories in hand. I like seeing all the different paths open to us. I find it makes it easier to mark them off and move on to the next one if they don't bear fruit, rather than having to go back to the blank drawing board and come up with new paths from scratch.

"Okay, we'll figure out what to do about Stein later," I say. "But what tells you this is a homicide and not a suicide?"

"The bruising," she explains. "It's not totally apparent but if you know what you're looking for, you'll see there are two distinct bruising patterns."

"Two?" Astra raises an eyebrow.

She nods and points to what just looks like one big mass of bruising around her neck. How she's able to discern one pattern from the other is beyond me. But that's why she's the medical examiner and I'm just the person assigned to figure out how she got the bruising in the first place.

Using the tip of her pen as a pointer, Rebekah traces a line that, upon closer inspection, is darker than the rest. She looks up at us.

"This was made antemortem," she says. "And if you look closely, you can see the impressions left behind."

I bend down and look closely. It takes me a minute to understand what it is I'm seeing and when I do, I stand up and look at Rebekah.

"Those look like fingers," I say.

She nods. "They do indeed."

She turns Madeline's head to the right, exposing the left side of her neck. And using the tip of her pen again, she points to a small area just below the ear. I look closely but can't see what it is she's pointing out. It's Astra, though, who grabs a magnifying glass and hovers it over the area, blowing up the section of skin, revealing what it was Rebekah wanted us to see. It's faint but in the skin, I can see the impression of what looks like letters.

"Letters," I note. "Like maybe from a ring."

"That's my guess," she says.

"I see part of what might be an M," Astra says. "And an A, maybe."

I nod. "That's what I see too."

Rebekah nods. "That's why I'm ruling this a homicide. That deeper level of bruising indicates manual strangulation. Not ligature."

"Then what's with the rest of the bruising?" Astra asks.

"That, my friends, was done postmortem," Rebekah tells us. "She was already dead when somebody hung her with a bedsheet."

"How can you tell that?" Astra inquires.

Rebekah shrugs. "Because I am really good at what I do."

I smile and nod. "That you are. And that is exactly why I wanted you to have a look at Madeline's body."

"So, it looks like not only do you have a murder, but you have a cover-up on top of it," Rebekah notes. "That sounds like fun."

Astra glances at me. "At least now we know why our little mystery was the locked-room variety," she says. "Somebody who had access to Madeline's room obviously killed her, then locked up on their way out."

"Seems that way," I nod. "So, all we need to figure out is who accessed her room."

"That I can't help you with," Rebekah says.

I laugh quietly. "No, but you've definitely put us on the path we need to be on," I tell her. "Now we know Dr. Stein is either lying or is totally oblivious to what's going on at the facility around him."

I frown and look down at Madeline's body. "I can't see the man killing her. He barely even acknowledged she was a patient, let alone dead. It seemed to me like he had a total disregard for her as a human being."

"Sounds like a charmer," Rebekah notes. "Terrific bedside manner."

"Which is probably why he went into research and drug-making," Astra says with a shrug. "He does come off as a bit of a misanthrope."

"Definitely. The man is smarmy and arrogant. Not somebody I'd choose to spend my time with," I add. "But I don't know that I'd go so far as to say he's a murderer."

"One thing you've always told me is that everybody's a suspect until they're not," Rebekah chimes in. "Just because somebody doesn't seem like a killer, it doesn't mean they're not actually a killer."

"Lots of people said Ted Bundy didn't seem like a killer," Astra notes. "They said the same thing about Dennis Rader too."

"Oh, I'm not discounting that possibility. He's definitely a suspect until he's not. And right now, he's at the top of the list," I tell them. "He just doesn't seem like a killer to me. But believe me, we will be doing a deep dive on this guy. He's at the top of the food chain at Whitehorn and has the most to lose. That gives him motive to cover it up."

"We just need to find motive for killing her to begin with," Astra says.

"To that end, I can tell you that she has been with child recently," Rebekah tells us. "It appears to have been terminated, but I found some of the telltale signs of a pregnancy."

"Way to bury the lead," I tease.

"And here I thought the lead was the cause of death," she counters. "Either way, I was coming around to this bit of news. I figured you'd want to hear it."

I laugh then share a look of astonishment with Astra. She's looking back at me with the same sort of dumbstruck expression on her face I'm sure is on mine. It's a good thing the Donaldson's okayed our request to exhume, because this case is getting deeper by the second.

"I did not see that coming," I say. "She's been locked up in Whitehorn for months."

"Which means she had to be having relations with the other patients. Or the staff," Astra muses. "Perhaps even Dr. Stein himself."

"Which would be motive to kill her, wouldn't it?" Rebekah asks.

"It might be. If it were known Dr. Stein, or any of his staff, were taking advantage of their patients, that would be a scandal that might cost them," I speculate. "I'm pretty positive they'd get all their federal funding pulled as well as the sweetheart lease I'm sure they have on that property up in Woodcreek."

Astra whistles low. "This case just got intriguing as hell all of a sudden."

I nod. "We've got a lot of work to do," I say, then turn to Rebekah. "Thank you for your help. Invaluable as always."

"Not a problem. I'll arrange to have her sent back to Pocatello and reinterred."

"You are a peach, Beks."

"Yeah, I know," she chirps, then shoots me a mischievous grin. "Hey, totally off topic but have you noticed how much Dr. Franz Stein's name sounds like—"

"Don't say it," I reply with a laugh.

Astra slaps me on the shoulder, snorting with laughter. "I told you. Didn't I tell you?"

"I'm leaving," I announce, and walk out of the autopsy suite, still chuckling to myself.

CHAPTER TEN

Criminal Data Analysis Unit; Seattle Field Office

"WELL, LOOK WHO IT IS," RICK CALLS OUT AS WE STEP into the office. "Mon Capitan and her faithful sidekick."

Astra gives him the finger as she sits down at her workstation, drawing a laugh from him. Mo grins as she turns to look at us.

"Didn't expect to see you two here today," she says. "Things up north going that well? Or that horribly?"

"Neither," I tell her. "We're just getting started."

"So, what, you two been on vacation these last few days?" Rick asks. "Take a couple spa days or something?

"You can see that I'm armed, can't you, Rick?" I ask.

He laughs and holds his hands up. "Don't shoot, don't shoot. No need for workplace violence today. Especially since we just had that seminar last month and all," he says. "That wouldn't be a very good look, boss."

"They'd have to find your body for it to be a problem," I say.

We all share a laugh as I step over our small kitchen area and pour myself a fresh cup of coffee. After I have it dressed the way I like it, I step to the front of the room.

"So, what's really going on up north?" Mo asks.

"We just got confirmation from Rebekah over at the ME's office that Madeline Donaldson is the victim of a homicide," I tell them. "Manual strangulation."

"Brutal," Mo mutters.

I nod. "What's worse is that somebody tried to cover it up."

"They tried to make it look like she hung herself," Astra says. "The Chief Science Officer up there, a Dr. Franz Stein, signed off on it being a suicide."

"Franz Stein?" Rick asks with a chuckle. "Dr. Franz Stein?'

I turn to Astra and shake my head, knowing she mentioned his full name just to get either Rick or Mo to make the same joke she had. She's trying to hold in her laughter and turns away, making me grin to myself.

"That's it, you're fired," I tell her.

"You don't have the guts!" she cracks in response.

"What did I miss?" Rick asks.

"Nothing," I reply, calming myself back down. "Anyway, listen up."

I fill them in on everything that happened while we were up in Woodcreek and what we've learned down here. Astra and I walk them through everything Rebekah told us. They both listen attentively and Mo jots down a few notes. When we're finished with our update, Mo is looking aghast at me.

"She was pregnant?" Mo asks.

"According to Beks, yeah. She said the pregnancy was terminated so there's no way to get DNA to prove paternity," I say. "But it definitely does add another layer to the events surrounding her death."

"And the conspiracy to cover it up," Astra notes.

"Right, that too," I say.

"This is getting deep," Rick comments. "Didn't expect it to break this way."

Mo shakes her head. "Me either."

"That makes four of us. But we're here now so we'll play the cards we were dealt," I say. "Mo, where are you with the rip crew?"

"Haven't been able to find much just yet, but I'm still looking," she tells me.

"I figured. It's like looking for a grain of salt on a beach."

"Pretty much," she admits. "But I'm going to nail them down. It's just a matter of patience and figuring out their habits."

"Right, well, put that on the back burner for now," I tell her. "I need you to start doing a deep dive into the backgrounds of the staff at Whitehorn. I need everything. Financials, socials, criminal records, anything that might lead us to some answers. Nothing is too small or insignificant."

"Specifically look for any link between the staff at Whitehorn and Madeline," Astra adds. "Has anybody posted about her on their socials? Has anybody sent her money?"

"Or money to her family," I add.

Astra nods. "Good call."

"Copy that," she replies.

"They've got a pretty lengthy roster. There are nearly a thousand men and women who work there if you factor in the administrative staff, orderlies, nurses, doctors, security, and the like," I tell her. "But I want you to start with Dr. Stein. Dig deep and turn over every rock you can. I want to know if there is anything shady about this guy that we can use to leverage him."

"Or tell us if he's our killer," Astra adds.

"Yeah, or that."

78

"You got it, boss," Mo says.

"Thank you," I say, then turn to Rick. "And have you been able to analyze the security footage and the keycard logs from the electronic locks?"

Rick nods. "I've reviewed them and, on the surface, I don't see anything amiss."

"But?" I ask. "What is it? I hear the 'but' in your voice."

He grins. "But I want to dig into it a little further. It's easy to fake or alter security footage and keycard logs if you know what you're doing. And I have to imagine a multibillion-dollar company like Whitehorn has people on staff who know what they're doing," he tells me. "I want to be absolutely sure everything is up to snuff, and nothing's been screwed with."

"That's good. Please do that," I tell him.

"Already being done. I'm running the footage through a program I designed. It should pick up on any abnormalities but it's going to take some time. It's a slow process," he responds. "And I'm going to need to go through the keycard logs by hand, which is an even slower process, so that's going to take some time as well."

"Fair enough," I nod. "Just keep me in the loop."

"You got it, boss."

"Sometimes, your anal-retentive diligence that borders on extreme paranoia is a blessing, Ricky," Astra replies.

"Everything about me is a blessing," he says with a laugh.

"Somebody's been lying to you again," Astra mutters.

"Don't make me hack into your digital life and wreak havoc on your world."

"Remember what Blake said about them never finding your body? She's too nice to actually go through with it," Astra tells him, a wicked grin touching her lips. "I'm not."

"Mom, she's threatening to kill me again," Rick whines.

"Play nice or I'll send you both to bed without dessert, children," I tell them.

Astra grins and turns back to me. "So, what's our game plan?"

"I figure we'll head back up to Woodcreek today and get settled in. We'll go back to Whitehorn tomorrow and start hitting them hard. Somebody has to know something and we're going to keep shaking trees until something falls out that we can use," I tell her. "And after that, we're going to find our killer and lock them up."

"I love it when she gets so ferocious," Astra cracks, drawing laughter from Mo and Rick.

"I'll go catch Rosie up on where we're at," I tell Astra. "Go see Benjamin and I'll swing by and pick you up in a couple of hours."

"Sounds good to me," Astra says as she gets to her feet and exits the room.

I turn back to Rick and Astra. "I'll stay in touch with you guys. I know I'm dropping a lot on you all at once and I'm sorry for that," I tell them. "But you're going to have some of the key pieces of evidence we're going to need to make our case."

"We won't let you down," Mo says.

"What she said," Rick chimes in.

"You never do," I tell them. "And I appreciate all the work you put in."

"Not to be the shallow, greedy weasel here," Rick starts, "but does that appreciation come with a monetary increase?"

Mo groans and shakes her head then looks up at me apologetically. "Sorry, boss. Apparently, when they were handing out tact, they ran out before they got to him."

"What?" Rick asks with a laugh. "In the immortal words of Michael Jordan, you miss one hundred percent of the shots you don't take."

"It was actually Wayne Gretzky who said that," I correct him.

"Whatever. It was one of those sports guys. I should get half-credit for that," he says with a wide smile.

"Fair enough. Half-credit it is. And if it were up to me, I would absolutely give you guys some monetary appreciation," I say sincerely. "But it's not up to me. However, let me see what I can do. If anybody deserves it, it's you two."

"Thanks, boss," they say in unison.

I give them a nod. "I'll check in with you guys soon."

I turn and head out, wanting to quickly update Rosie then get out of here. I want to grab some things from home before we hit the road again.

CHAPTER ELEVEN

Whitehorn Mental Health and Research Foundation; Woodcreek, WA

"OH. YOU'VE COME BACK," DR. STEIN SAYS.

"We have," I tell him. "We need to begin interviewing your staff."

"Interviewing my staff?" He arches an eyebrow, somehow managing to keep the rest of his face stone still.

"Yes. We need to speak with anybody—well, everybody actually," I tell him. "Turns out Madeline was murdered, Dr. Stein. This wasn't a suicide."

His eyes widen slightly, but he quickly gets himself back under control. He shakes his head, an expression of irritation flashing across his features, as if Madeline's death is somehow an inconvenience to him. I have no doubt that's how he sees it. The man is one of the most self-centered, narcissistic people I've ever come across.

"Are you certain?" he asks.

I nod. "I had Madeline exhumed then examined by our ME," I tell him. "The results are conclusive."

"Wonderful," he mutters darkly. "This is going to take days."

"Probably a couple of weeks, to be honest. But it's an unfortunate necessity in conducting our investigation," I tell him. "Believe me, I'm not looking forward to this any more than you are. But all I can do is follow up on this to the end. Every T needs to be crossed and every I dotted."

His face morphs into an expression of intense displeasure. He obviously wants us out of here. What I'm not totally sure of is whether he wants us gone because he fears what we might uncover or because we're simply a nuisance he doesn't want to deal with.

"We're also going to need a room we can use," Astra tells him. "A private room that can't be accessed by anybody but us."

He sighs. "Anything else, Agents?"

"No, I think that'll do for now," I say. "We'll let you know if we need anything else though. Thank you, Doctor."

He glowers and shakes his head. "This seems a lot of rigamarole for a woman who took her own life. It's sad but there is no need to make a federal case of it," he says, and frowns as he realizes what he said. "No pun intended. Obviously."

"Obviously," I echo him. "But here we are anyway. We'll do our best to stay out of your hair and have as little impact on your operation as possible, so long as you stay out of our way and let us do our job."

He grumbles under his breath. "Fine. Whatever you require."

"Thank you."

"Just wait here. I'll send Jonathan to fetch you," he grouses. "He will escort you to the room you will be using."

"Thank you, Doctor," I say.

He turns and strides off without another word, leaving us standing in the main lobby. It's circular, with doors to our left, right, and directly across from us. A currently unattended reception desk is situated near the door across from us—the one Stein disappeared behind. And the doors to the left and right stand open, leading to hallways that will take us deeper into the corridors of the Foundation.

The walls of the lobby are stark white and filled with pictures of the staff as well as a plaque that denotes the various donors. There are also framed newspaper articles showcasing some of the breakthrough miracle drugs manufactured by Whitehorn. And one entire wall is dedicated to framed photos of the Kinzinger family, the founders of the company.

The door Stein disappeared through opens and a woman with auburn hair and green eyes comes out. She's wearing a dark skirt that falls to her knees and a white blouse beneath a dark jacket. She's wearing minimal makeup and has her hair pinned up. I'd put her somewhere in her forties, and she has a very crisp, professional demeanor. She gives us a cursory glance, then seems to dismiss us as she takes her seat behind her desk. The woman clearly knows who we are and doesn't appreciate us being here any more than her boss does.

"Is it me or did the temperature just drop about fifty degrees?" Astra mutters.

"It's definitely not you," I reply.

Jonathan, the orderly who'd escorted us last time, comes through the door to our left and gestures for us to follow him. We do. He leads us through a maze of winding corridors that pass by a host of patient's rooms, day rooms, and smaller suites probably used for therapy sessions. We also pass by a number of locked, windowless doors and I can only speculate about what goes on in those rooms.

"Where is the medicine made?" I ask, trying to break through Jonathan's icy exterior.

"Lower levels," he says.

He falls silent again as he leads us down a long hallway with a door at the end of it. Jonathan slides a keycard through the lock and a moment later, there's an audible beep and the heavy clunk of the locks disengaging. He opens the door, then turns around and hands me the keycard. I take it and give him a smile. But his face remains about as expressive as a stone.

"Thank you," I say.

"Dr. Stein says you are not permitted to wander around the facility on your own," he says and hands me what looks like the key fob for a car alarm. "If you need to go anywhere, press this button and I will come and retrieve you. I will escort you where you need to go. Is this all understood?"

"Got it," I say and snap him a small salute.

He nods and starts to walk off but pauses and turns around. For the first time since we met, I see a hint of emotion on his face. He quickly swallows it down though, and his face is as blank as slate again.

"You will find out what happened to Madeline?" he asks.

It strikes me as an odd question coming from him, but it shows me that he's a human being under all those layers of stone. That he has some sense of compassion and responsibility for those people he's charged with taking care of. But it also makes me wonder if he knows something more about it.

"Do you think there's more to the story than what we're being told?" I ask. "Do you disagree with Dr. Stein's conclusion that Madeline took her own life?"

He shrugs his broad shoulders. "I don't know. I wasn't here the night she died. She was a nice girl, though. She didn't deserve to die that way," he says, his voice a deep bass rumble. "I try to take care of the patients as best as I can. They're not bad people. They're just... troubled. I don't like seeing them hurt."

I nod. "Well, we're going to find out what happened to her. I promise you."

He purses his lips and nods then turns and walks away without another word. It was an interesting exchange, to say the least.

I hadn't expected somebody who looks like a walking building to feel so deeply for his charges. It's sweet though.

"No rings on his fingers," Astra notes.

I nod. "I noticed that. Still, somebody we're going to need to take a closer look at. There's obviously a connection there. Might be nothing—"

"But it might be something," she finishes for me.

"Right," I nod. "All right, let's get our room set up."

We walk in and find a small conference room painted the same stark white as the lobby. There are only two narrow windows at the top of the wall that don't open, leaving the room stuffy. A door in the far corner leads to a small bathroom and a credenza against the wall beside the door holds a coffee maker that looks like it hasn't been used in a decade. At least.

"Yeah, I'm not using that," I say.

"Snob. It just needs a little cleaning," Astra replies.

"There's a dried spider carcass in the bottom of the pot," I protest.

"Yeah, we'll bring in our own."

I walk over to the thermostat and turn it on to get some air circulating. The fluorescents overhead spring to life when Astra turns them on, making the walls glow so white it's almost blinding. Unlike the lobby, though, there are no photos or anything warm and comforting in this room to tone down the stark whiteness of the place.

It's a rectangular box with a table in the middle of the room that might seat six if you were lucky. We might be able to get twelve people into the room in total. We do however have an empty shelving unit and a rolling whiteboard with an assortment of dry-erase markers that are dried up and useless, so we've got that going for us.

"Very gracious of Dr. Stein," I comment as I drop the pens into the trash can.

"He's the living embodiment of grace," Astra adds.

We set our bags down, pull out our files and notebooks, and get ourselves set up. When we're done, we look at each other and nod.

"Ready?" I ask.

"Let's get started."

∽

"And did you have any personal dealings with Ms. Donaldson?" I ask, fighting to keep from sounding as bored as I feel.

The man sitting across the table from us is a large, bulky guy with shaggy brown hair, deep-set dark eyes, and a prodigious beard that even Rick would envy. He's an orderly named Harley and shakes his head at my question.

"Nah. I ain't have nothin' to do with her," he tells us. "I'm always stationed in the east wing of the buildin'."

I nod. The information lines up with what we have in the personnel records and folders Dr. Stein provided for us. We divided up all the files into classes—those who didn't have any contact with Madeline, those we think might have had contact with Madeline, and those we know had contact with Madeline. We have to interview everybody of course, but having them in priority piles like this allows us where to put most of our emphasis. We're obviously not going to spend as much time on somebody who's never had a conversation with Madeline as somebody who worked in her ward daily. But just for due diligence's sake, we're talking to everybody like Harley here.

"So, you've never been to Madeline's wing?" Astra asks.

He shakes his head. "Nah. Never. Always the east wing."

The east wing is where the Foundation's most violent patients are housed, so it makes sense to have a guy who looks like he could be the Hulk's stunt double on staff and stationed there. We ask him a few more perfunctory questions just to gauge his honesty and he passes with flying colors. Not so much as the hint of a lie, which is good.

"All right, well, thank you for talking to us, Harley," I say.

He gets to his feet and grunts before turning and walking out of the room. The door closes behind him and I slump forward dramatically, beating my head against the table. Astra laughs as I sit up.

"I guess all you need to work in this place is to be built like a brick crapper," Astra says.

I shrug. "Don't need to be able to understand quantum physics to physically control an unruly patient."

"Yeah, I suppose so," she replies. "It'd be nice if they could string a few coherent words together though."

"I don't disagree," I grumble. "We've been at this now for three days, but it feels like three weeks—and we've barely made a dent in the employment roster. There has to be a way to streamline this process."

Astra frowns. "I can't see any way. Not if we want to make sure we've accounted for every employee," she says. "We could flip the order though and start talking to the people we know have had contact with her first. Maybe we get lucky and hit on some suspects."

"If only we could get so lucky."

"We might."

I arch an eyebrow at her. "Have we ever been that lucky?"

"There's a first time for everything," she says with a laugh. "When are we going to take a crack at Stein?"

"When we have something more to hit him with. He's slippery and I want to be able to box him in," I reply. "We need something concrete."

"That's fair."

We've been working through the roster starting with the low to no known contact employees first, figuring we'd be able to get through them quickly. I just didn't stop to think about the sheer number of them. I horribly underestimated how quickly we were going to get through them all. I mean, we need to be able to rule everybody out, but maybe Astra's right and we should flip the order.

Just because somebody saw her every day doesn't mean they had anything to do with her death, though. We might spend as much time on the pile of people who worked on her ward as those who didn't and still not get any answers. It very well could be somebody who's only worked a couple of shifts on Madeline's ward who was responsible for her pregnancy—or for her death.

Then there's the ever-present possibility it was one of the other patients who got her pregnant and killed her. Patients having sex with each other isn't unheard of, but it is something that's frowned upon. In fact, it's strictly against the rules in most every hospital I've ever been around. If one of the patients got Madeline pregnant, she may have been forced to terminate.

Dr. Stein and his staff would have every reason to cover it up. It is entirely possible that some of the pearl-clutching bean counters in DC would be so freaked out about the impropriety of sexual relations between patients that they could pull his funding. In this day and age, accusations of sexual misconduct are not taken lightly. Nor should they be. And knowing that, I can see why it might be possible that Madeline was forced to terminate her pregnancy. I can see why they might possibly go to great lengths to cover it up.

But did that cover-up extend to murder? Would they actually kill somebody to cover up the fact that one of their wards had gotten pregnant?

Those are just a few of the many questions we have to find the answers to.

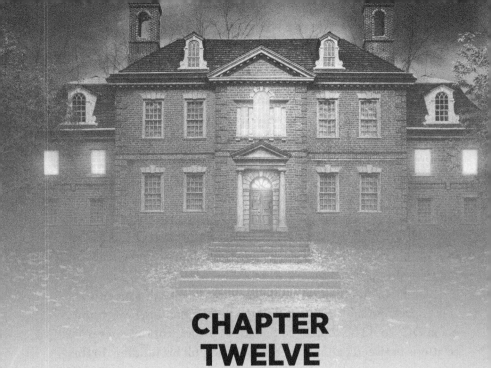

CHAPTER TWELVE

Whitehorn Foundation, Conference Room 12-A; Woodcreek, WA

"GHOSTS?" I ASK.

Alice Meyer, one of the nurses on Madeline's floor, nods, her expression serious. Astra and I glance at each other, both of us doing our best to keep from rolling our eyes. This is the third person in the last couple of days we've spoken with who's mentioned the ghosts that supposedly haunt the hospital. They've all been otherwise rational people but the fear I see in their eyes when they talk about the supposed ghosts is real. I have no explanation for it.

It's the second day of interviews after we flipped the order of the people we're speaking to. And in terms of results, it has been every bit the dry hole doing things the other way was. We haven't gleaned a single bit of useful information. Not one person we've interviewed has set off our radar and emerged as a suspect.

"Sometimes, late at night, I hear them walking around. I'll hear sounds like when rubber shoe soles squeak on the tile. Other times I'll hear a cough or the sound of somebody clearing their throat," Alice says. "But when I look, there's nobody there. It's just the sounds."

Astra is tapping the point of her pen on her notepad. Her jaw is clenched and she's refusing to look at Alice. She's obviously doing her best to keep her mouth shut so she doesn't say something snarky. It's a struggle I'm finding myself relating to. But one of us has to be the adult in the room and I guess since I'm the boss, that burden of responsibility falls to me.

I clear my throat. "So, just to clarify, your position is that Madeline was strangled by the spirit of a former patient. Is that about right?"

Alice shrugs. "Believe me, I know how this sounds. I know I must sound like an absolute crackpot to you," she says. "But things happen around here that defy explanation, Agents. Things have happened that we can't find a reason for."

"Such as?" Astra finally asks.

"Things going missing. That happens all the time—"

"And what's gone missing, Alice?" Astra presses.

"Small things. Pens. Pillows. Blankets. Aspirin," she tells us. "I came in one morning to find one of the nurse's stations on the third floor completely torn apart. Those stations are always locked up tight, but it was like somebody got in and ransacked the place. And I've read that sometimes angry spirits do that. I've read that they will turn a room inside out."

Astra grimaces, doing her best to hide her annoyance. "So, what you're saying is that a ghost—like the actual spirit of a dead person—has been ransacking nurse's station and lifting things like pillows and blankets and aspirin."

Alice's cheeks flush with color and she looks down at the table. "Like I said, I know how this sounds. But I can't think of another explanation. All the staff is accounted for, and yet, these things still happen," she tells us. "You don't know the history of this place. When it was first opened, they conducted terrible experiments on people. Dozens died. Maybe hundreds. And I'm not the only one who's seen and heard strange things around here."

"Yeah, we know," Astra says. "We've talked to a few of your colleagues who share your enthusiasm for ghost stories."

"Well, it's a big topic of conversation around here," she tells us. "I mean, after all, this place has a fairly blood-soaked history."

"I don't doubt that," I chime in. "But my question is, simple… what does a ghost need with pillows and blankets?"

The question is simple but seems to catch Alice off guard. She sits back, her mouth open as if to reply, but then she thinks better of it and closes it again. A moment of strained silence passes between us all as if she is searching for an answer. Not finding one, she shrugs.

"I don't know. Perhaps it was one of the orderlies giving the comfort items to other patients," she says, still unwilling to give up the ghost story angle. "But unexplained things happen around here all the time. There's a reason why nobody goes into the south wing."

"And what is that reason?" Astra asks.

"It's being renovated. Everybody knows that renovations stir up the spirits," she says. "It's probably why there's been more… activity… lately."

"Activity?" Astra raises an eyebrow.

Alice nods soberly. "Paranormal activity."

I frown and bite back a heavy sigh. "And you believe it's this increased paranormal activity that led to Madeline's death?"

"Maybe," she replies. "I mean, she was seeing her dead boyfriend. It wouldn't be the first time an angry spirit took revenge upon the person who ended their life."

I cock my head. "Seeing her dead boyfriend?"

Alice nods. "She and I spoke about it a few times. She said she kept seeing him here," she says. "She saw him in the day room. In the cafeteria. Out on the grounds."

"This would be the boyfriend she shot and killed?" Astra asks.

"Yes. Him," she tells us. "And yet, she kept seeing him everywhere."

Astra laughs softly to herself. "Don't you think it's possible she was seeing things? I understand she's a schizophrenic and as you know, hallucinations—"

"I know that, Agent," Alice snaps. "But Madeline was on her meds. She was stable and wasn't experiencing any symptoms."

"I'd argue that seeing her dead boyfriend might count as a symptom," Astra counters.

"If you don't believe then yes, I can see how it might look like that," Alice says. "But I'm a trained nurse and I'm telling you, once she balanced out on her meds, she was right. She wasn't experiencing any symptoms."

I feel like this interview is starting to come off the rails and head in a direction I don't want it to go. The last thing I want is to get into a conversation about the paranormal. I want facts. Solid evidence. I don't deal in spooks, spirits, and stories of the unexplained. I broker in things that can be seen, felt, and most importantly, can be proven. I know to get back on track, I'm going to need to steer this conversation back.

"Okay, you were working the floor the night of Madeline's murder," I say.

Alice nods. "I was."

"And did you see anything out of the ordinary?" I ask then quickly realize my mistake and add quickly, "What I mean is anybody who shouldn't have been on the ward. Any strange or suspicious people lurking around you hadn't seen before?"

She shakes her head. "No, the floor was quiet that night. I didn't see anybody."

"That's a beautiful ring," Astra says, gesturing to the ring on her hand.

Alice smiles. "Oh, thank you. It belonged to my mother."

"May I see it?"

Alice slips it off and hands it to Astra. She looks closely at it, pretending to be admiring the craftsmanship, but she cuts a glance at me and gives me a small shake of the head. It's not the ring we're looking for. She hands it back to Alice with a smile.

"It's gorgeous," she says.

"Thank you," Alice replies. "It's very sentimental to me."

There is nothing in the background Mo ran for us that raises any red flags for me. Her financials are clean, she's got no criminal history, and she has a solid, stable marriage and two kids. Other than an apparent obsession with the paranormal, there's nothing about her that makes me think she murdered Madeline or knows anything about it.

"All right, well thanks for speaking with us, Alice," I tell her. "If we have any follow-up questions, we'll be in touch."

She frowns and bites her bottom lip for a moment, looking down at the table. She eventually raises her eyes to us though.

"If... if this really was a person who killed Madeline, please catch them, Agents," she says, her voice suddenly shaky. "Madeline was a sweet girl. She didn't deserve to die that way."

"We're doing everything we can," I assure her.

Alice nods and gets to her feet then leaves our makeshift shop. When the door closes, Astra and I both let out deep, dramatic breaths in unison... which makes us both laugh.

"I swear to God, if I hear one more campfire ghost story, I'm going to scream," Astra says, her tone exasperated.

I nod. "Yeah. That makes two of us."

She sighs and picks up the next file we have. "Damon Renfrow is our next contestant."

"I need a break," I tell her. "Let's take a walk."

Astra arches an eyebrow at me. "You have that look you get when you're about to cause a little mischief."

I grin. "I have a mischief face?"

"Oh God, yes. And you never do a good job of hiding it. Sorry to say but your poker face sucks," she says with a hearty laugh. "So, what sort of trouble will you be getting us into this afternoon?"

"Well, I want to see what has these people on edge in the south wing."

"I was so hoping you'd say that," Astra grins. "Will Jonathan be joining us on our little impromptu adventure?"

"God, no. The last thing I want is one of Stein's people breathing down our necks."

"Even better."

⁓

We somehow managed to make it to the south wing of the Foundation without attracting any unwanted attention. We step out of the elevator on the third floor. Plastic sheeting is hanging down from the ceiling all over the place. There are exposed wooden beams as new walls are being built and some others are already drywalled. The lighting on the floor is dim and thick pockets of shadow loom in the corners, hiding unknown depths. With rubble all around, tables littered with tools, and empty soda cans and food wrappers scattered all over the floor, the place is a wreck.

"Looks like they're building more rooms," Astra observes.

"Business must be booming in the mental health care field."

"Or in the human experimentation field."

I shrug. "They have to run trials to see if the drugs they're developing work. It's like any medication. And the trials are all so heavily regulated, it's safe—more or less," I say. "It's not like it was back when this place first opened. They're not cutting people open just to see what's inside or offering icepick lobotomies."

"Are you sure about that?"

I laugh softly. "I'm pretty sure. If they were just cutting people up, I'm sure there would have been something on TMZ about it. It's not like people can keep secrets anymore," I say. "Somebody would have posted a selfie with one of the corpses."

Astra grins. "Yeah, that's probably true."

We prowl through the upper floor of the south wing, looking around and poking our heads into every room that's been completed. I don't know why I felt the need to check out the south wing other than I just had a need to prove these people wrong. It's stupid, I know. How can you disprove the idea that a ghost murdered somebody? I shouldn't be giving their ridiculous theories the least bit of oxygen. But for some reason, I felt compelled to come up and have a look around for myself.

"Did you hear that?" Astra asks in a hushed whisper.

"Hear what?" I reply.

Astra holds her hand up, telling me to be quiet as she cocks her head and listens. I hold my breath and listen for several long moments but hear nothing. I look over at Astra and she frowns with a shake of her head.

"I thought I heard something," she tells me.

We walk on, moving deeper into the wing. The air around us suddenly feels saturated with a tension that wasn't there a moment ago. Neither one of us is speaking as we both have our ears perked, listening intently. As we move, I feel a heaviness in the atmosphere. The hair on the back of my neck stands up and I feel a finger of ice slide down my spine. It's the unmistakable feeling of being watched. I glance over at Astra and can tell by the look on her face that she's feeling the same thing I am.

Picking up my foot, I'm about to take another step when I hear the soft scuff of a foot on the concrete flooring. We both freeze and pull our weapons, turning toward the direction I'd heard the sound coming from. My eyes dart left and right, looking around the half-completed floor. My heart beats a bit harder and I feel my stomach churn as I wait for somebody—or something—to come hurtling at us from the thick pockets of shadow and gloom. Nothing comes rushing out at us, but I'm still walking around on red alert.

We keep moving, weapons drawn and senses strained as we listen for the slightest sound and look for the subtlest movement. As much as I hate to admit it, I'm feeling creeped out up here because that feeling of being watched persists. I pause and swing to my right, my weapon leading the way when I hear what sounds like a furtive footstep. Beside me, I hear Astra chuckling softly. When nothing leaps out of the gloom at me, I turn back to her.

"What are you laughing at?" I ask.

"I was just thinking that we just spent like half an hour mocking poor Alice about the idea of ghosts running around this place," she says. "And here we are jumping at every sound like a couple of idiots."

I look down at my weapon, pointed and ready to go, and just shake my head. Feeling like a fool, I holster my weapon and laugh softly at myself.

"Yeah, I guess these really aren't going to do a lot to a ghost either, huh?" I ask.

"Yeah, probably not."

"Power of suggestion," I offer. "Alice put the thought in our heads, and we absolutely let them take root."

She nods and holsters her own weapon. "Yeah. I'm feeling like an idiot, how about you?"

"Big time."

We walk through the last section of the floor we haven't cleared yet, laughing at ourselves for being so foolish and giving into Alice's suggestions so easily. We stop at a room near the back of the floor. It's one of the finished ones, lacking only a door. But in the corner is a pile of pillows and blankets. A pile of trash sits on the other side of the room—empty beer and soda cans, food wrappers, and the other detritus that tells me somebody's been living in here.

The realization that somebody's been living here triggers the sound of furtive footsteps I'd heard out there on the floor. Suddenly, the feeling of being watched makes sense. It wasn't a ghost watching us. It wasn't the angry, avenging spirit of Madeline's dead boyfriend shadowing us around the floor. It was a homeless man keeping an eye on his things.

"Well, I think this explains a lot," I say.

Astra nods. "So much for the ghosts running around the place. Nothing more than your garden variety homeless person."

"Looks like it."

"You want to break it to Alice or should I?" she asks.

"I think you'd enjoy it more."

Astra nods. "Yeah, probably."

We laugh as we make our way back to the elevator. One mystery solved. A hundred more to go. As we climb into the elevator car though, I still can't shake that feeling of being watched. Only, it's worse this time. More intense. Even creepier. Homeless guy or not, something feels sinister and hostile about it. And it kills me to say but something about that intense blast of emotion feels almost otherworldly.

Damn Alice for putting those thoughts in my head.

CHAPTER THIRTEEN

Bayview Motor Lodge; Woodcreek, WA

"FOR BEING A TOWN OUT IN THE STICKS LIKE IT IS, THEY have got some killer Chinese takeout," Astra says through a mouthful of fried rice.

I nod as I stuff some noodles into my mouth. I chew it up then wash it all down with a swallow of soda.

"They really do. I'm shocked," I say.

I'm sitting in the middle of my bed surrounded by my food and stacks of files while Astra is perched on the chair at the small round table by the window. After wrapping up at the Foundation today, we got some takeout and came back to our motel to eat and go over what we have... which isn't much. So, we've moved on to strategizing how to attack our interviews the following day.

"We're eventually going to have to talk to this US Attorney," Astra points out, then takes a bite of her BBQ pork.

I nod. "Craig. James Craig. Yeah, I was thinking about that too," I say. "If for no other reason than to read him the riot act for how badly he bungled this whole case."

"I've honestly never heard of a prosecutor signing off on a case without doing any actual legwork on it and simply accepting the supposed evidence from the target of an investigation," Astra huffs, giving voice to my exact frustrations. "I mean, I get that he's probably busy, but this is either sheer incompetence or absolute laziness."

"Yeah. I'd really like to know what was going through that guy's head. If it's as bad as I fear it might be, we're going to have to ask Justice to remove him from that post, then review his entire case history," I say. "There's no telling how many other cases he's screwed up this badly."

"Where there's one, there's bound to be many more," Astra notes.

I pop some more noodles into my mouth then pick up the file that has the notes from Dr. Langenkamp's sessions with Madeline. They feel incomplete to me. Like perhaps she knew we would get the confidentiality waived and preemptively edited her notes. I'm obviously no therapist, but Madeline had been in Whitehorn for well over a year, and to me, the folder with all her session notes feels woefully thin.

"What is it? You've got that look on your face," Astra asks around a mouthful of pork.

"What look is that?"

"The one that says something's bugging you."

I nod. "Well, it is. Not that I have a special face for that—"

"You do. Trust me."

"Fine, whatever," I relent. "But Dr. Langenkamp's session notes don't feel right to me. It feels like they're missing something."

"Like what?"

I shake my head. "Well, for instance, there is nothing in this file about Madeline seeing her dead boyfriend," I say. "I mean, there's plenty about killing her boyfriend. But nothing about seeing him walking the halls of Whitehorn."

"Maybe Madeline never mentioned it to Langenkamp?"

I frown. "It's possible. It's definitely possible. But I can't see it," I say. "I mean, based on our interviews, she mentioned seeing his ghost to a few of her ward nurses. To a couple of orderlies as well. I have a hard time believing it never came up with her therapist once in all the time she was there."

"So, Langenkamp is falsifying records then."

"Maybe. But it's not something I can prove," I say with frustration in my voice. "They have no audio or video of their sessions so I can't back up the claim."

"But why would Langenkamp remove references to that?" Astra asks, playing the devil's advocate.

I shake my head. "I don't have an answer for that."

"All right, so what do we have that we can prove?"

I purse my lips and look at the files scattered all around me. "We know she was pregnant. We know she was made to terminate and that was covered up by the hospital," I say. "We know for a fact that she was murdered, the US Attorney signed off on it as a suicide, and everybody seems to be hoping we're just going to go away."

"Fat chance of that. Not now. Not with what we know... as little as it may be right now," Astra says.

We both fall silent as we take a few bites of our meals. All the while, my mind is spinning with theory after theory. Sadly, most of them seem straight out of tin-foil hat country. I don't think I can be blamed though. There are a host of disparate parts scattered around the table right now and if you look at them as they are, without any sort of context, it certainly seems like a large-scale cover-up of a young woman's murder.

I take a drink of my soda and try to clear my mind of all the noise. We're in short supply of facts right now. But we're not completely without them. One thing I've learned is that one fact can lead to another. And another. And it can paint the entire picture for you if you let it. But you just have to get that first piece of the puzzle to fall into place. And that means I need to go back to the basics of any investigation.

"Okay, who benefits most from Madeline's death?" I ask.

"Stein," Astra replies. "A murder in his hospital could put a serious cramp in his style."

"True. But his wouldn't be the first hospital with ties to the government who have had patients murdered," I say. "In truth, it would likely be a minor inconvenience that's swept under the rug because, in the grand scheme of things, Madeline was a nobody."

Astra purses her lips and chews on that for a moment. "Okay, so maybe Stein didn't kill her himself. But he definitely participated in the cover-up, either through his own negligence or to protect somebody else."

I nod. "Better. Let's play that out a little bit because I, for one, don't think Stein has the stomach to actually kill somebody. He's a weasel of a man but he doesn't give me the cold-blooded killer vibe," I say. "I just can't see him actually putting his hands on Madeline and choking the life out of her. I don't think he has the stomach."

Part of solving cases when you have next to nothing to go on boils down to knowing people. Profiling them. And I've been profiling Stein since the moment we met him. He's arrogant. Smarmy. He thinks he's the smartest man in any room he walks in—and to be fair, he probably is. But he's also got a superiority complex and has to make sure everybody knows he's the smartest man in the room. He's also a control freak. Stein has to have control over everything and everybody around him.

All of that adds up to a very annoying person. One I wouldn't personally choose to spend a minute of my time with. But even his annoying personality and irritating quirks don't mean he's a killer. In fact, underneath that arrogant swagger, I see Stein as something of a coward. He hides behind his intelligence and uses it to bludgeon others into submission. But it's a shield he uses to hide, and if he were to actually be confronted by somebody, he'd cower. He strikes me as the sort of man who thinks physical violence is abhorrent and that's why I don't see him putting his hands on Madeline. He'd never get his hands dirty that way.

"He's an annoying little weasel but he's not a killer," I say.

"All right, so let's circle back to the idea that whoever knocked Madeline up is the one who killed her," Astra muses. "And that Stein helped cover that up just to keep the feds, who are always sensitive to scandal, from shutting him down or pulling his funding."

"I honestly doubt it would be a blip on anybody's radar. As long as he's making them money at the rate he has been, he's the golden child," I counter. "He could stand in the middle of Fifth Avenue in Manhattan and shoot somebody, and he wouldn't lose a nickel of funding."

"Yeah, but he probably doesn't know that," Astra says. "The optics would be bad for him—pregnant women forced to terminate then murdered. I'm sure all he'd see would be the headlines. And given the times we're living in and the way the media handles things, I bet that'd be enough to freak him out."

I nod as I chew on a piece of egg roll. "Yeah, you very well might be right about that," I tell her. "That's a really good thought."

"See? Not just a pretty face."

I laugh and take another bite, letting the entire scenario play out in my mind. All the pieces fit and form a very plausible picture, but to me, it still feels incomplete. Like we're missing something. I just don't know what it is yet.

"All right, so who was the father of Madeline's child?" I ask. "If we can figure that out, we'll be on a good path."

"Stein?"

"It's possible but I'm thinking not," I shake my head. "If he were the father and had forced her to terminate, why kill her? And like I said before, I don't think he killed her."

"Fair point," she replies.

Astra leans back in her chair as she munches away on her meal in silence as we think it over. I eat some more noodles as I let my mind spin. As I chew, a thought occurs to me that seems completely outlandish but is still intriguing. I sit up and take a drink as I let the different pieces fall into place before I give voice to it.

"I've just had a thought," I say.

"Well, there's a first time for everything. Congratulations."

I laugh and give her the finger. "Shut up and listen to me."

"I'm all ears."

"Okay, this is going to seem out there. Like really out there," I say, trying to prepare her. "And I've got nothing to back it up."

"We've cracked cases when you've had these out-of-left-field theories before though, so lay it out for me."

"What if the father of Madeline's child was none other than US Attorney James Craig?" I ask. "What if he knocked her up and Stein terminated the pregnancy to cover it up for him?"

"Then why kill her?"

"Because Stein, who is an absolute control freak, has leverage on Craig. He probably kept records," I go on. "To eliminate the leverage, you eliminate Madeline."

"Except that Stein still has this proof you're talking about."

"Maybe. But the second Craig signed off on the suicide, he took that leverage away from Stein," I press. "Officially, Madeline took her own life. And it would have stayed that way except for us exhuming her."

Astra looks off for a long moment, processing what I said. She finally nods and turns her eyes back to me.

"Okay. I can dig it," she says. "But what does Stein get out of this arrangement?"

"A powerful friend in a high governmental position."

Astra whistles. "That makes sense."

"And that means we need to talk to Craig as soon as possible."

Astra nods, agreeing with me as my cell phone chirps. I look at the display screen and see it's Rick calling. It's odd that he's calling given that it's well after business hours. Rick has never so much as spent an extra two minutes in the office that he doesn't have to. Whatever this is about must be huge. I connect the call and put it on speaker.

"Hey, Rick. What's up?" I ask.

"Hey, boss," he replies. "How are you guys doing up in the sticks?"

"Knee-deep in a mystery," I say. "But I think we're coming up with a workable theory."

"Yeah, well, you might want to hold off on that," he tells us. "I'm about to destroy any theory you might have."

Astra and I exchange a glance. "Okay, what do you have?" I ask.

"I did some deep digging and your vic, Madeline Donaldson, isn't who you think she is."

"You really going to drag this out?" Astra asks.

"A master storyteller draws his audience in before giving the big reveal," Rick says. "Do you really know nothing about story-craft, you heathen?"

I laugh. "Spill it, Scanlon."

"Heathens. Anyway, Madeline Donaldson has a file sealed by the US Marshal's Service. It was completely buried, and no mere mortal would have been able to even find it," he says. "I tried to crack the file but couldn't get through their security, which is slightly embarrassing. But it looks to me like she's a witness, and they stashed her at Whitehorn to keep her out of sight until trial."

Astra and I both sit back and whistle in unison. We take a moment to digest what Rick just told us and how it fits in with everything we've learned and gathered to that point.

"Big, nasty plot twist, right?" Rick asks with a chuckle.

"I did not see that coming," Astra notes.

"Glad I can manage to surprise you even after all this time, buttercup," Rick says.

"You call me buttercup again and you'll be breathing through a tube," Astra tells him.

"You say the sweetest things."

I get my feet back under me and run a hand through my hair as I try to figure out what our next steps are going to be.

"Thanks for the heads up, Rick," I tell him. "Keep digging but stay away from that file. I'm sure they'll flag it the moment you crack it, and right now, we want to move in the shadows. We don't want to tip our hand until we figure out how to use this."

"Will do," he says.

"Good work, Rick."

"Thanks, boss."

I disconnect the call and drop my phone onto the bed then turn to Astra.

"This changes everything," I say.

CHAPTER FOURTEEN

US Marshal's Office, Western District of Washington; Seattle, WA

ASTRA AND I WERE UP HALF THE NIGHT TRYING TO FIND A way to come at this whole thing sideways. We didn't want to tip our hand or let anybody know we were sniffing around, but there didn't seem to be any way to avoid it. So, the only thing we could think of was to come at it straight on and ask for some professional discretion.

That led us to jumping in the car at first light and heading back down to Seattle to meet with Assistant Chief Deputy US Marshal Wendy Voight. That's the name Rick gave us that was associated with the case file he'd found. It struck me as odd that an Assistant Chief would be handling the case rather than one of the deputy marshals who are normally assigned to handle specific witnesses. The fact that an Assistant Chief is overseeing it tells me that Madeline was a high-value witness.

The Seattle Courthouse for the Western District of Washington is a tall building made of steel and glass. The design is modern and sleek, but to me, it's a bit cold and sterile. It doesn't have some of the stateliness or gravitas as some of the old courthouses back east. There are no fluted columns, arched doorways, marble foyers, or any of the nineteenth-century features that make those old courthouses charming and dignified.

We step into the lobby and everything is shiny and reflective. It may as well be a high-rise office building. We check the directory then take the elevator up to the eighth floor where the Marshals office is located. We step out of the car and find ourselves in a lobby with hardwood floors and walls painted a soft, neutral tone. Pictures of the President and Vice President along with the director of the Marshals Service hang on the wall to our right and the left is adorned by pictures of deputy marshals who've fallen in the line of duty.

A chest-high counter stands in front of us and is staffed by a severe-looking woman. She's probably in her mid-forties and has dark hair shot through with gray pulled back into a tight bun. She's wearing a natty dark blue pantsuit that was obviously expertly tailored with a cream-colored blouse beneath the blazer. She just gives off a vibe of efficiency and competence that I like about her instantly.

"Can I help you?" she asks.

We badge her. "SSA Wilder, Special Agent Russo," I say. "We need to speak with Assistant Chief Voight."

"Do you have an appointment?"

"We don't," I reply. "But it's important we see her."

"What is this regarding?"

"It's official business," I tell her.

"I'll see if she has time for you."

The woman picks up the phone and turns away, speaking in low tones to keep us from overhearing her. I turn to Astra and roll my eyes, making her grin. The desk agent turns around and hangs up the phone.

"Assistant Chief Voight will see you," she says and points to the hallway to the left. "Follow that hallway and take the first right then the first left. The Assistant Chief's office is at the end of the hall."

"Thank you."

We follow her directions and find our way to Voight's office. The hallways are all hushed and there isn't the sort of buzz and commotion we have in our field office. I don't know that I could work in a place this quiet.

"Come," she says, her voice muffled.

I open the door and let Astra go through before me. I follow her in and close the door behind me. The woman behind the desk is on the phone and gestures to the two chairs that sit in front of it. Astra and I take our seats and I look around. Voight's office is clean. There isn't a thing out of place. All the furniture is done in a red wood polished to a near mirror shine and the walls are earth tones. The bookcases are filled with binders, all of them tagged with handwritten cards I assume are case numbers. There's a large window on the wall behind Voight that has a stunning view of downtown Seattle.

Voight herself is a tall woman. I'd put her at about five-ten, with short, dark hair that's flecked with gray, green eyes, and is solidly built. She has perfect posture and speaks in short, clipped sentences. She's got a military bearing about her and it wouldn't surprise me to learn she served. As she starts to wrap up her call, my eyes drift back to the bookcase. I keep thinking about the binders. That and the shadow box I see on the wall beside the bookcase that holds the fruit salad of her medals and citations from her time in the military.

Most people when they get into upper management, such as an Assistant Chief, become bureaucrats. They spend their days in meetings, filling out reports, playing politics, and dealing with all the red tape that comes with their advanced position. But Voight seems like she's actively working with witnesses. It's unusual, to be sure. In the Bureau, people like Rosie don't often work cases—they delegate them. The fact that she is apparently still working with active cases tells me a lot about Voight's work ethic. It's interesting.

She hangs up the phone and turns to us, her cool green eyes taking us in. I can see her taking our measure and assessing us. No doubt she'll find us wanting. If I were her, I'd probably find us wanting as well.

"What is it I can do for you, Agents?" she asks crisply.

She's blunt. Straight and to the point. That tracks. "We're here about Madeline Donaldson," I tell her. "She would be your case number four-one-alpha—"

"Two-seven-echo-three," she replies curtly. "Yes, I know her case number. She took her own life. Other than that, I can't discuss her case with you."

"With all due respect, Chief, Madeline is dead," I say. "And we want to find out who killed her."

"I understand that but..."

Her voice trails off and she turns away, seeming to be staring out her window for a long moment. I can see her grappling with the decision in her mind. The witness is dead so there's no reason for her to protect Madeline's whereabouts anymore.

"Hell, it doesn't matter anymore, I guess. Without Madeline, they don't have a case anymore anyway," she mutters to herself then turns her eyes to us. "But I don't know why you're looking into this. My understanding is there is no case. She took her own life. I can give you the case file the US Attorney provided to me if you don't have a copy."

"We have a copy, thank you," I tell her. "But the case file is incorrect and the conclusions that were drawn in Madeline's death are wrong. Madeline didn't kill herself. She was murdered, Chief."

She leans back in her chair and steeples her fingers in front of her, a considering expression on her face. I can see the surprise in her eyes. It's obviously news to her and judging by the scowl that crosses her face, it's news she's taking personally.

"Who told you that?" she finally asks. "What makes you think she was murdered? And why were you even looking into her death in the first place?"

"Because of the nature of the work being done at Whitehorn along with the government funding and contracts, my team was asked to look into this by the Director of the FBI," I explain. "We spoke with Woodcreek's sheriff who had received a call from Whitehorn reporting the murder. And when we began investigating, we found that the US Attorney signed off on the suicide based on evidence provided by Whitehorn itself."

Voight frowns. "I wasn't told any of this," she says quietly. "Using evidence provided by an investigative target is problematic."

"That's one way to put it," Astra chimes in.

"Are you certain?" Voight asks.

"We had Madeline exhumed and examined by our ME," I tell her. "It's conclusive."

"Jesus," she mutters.

"Did you know she was pregnant, Chief? Or that her pregnancy was terminated?"

Voight's eyes widen and her mouth falls open. She looks absolutely stunned by what we're telling her. I know it's premature but I'm mentally crossing Voight off my suspect list. Or at least, moving her to the back burner. I clock her as honest to a fault and I don't think she's that good of an actress. I'm satisfied, at this point, that Voight had no knowledge of or participation in Madeline's death.

"So, you didn't know she was involved with somebody up at Whitehorn?" Astra asks.

Voight shakes her head. "I had no clue."

"How often were you in contact with her?"

"Weekly," she says. "I visited her every Friday just to check in with her. Bring her anything she wanted. Just to let her know she wasn't alone."

"You cared about her," I note.

She nods. "Madeline had her issues. I'm not going to lie and say otherwise," she tells us. "But when her mind was straight, she was a good girl who got stuck in a bad circumstance. She was bright. Funny. Yeah, I cared about her."

"Did she ever mention having trouble with anybody?" Astra asks. "Anybody threatening her or bothering her in any way?"

A wry smile touched Voight's lips. "The only person she told me she was having trouble with was the man she killed," she said. "She was on her meds and her mind was otherwise straight. But she kept telling me she was seeing Pasha in the hospital."

"Chief, can you tell us why you stashed her at Whitehorn?" I ask.

"Well, part of it was that I hoped they'd be able to help her. I wanted her mind right for trial," she explains. "But also because it seemed like a safe place. I didn't think anybody would be able to find her there. I thought she'd be safe. Guess I was wrong."

"Can you tell me what the case was?" I ask. "Who is Pasha and why did she kill him?"

She nods. "Pasha Sobol. He ran a Russian mob outfit here called *Chlopciki*. It translates roughly to, 'the boys'. They have ties to the Odessa Mafia, who are the largest, most brutal Russian mob in the States," she tells us.

I've heard of the Odessa Mafia. They aren't just the most brutal Russian mob outfit around, they're the most brutal mob outfit period. Nobody is harder than the Russians. Not the Italians. Not the Serbians. Not the Armenians. When it comes to sheer savagery, the Russians are kings of that particular hill.

"Anyway, the *Chlopciki* was doing business with one of the Chinese Triad groups in Seattle," she goes on. "My understanding is the Bureau has been trying to infiltrate both groups for a long time but have had no success."

I nod. I've heard some of this when I talked to my friend Jonas over in Organized Crime. He told me they'd lost three agents trying to get inside the Russian and the Chinese outfits and their investigation was dead in the water.

"Sounds like Madeline offing one of the heads of this Russian group was a blessing in some ways," Astra says.

"It was. Madeline had the goods on everybody. And she was going to get full immunity for her testimony. With her, they were going to be able to cut the heads off a lot of snakes," she tells us. "Which obviously meant she had a lot of people looking to take her head off first."

"When you went to visit her at Whitehorn, you made sure you weren't being followed, right?" I ask.

Voight gives me a sour look. "I've been doing this for a long time, Agent Wilder. I know how to look for tails. And no, I was never followed to Whitehorn."

"I just had to ask. No offense," I say.

"None taken," she replies and runs a hand over her face. "What a mess. I'm tempted to go up to the tenth floor and rip James's head off for this."

I cock my head. "You don't think he had anything to do with her death, do you?"

She shakes her head. "Craig? Definitely not. He faints if he sees blood when he cuts himself shaving," she says. "He wouldn't have the spine to kill somebody. Besides, he'd have no motive to kill her. He was going to use this case against the Russians and the Chinese as a springboard to higher office."

"He's a climber," I note.

"He redefines climber. I've never met a bigger political animal," she tells us. "The man chases headlines like his life depends on it."

"Great. A showboat," Astra comments.

Voight nods. "The man is most definitely a peacock. And he's in love with the sound of his own voice."

"Did Craig know where you'd stashed her?" I ask.

Voight nods. "Unfortunately, yes. I had to take him up there a few times recently," she says. "He was working with Madeline on her testimony because the trial is coming up. Or at least, it was coming up."

I frown and look away for a moment. I can't think of any more questions for the Chief right now. It seems obvious to me that she's in the clear.

"Chief, I need to ask for your discretion," I tell her. "This conversation should remain between the three of us while our investigation is ongoing."

"My lips are sealed, Agent Wilder."

"Thank you."

"Catch this guy and stick him in a cage, Agents," she says. "Madeline didn't deserve this. She didn't deserve any of this."

"We're going to do our very best, Chief."

CHAPTER FIFTEEN

Office of James Craig, US Attorney, Western District of Washington; Seattle, WA

A S LONG AS WE WERE IN THE NEIGHBORHOOD, WE DECIDED to take the elevator up to the tenth floor to drop in on US Attorney James Craig. I figure we'll rattle his cage and see what comes of it. If anything. Before the doors even slide open though, I already have a feeling I'm not going to like this guy. Not one bit.

"So, that was an enlightening conversation with Voight," Astra comments as we step into the elevator car.

"It was," I confirm. "It's made an even bigger hash of things now."

"You can say that again," she says. "I'm going to blame Rick though, since he's the one who threw a wrench into our plans to begin with."

"That's fair. We'll flog him when we get back."

"Can't wait."

The door opens and we turn right then walk down a short hallway and come to a glass door marked with the embossed seal of the Department of Justice. I pull it open and we step into a lobby that's got a floor made of marble and seems to be trying to drum up a little bit of the gravitas the rest of the building lacks. The room has one door across from us that's also glass and embossed with the seal, and I'm guessing is bulletproof. An electronic keypad sits to the right. You obviously need the combination to access the rest of the office.

The walls in the lobby are all a light gray, and like the Marshals Office, photos of the President and Vice President flanked by the Stars and Stripes adorn one side while the Washington state flag on the other. Set below the photos, there's a third framed picture of US Attorney James Craig. It's a subtle, subliminal message he's sending though. It tells anybody looking at that wall Craig thinks he deserves to be mentioned in the same breath as the President and Vice President. It tells me Voight was right about Craig having a high opinion of himself and that he's a climber. And a peacock.

Framed, generic artwork hangs on the other walls and the atmosphere is very staid and solemn. It's as if anybody who walks through those doors needs to understand the weight of the work being done there. To our right is a mahogany desk occupied by an attractive blonde woman. Her hair is pulled back into a twist and under the desk, I can see she's got long athletic legs. She's wearing a blue pencil skirt, a white blouse, and a matching jacket. She's got stylish, black-framed glasses and looks like her makeup was done professionally. Apparently, US Attorney Craig prefers that his receptionists look like lingerie models, which I find a little misogynistic. Yeah, I'm really not going to like this guy.

"Hi, may I help you?" the woman asks.

We flash her our badges which makes her perfectly plumped

and lined lips pull down into a frown. She looks from our creds back up to us.

"SSA Wilder. Special Agent Russo," I tell her. "We need to speak with Mr. Craig."

"Oh, I don't believe he's receiving visitors today—"

"Visitors? We're not visitors. This isn't some high school field trip," I demand. "We are federal agents here on official business— business that involves Mr. Craig. So, I suggest you pick up that phone, dial his extension, and tell him that we are out here at the direction of the Director of the FBI, and he better carve a couple of minutes out of his busy schedule for us."

As she picks up her phone, Astra and I step away from her desk to give her some privacy. We turn our backs to her to keep her from seeing us grinning.

"Wow. You were like all authoritative and stuff," Astra says. "How'd that feel?"

"Pretty good, actually. Thought I might try it out for a change," I tell her.

"I think you may have taken ten years off that poor girl's life."

"I'm tired of getting the run-around," I say. "And there is no way in hell I'm going to let Craig weasel his way out of a chat with us."

"Yeah well, he still might."

"He can try," I growl. "I scared the girl into making the call. If needs be, I can scare her into giving us the code for the door."

"Remind me to avoid getting on your bad side."

"You're a big girl. You can remember that on your own."

Astra laughs softly. Behind us, the sound of a phone being hung up draws our attention and she turns around. The young woman clears her throat and gets to her feet, avoiding eye contact with us, and walks over to the door.

"Mr. Craig will see you now," she says as she punches in the code. "Just go straight back and take a left at the hallway. Mr. Craig's door is at the end."

There's a loud buzz and the girl opens the door for us. Astra goes through and before I follow, I turn to the girl and give her a smile.

"Sorry. Didn't mean to be so gruff," I tell her honestly. "And thank you."

"Y—you're welcome."

I follow Astra through the bullpen. It's a hive of activity as the paralegals and other assorted staff are doing the work that makes the actual attorneys look good. I catch the curious looks at us as we pass by as well as the guys openly gawking at Astra's backside. Some things will never change. We get to the hallway and take a left, then walk down to the door which is propped open.

"Come in, Agents," he calls before we even knock.

I see the camera discreetly mounted high in the corner. Mr. Craig apparently likes to see who's coming to his office door before they arrive. My cynical but oftentimes realistic mind makes me think it's because he doesn't want to be caught off guard doing something a man in his position shouldn't be doing.

We step through the door, and I close it behind us. Craig is sitting in his oversized captain's chair behind his very oversized desk. The furniture in his office all looks to be made of oak or walnut. All handcrafted, showroom-style pieces. Like Assistant Chief Voight a couple floors down, the wall behind his desk is glass and overlooks the city—only from a higher vantage point. There's a sitting area off to the side of the office with matching sofas sitting across from one another, separated by an oval-shaped coffee table made of the same wood as everything else.

Craig has a giant ego wall to the left of his desk. It's covered in his framed diplomas, letters of commendation, photographs of him with various celebrities and other dignitaries. Everything about that wall screams, "look at me, look at me." It's the exact opposite of Voight's wall, and to me, is far less impressive. The other wall is dominated by a bookcase filled with various books of case law on the lower shelves while the top couple of shelves are littered with personal mementos.

As for US Attorney James Craig himself, the man is all style, and from where I sit, little substance. He's wearing a personally mono-grammed shirt with cufflinks that look like they cost more than I make in a year. His hair is perfectly coiffed, his teeth are so white they practically glow, and despite living in Seattle, he has an all-over golden California tan. The guy looks like he spends more time primping and preening than on matters of law.

"Please, have a seat, ladies," he says, gesturing to the plush wingbacks.

"It's Agents," I reply as we take a seat, setting my folder in my lap.

"Apologies," he says with a condescending chuckle. "Can I offer you coffee? Tea?"

"No, thank you," I reply.

"All right, so what is it I can do for you la—Agents?"

"We're here investigating the death of Madeline Donaldson."

A sour expression crosses his face. "Yeah. That stinking mess," he grumbles. "Couldn't have come at a worse time. A year of work down the damn drain. And even worse, we have nothing anymore. Our case is dead."

"Yeah. I'm sure being killed was pretty inconvenient for Madeline too," I fire back.

"Killed? No, she killed herself."

"And where did you come by that information, Mr. Craig?" Astra asks.

"It's all in the file—"

"No, you're not answering my question," Astra interrupts. "Where did you get the information you put in that file?"

He glowers at her for a moment. "I looked at the postmortem forms filled out by Dr. Stein. He concluded that Ms. Donaldson died of self-inflicted asphyxiation."

"So, you are just accepting the word of a man whose organization would be the target of any investigation?" I raise an eyebrow. "That is, if an investigation were actually conducted."

"I know you're not here to lecture me or tell me how to do my job, Agents."

"Somebody should," I shrug. "Because from where I sit, you're not doing your job. Not even close, Mr. Craig."

"Please tell me you can see the conflict of interest in accepting the findings of a person who might be culpable in Madeline's death, Mr. Craig," Astra chimes in.

"Look, does it really matter?" he snaps. "She's dead and my case, what was going to be the biggest case of my career, died with her."

"Your compassion is really something to behold," I say.

"Way to make somebody's death all about you," Astra snipes.

"You can't come in here and talk to me like that. Do you even know who I am?" he almost shouts.

"I do know who you are," I say. "You're the guy who made the mess we have to come in here and clean up."

"I don't appreciate your tone, Agent Wilder."

"Sorry about it," I say. "But by accepting Dr. Stein's findings sight unseen, you made one hell of a mess."

"What are you talking about? She killed herself—"

"No, Mr. Craig. She didn't," I cut him off, my voice hard with anger. "She was murdered."

"That's garbage. She hung herself."

I pull a copy of Rebekah's report out of my folder and slide it across the table to him. Craig looks at the page like it's a snake, coiled and ready to strike. I sit back in my seat though, content to wait him out. He sighs dramatically and picks up the report. I give him a few minutes to look it over and watch as he fights to control his expression. He all but blanches as he reads the report, and I can only imagine he's having visions of his career circling the toilet bowl. He drops the page and glowers at us.

"And who gave you the authority to have her exhumed and autopsied?" he demands.

"Yeah, because that's what's important here," I crack.

"It is important. Who gave you the authority?"

I struggle to keep my composure but he's really trying my patience. "Our authority comes from the Director of the FBI by way of main Justice and the Attorney General of the United States—who, if I'm not mistaken, is your boss."

"You're welcome to call the Director to verify if you'd like," Astra adds.

Craig frowns knowing we've got his boy parts in a vise. He says nothing for a long moment, obviously struggling with the situation. If what Voight said about him is true, I'm sure he's calculating the damage that will be done to his reputation and political ambitions if this gets out. I'm no expert but I'd guess the damage would be pretty substantial.

"What do you want?" he growls, all pretense of civility gone.

"For starters, I want to know how you screwed this up so bad?" I ask. "How could you sign off on a suicide when it was very clearly a homicide?"

He says nothing but looks down at the top of his desk, a frown stretching across his lips. He's struggling with the answer, but I think I know what it is. And it infuriates me.

"It's because she didn't matter to you. Not as a person," I state. "All you cared about was racking up a big win in court. Making the case. You didn't give a damn about Madeline so when she died, you didn't care enough to do the work that needed to be done."

He raises his head and glares at me. "Please. Like you're any different," he spits. "You have CI's. You use them and don't think about them beyond what they can do for you."

"That's where you're wrong. They're people to me first," I say. "And if I screwed up and got them killed, I'd sure as hell do what was necessary for them. You and I are not alike, Mr. Craig. Not even close."

"Got her killed? What are you talking about?"

"Nobody knew she was there but Chief Voight and you," I say. "You knew what she was up against. Knew what sort of animals were hunting her."

"What are you saying?"

"That you have a mole in your office," Astra says bluntly.

"That is not only outrageous, it's offensive," he sneers.

"But it's true," Astra presses.

"I assume you have some proof to be throwing out allegations like that," he growls indignantly.

"Nobody but Chief Voight and your office knew where Madeline was being stashed," Astra doubles down. "And I'm relatively certain Chief Voight wouldn't have told if somebody was peeling the skin from her bones. That leaves your office."

"She makes a compelling point," I say. "So, I'm going to need a list of all your employees who have so much as looked in the direction of Madeline's case file—"

"Let me stop you right there," he interrupts. "I won't be turning over the names of my employees. And you may have the authority to reopen this case, but you do not have the authority to demand the sensitive information you want. I am the US Attorney for the Western District of Washington. That's not nothin'. I have friends in high places of my own. You really don't want to push me, ladies."

"You're awfully defensive, counselor," I observe. "It's a simple request."

"It's an invasion of privacy."

"Tell me, Mr. Craig,' Astra says. "Are you simply afraid of this getting out? Are you really going to deny an innocent woman justice—"

"We're done here, ladies," he says just to get under my skin. "I'm afraid I have a meeting to attend so I must ask you to leave."

Astra and I look at each other for a moment, then get to our feet. This is obviously a waste of time. I just can't imagine being so worried about my reputation that I'd try to defend my negligence. It's arrogant. It's hubristic. It's infuriating. And it's also a waste of time because Craig isn't going to ever think, let alone admit, he'd done something wrong.

"We'll be back, Mr. Craig," I warn him. "This case is getting deep and I kind of feel like you're up to your butt in it. We'll find out if it's just your negligence and incompetence—"

"Or something more," Astra finishes for me.

"You two may go now."

I stand where I am for a long moment, my eyes burning holes into him. He looks like he wants to say something, wants to verbally thrash us. But he's smart enough to know there are times when silence is the right way to go. And he seems to believe this is one of those times because he closes his mouth and looks away. He pointedly picks up his phone then gestures vaguely to the door, as if to dismiss us.

Astra and I exchange a look and I can see the annoyance on her face. But she holds it together and we turn then walk out of his office. We make our way back through the bullpen and out to the elevator, stepping in just before the doors slide closed. As the car descends, Astra turns and looks at me.

"He seems nice," Astra says.

I laugh softly. "He got defensive pretty quick."

"I probably would too," she replies. "I mean, he's either negligent and incompetent—"

"Or he's hiding something," I finish.

Astra nods. "Exactly."

"Well, let's find out which it is."

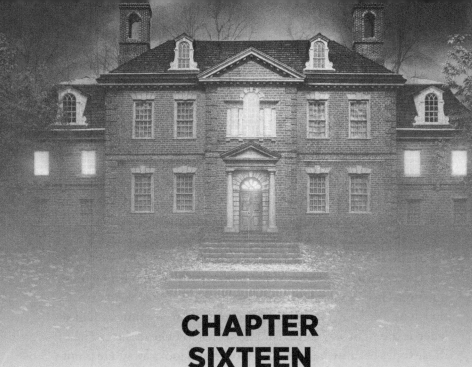

CHAPTER SIXTEEN

Bayview Motor Lodge; Woodcreek, WA

I PACE THE FLOOR OF MY BUNGALOW, TAPPING A PEN AGAINST my bottom lip as Astra sits on my bed with her back up against the headboard and her laptop sitting open on her lap. She's focused on something and I can see her eyes moving back and forth as she reads.

"The Russian mob. The Chinese Triads," I muse aloud. "A doctor who thinks he has everything to lose. A US Attorney who has even more to lose than that. The man who got her pregnant—"

"And a partridge in a pear tree," Astra jumps in. "We also shouldn't rule out some garden variety freak who gets off on murdering people."

"Fair. But I don't think your garden variety freak would have the skill to get into the hospital and then into Madeline's room without being seen or leaving any trace," I say.

"You never know. Our garden variety freaks are getting more sophisticated by the day."

I laugh. "Why can't they just be stupid for a change?"

"That would be nice, wouldn't it?" she says.

"So, we've got a list of suspects that has suddenly grown as long as my arm. I'm pretty sure more people wanted to kill this girl than want to kill my sister."

Astra laughs softly. "That's dark."

I shrug. "But true."

Astra sighs. "So, we find a way to narrow that list down," she says. "One pertinent question, do we think Stein or Craig have any involvement in Madeline's death?"

I shrug. "Hard to say at this point. We know they had a hand in the coverup. Which to me, suggests they might have had something to do with her death," I say. "But that is far from definitive. I mean, they certainly had the means and opportunity. But I'm lacking any sort of a motive from either of them to kill her."

"Well, now that we know the Russian mob and the Chinese Triads are in play, it could come down to something as simple as money. Greed," she offers. "Maybe they were paid a healthy sum to get the job done."

"It's a good thought and one worth looking into. But as far as Stein goes, I would bet he makes far more running Whitehorn than the Russians or the Chinese could have given him," I say. "Craig makes a pretty decent sum, but probably not as much as he would in a private law firm. He might be tempted to cash in on a big payday, but he'd have to balance that against his political ambitions. Any hint of being connected to a murder and his obvious desire to sit in the Oval would be down the drain."

"Maybe somebody has some leverage over either Stein or Craig—or both—and used it to squeeze them to kill her then cover it up."

"That's a possibility too. I mean, they definitely covered it up,"

I acknowledge. "Whether that was intentional or just plain negligence we don't know."

Astra shakes her head. "There are just so many maybes and what-ifs. Nothing is making sense right now."

I pick up my phone and dial then put it on speaker. Rick picks up the call on the second ring, sounding like he's half-asleep.

"You awake?" I ask.

"I am now, thanks," he replies with a chuckle. "Sorry, I must have nodded off for a minute going through all this code. What's up?"

"I need your magic," I say.

"That's what all the ladies say."

"Let's leave your cousins out of this, Scanlon," Astra pipes in.

"Oh, somebody's feisty today," he cracks. "Anyway, what do you need, boss?"

"I need you to dig up the financials on Stein and Craig," I say. "I mean, I need everything. Shell corporations they might be routing money through, any hidden accounts—I need you to dig deep, Rick."

"Go full truffle pig on them, Scanlon."

"Got it. I will start getting deep in their backside immediately."

"Good. I want you to give what you dig up to Mo and have her run through them for abnormalities, any recurrent patterns—anything unusual."

"Yes, ma'am," he says. "Are these two suspects?"

"We suspect them of something," I tell him. "We're just not sure what yet."

"That's cryptic."

"Well, we're still trying to sweep up the mess you left behind when you dropped that bombshell on us," I say. "This is where we're at."

"Which is basically nowhere right now," Astra adds.

"Hence, the grumpiness and feistiness," Rick chirps. "I get it now."

"When we get back, I'm going to beat you bloody," Astra promises.

"Remember what I said about the workplace violence seminar we just took?"

"Who said anything about the workplace?" Astra asks. "I know where you live, fool."

Astra is grinning and all I can do is roll my eyes and shake my head. They're like siblings, I swear to God. But the camaraderie between them is a good thing. It's how I always envisioned my team to be—a family. So, if there's anybody to blame for their constant back and forth, it's me. They make me laugh.

"Let's stay focused, children," I tell them.

"Right. I'm going to dig up every piece of financial dirt on these two cats that I can," Rick says. "I got it."

"There's more," I say. "I need you to dig up a roster of people working in the US Attorney's office. Specifically, the names of those people working directly under James Craig."

"James Craig? Wow, you two really are going big game hunting, aren't you?" he asks.

"Just going where the breadcrumbs lead us. We need a full list of staff and personnel."

"You realize that's public information, right? You could get it yourself," he says.

"I pay you to get it for me, Rick."

"All right, all right. Anything else?"

"Just forward us those names when you get them. In fact, prioritize that list," I tell him. "And have Mo do a deep dive on those people. I want to start knocking names off our ever-expanding suspect list."

"You got it, boss."

"Thank you, Rick."

"Always a pleasure," he replies.

I disconnect the call and drop my phone on the table then start to pace, folding my arms over my chest as I let my mind work on this Gordian knot. It's like all we have are "flap As" with no "slot Bs" to put any of these disparate parts into. And that is keeping us from making any headway on this investigation. We've got a rogue's gallery of bad guys who would have likely lined up to kill this girl, but no indication who actually did it. We've also got two powerful men who seem to have covered up Madeline's death but no real motive for them doing so.

It looks bad. It absolutely looks like they were complicit in covering up a murder. But if you turn that picture ever so slightly, it could also look like simple negligence. Stein would definitely make more money pumping out his pharmaceuticals than the mob would have offered him, so I can't see him risking his golden goose to do a solid for them. A one-time payment of even tens of millions of dollars doesn't trump the ongoing payment that will total hundreds of millions he stands to make over the course of his life.

Then there's Craig. His ambition makes him ultra-sensitive to even the barest hint of scandal or whiff of impropriety. Craig doesn't see other people as human beings. He sees them as commodities. He uses people and their value to him extends only as far as their usefulness. When Madeline died, so too did her usefulness to him. It seems to track with his personality that with no further use to him, Madeline ceased to be. I can absolutely see that he'd be so disinterested in her that he'd sign it off as a suicide simply because he no longer cared enough about her to pay attention to the details.

However, if he were involved with Madeline's death, it would more than likely only be if he was well insulated from it. But I have to question why he'd be involved in the first place. Again, the lack of a motive for Craig—and Stein for that matter—makes me really question whether they were actively engaged with her death or simply negligent after the fact. Were they, as Astra had suggested, being leveraged by something? I know that Stein has no family that can be used against him. Nor does he have any obvious pressure points. Nothing that can be squeezed hard enough to make him squeal.

"Hey, Craig doesn't have family, does he?" I ask.

Astra taps a couple of keys on her laptop and shakes her head. "Only child. Mother died about ten years ago," she tells me. "His father is in a nursing home back east. Advanced case of Alzheimer's apparently."

"So, it's not like he's got family that can be used as leverage," I mutter to myself as I continue to pace.

"All right, so neither Stein nor Craig have family being used to leverage their cooperation," Astra muses. "So why cover up her murder?"

"That's the million-dollar question," I reply.

A moment of silence descends over the room as I continue trying to crack that particular nut. I keep coming back to the idea that it was simple negligence and a dereliction of duty on both of their parts. Neither one of them gave a damn for Madeline. I personally feel it's established as fact neither of them cares about anybody who isn't useful to them. It's established as fact in my mind anyway. I watched them both closely. The disregard, even contempt, they have for others who have no practical use to them isn't that hard to see.

So from that perspective, it's not hard to subscribe to the idea that they didn't care enough to get the details on her death right. They simply signed off on whatever was most expedient to get it off their plates so they could move on to something else. Madeline's death inconvenienced them both and they wanted to take the easiest route to washing their hands of it—and her—completely.

As I pace, I turn that over in my mind again and again. On the one hand, it feels right. It feels very much in line with how I've profiled them both. Everything lines up. Everything fits. I still can't help but feel like it's too simple of an explanation though. Something niggling in the back of my mind is making me think there's more to the story. That I'm missing something. For the life of me, I can't figure out what it is though.

I shake my head. It's also possible that I'm not missing anything and that I'm just searching for answers and meaning when there is none to be had. Not everything is going to make sense. Not everything can be wrapped up with a bright, shiny bow. Sometimes, people are just... bad. Sometimes, people have no care or compassion for anybody. Some people are definitely narcissistic enough to believe other people are there simply to serve some purpose to them. And when that purpose has been served, those people can simply be thrown away like a piece of garbage.

"So, I've been doing some digging into this group... this *Chlopciki*. They're definitely an offshoot of the Odessa Mafia. And they're Ukrainian, not Russian," Astra says. "That's actually a Ukrainian word."

"Last I heard, the Odessa Mafia was operating out of New York, Miami, and San Francisco," I say.

"They've branched out, I guess. There are identified branches in Los Angeles, Chicago, Dallas, and you guessed it, Seattle," Astra tells me.

I nod as I process it all. The Odessa Mafia is historically one of the most secretive criminal organizations around. It's proved next to impossible to infiltrate, and although they've got their tentacles in everything from human trafficking to narcotics to loansharking, making cases against them has proven as difficult as infiltrating them. They're tight-knit and organized. Paranoid, even. And not even the Armenians, who have made brutality an art form, are half as violent and savage as the Ukrainians.

I stop pacing and lean against the low chest of drawers, my arms still folded over my chest. Pursing my lips, I look down at the carpeting, which is dark and patterned. Like the bedspread, it's designed to cleverly hide the stains. I look up at Astra as a question hits me like a lightning bolt out of a clear blue sky. She gives me a grin, telling me she's already arrived at that question and was simply waiting for me to catch up.

"What is an international organization like the Odessa Mafia doing in a small, backwater town like Woodcreek?" I ask.

"Bingo," she says.

"I say we go find out."

"I'm two steps ahead of you," Astra says. "As usual."

CHAPTER SEVENTEEN

Little Kiev District; Woodcreek, WA

"WELL, IT'S NO BRIGHTON BEACH, BUT IT'S SIZEABLE," I remark.

"Fun fact, Woodcreek has the largest population of Russian and Ukrainian immigrants on the West Coast," Astra informs me.

Over the years, as Woodcreek has grown and prospered, different cultural enclaves have sprung up around the city. There is a section of the city that's mostly Chinese immigrants. One small section dominated by Italians. And of course, Little Kiev. As we walk down the street, I can feel the eyes on us. We stand out like sore thumbs. These cultural enclaves being as insular as they usually are, strangers are not usually trusted. Or welcome, really. Especially ones like us, who apparently have 'cop vibes', as Astra likes to so eloquently put it.

We pass a bakery that has the most delicious aromas flowing

from it. But the table out in front has three men, all in nicely tailored suits and fedoras sipping espressos and talking quietly among themselves. It couldn't look more like a scene out of a mobster movie if there were cameras and a director shouting "action" nearby. As we pass by, I see all three heads turn, their gazes following us down the street. This time though, I don't think they're admiring Astra's posterior. They're obviously tied to Odessa, and since we're strangers in Little Kiev, they're obviously sizing us up.

Astra leads us down a narrow side street and we pass a small group of boys on skates playing street hockey. I watch as they streak toward the goal, bumping and jostling each other. I've always been amazed that hockey players can do the things they do on blades. Skating is difficult enough on its own. But when you add in all the elbowing, shoving, and hard checking going on, it makes it even more difficult. Their skill is impressive. The boys stop their game and turn, openly staring at us as we pass by. Apparently, the hostility and suspicion of strangers is taught from an early age here.

"You two don't belong here," shouts one of the boys.

He skates over to us and stops a couple of feet away. He's tall and brawny for his age, with wide shoulders but a narrow waist. His features are sharp and angular, his skin pale, and his eyes a light shade of green. All the other boys look to him, marking him out as the leader of this little group. He can't be more than thirteen or fourteen, but he looks us up and down, giving us a hard stare. Somehow his eyes are tinged with steely resolve, even through his youthful face.

"You two don't belong here," he repeats, his voice tinged with a hint of a Russian accent.

"No?" I ask.

He shakes his head. "No."

"And why is that?" I ask.

"You're not Russian. You're not Ukrainian," he says. "This place is ours. Not yours."

I give him a smile. "And who told you that? Your father?"

He nods. "Yes. And my uncles."

"Oh? And who are they?"

He opens his mouth to reply then closes it again, obviously thinking better of it. He glares at us like he hates us though, and the only thing I can think is that he's being taught to hate outsiders, likely by the very father and uncles he just mentioned. It's a shame, really. A kid like him should be free to enjoy playing with his friends, not aggressively posturing like this to two women twice his size. I would almost prefer that he and his friends were actively ogling me and Astra instead of this—better to be a normal thirteen-year-old boy gawking at women than to find yourself tangled up in international turf wars. But something tells me the streets of Little Kiev are filled with lots of boys his age being fed the same toxic nonsense from their elders.

"You should go," the boy finally says. "Before something bad happens."

I hold open my coat and show him my badge and my weapon. He eyes them, totally unimpressed. Like he's seen guns a million times before. I give it some thought and figure he probably has.

"It's not smart to threaten federal agents," I tell him. "Not smart at all, kid."

"I'm not threatening you. Just telling you a fact."

I look at him for a long moment. "You ever hear of the *Chlopciki*?" I ask.

"You shouldn't mention the *Chlopciki*. You should never mention them again," he says. "They'll come for you if you talk about them."

I grin. "Like the bogeyman?"

"Worse," he says, his tone grave. "Much worse."

"Uh-huh," I reply. "You should go back to your hockey game. You look good out there. Got some speed and nice moves with the puck."

He smiles briefly but then seems to remember that I'm a

stranger—and a cop to boot—and the smile quickly vanishes, replaced by that hard scowl that sadly, seems to be his default expression. Then he turns and skates off to rejoin his friends. They all huddle together though and keep looking at us suspiciously.

"It's sad they learn to hate so young," I say.

Astra nods. "It really is."

We turn and continue on down the street. We could have driven, but I wanted to get a feel for this community. Wanted to see what it was like, and more importantly, what the people are like. It's honestly about what I expected. About fifteen minutes later, we come to our destination. We stand on a small rise that overlooks the docks and the sprawling complex of warehouses, most of them owned by different business entities. And undoubtedly, there are a large number of those business entities are owned and operated by the *Chlopciki*.

"This makes sense now," I say. "I see why this mob offshoot would set up shop here in Woodcreek."

Astra nods. "Little to no oversight. No prying eyes watching what they're doing."

It's smart, I have to say. A small town like Woodcreek isn't going to have the sort of security that a major port like the one in Seattle would have. In theory, a group like the *Chlopciki* would have free rein to bring in whatever they wanted—especially since it seems like they control a good chunk of the docks down here. All around us, I see signs in Cyrillic. There is another, smaller port on the other side of town that services the fishing fleet we saw earlier, but this one looks like it's bringing in commercial goods. And it's controlled by the Ukrainians.

"What do you think?" she asks.

"I think you're pretty brilliant."

"That goes without saying," Astra says with a grin.

I laugh softly. "This would be the perfect place to smuggle in contraband goods," I say. "The Ukrainians control the port on this side of town, obviously. Nothing stopping them from bringing in anything and everything they want."

I spot a small building marked US Customs and Port Authority tucked between some of the larger warehouses.

"Let's go have a closer look," I say as I gesture to that building.

We head over to the Customs building, watching the activity all around us. Forklifts rumble, carrying pallets of goods from marshaling yards to their warehouse destinations. The markings on the crate are in Cyrillic but also have English translations below that. I see rugs, furniture, and a variety of other mundane things being transported to the various warehouses and can't help but wonder what's really in the boxes.

Chances are most of it is just what the markings say they are. But I'd bet a year's salary that some of those boxes contain anything from coke, to oxy, to fentanyl. Unfortunately, I don't have nearly enough to get us a warrant, so as much as I'd like to, I can't go cracking open crates all willy-nilly. There is no judge in this country who'd sign off on my gut instinct. But this gives us a very good, very important place to start.

We step into the Customs office. It's small. There is a row of six hard plastic chairs lined up beneath the front window with two more on the wall perpendicular to that. The floor is covered in a white linoleum that's scuffed and dirty, and the walls are covered in informative posters. A plastic plant stands in the corner beside a water cooler and the fluorescent lights overhead cast the office in a harsh, sharp glare.

Directly in front of us is a chest-high counter. A bored-looking man is standing behind it; he barely flicks his eyes up from his magazine as we walk in. He's got warm, tawny skin, dark eyes, and dark hair. He's a man of average height and weight, looks to be in his early twenties, and doesn't have anything too exceptional about him that I can see. He's good-looking, I guess, but also looks like the sort you'd forget five minutes after meeting him. He's dressed in the dark blue work shirt with the patches of his agency on the sleeves and a name patch above his breast pocket that says, "Sanchez."

"Can I help you?" he asks.

We approach the counter and badge him. "SSA Wilder, Special Agent Russo of the FBI," I announce. "Seattle Field Office."

He stands up a little straighter and more interested than he did when we first walked in. Sanchez closes the magazine and pushes it to the side.

"What is it I can do for you, Agents?" he asks.

"I'd like to see your receiving logs for the last month," I say.

"Uh, sure. Was there a specific company you wanted to look at?" he asks.

"Give us the two busiest companies to start," I reply. "I'd like to see how often they take deliveries."

"Oh, that would be Ural Furnishings and Brighton Imports and Exports," he tells us. "They do a brisk business around here."

"Great. We'll start there."

"Umm… all right," he says uncertainly.

He steps back to a file cabinet and opens a drawer, then starts pawing through the papers inside, looking for the right files.

"Can I ask what this is about?" he asks.

"Routine inspection," I tell him. "We just want to make sure everything's up to snuff around here."

"Oh, we're pretty diligent with our paperwork, I can assure you," he says.

"We're sure you are," Astra tells him. "But we have to be just as diligent with our paperwork too, so we have to make these trips."

"Huh, he says. I honestly can't recall the FBI ever coming in here," he tells us with a nervous laugh. "Guess not everybody's as diligent as you two."

"Well, they should be," Astra replies. "There's a right way and a wrong way to do the jobs we do."

"Amen to that," he says. "Oh, here we are."

He's just started to pull a thick file out of the drawer when a door behind the desk opens and a tall, authoritative man steps out. He's wearing the same uniform as Sanchez and has short gray hair and light blue eyes. He's got broad shoulders, a barrel chest, a comfortable paunch around his midsection, and a thick mustache on his top lip.

"What's going on out here?" he asks, his voice deep and gravelly.

"Agents Russo and Wilder," Astra says. "We're just doing a routine paperwork check."

The man, whose name patch identifies him as Hartman, looks over at Sanchez, who immediately freezes in place. He looks from us to his superior, an expression of uncertainty on his face. Hartman walks over to Sanchez and plucks the folder from his hands. His mustache twitches as he looks at the tag.

"I'll take it from here," he tells Sanchez. "Go take a break."

Sanchez offers us an apologetic glance before turning and scurrying through the door in the back of the office and out of sight. Hartman turns to us and very deliberately slips the file back into the drawer then closes it.

"Afraid I can't give this to you," he grumbles. "The companies who do business here expect a modicum of privacy."

I clear my throat and frown. "I don't see how giving us a look at their shipping manifests violates that privacy in any way."

"Unless there are things on those shipping manifests they don't want us to see," Astra adds. "Is that the case, Agent Hartman?"

A small grin quirks a corner of his mouth upward. "Yeah, those fancy feebie interrogation tricks don't work on me. Nice try, though."

"Why are you opposed to letting us see the manifests?" I ask.

"Because they're not your business. They fall under my purview, not the FBI's," he says. "You want to see them, you go through the proper chain of command. Or you get a warrant. One of the two. I don't know how they do things at the FBI, but we don't cut corners around here."

I pinch the bridge of my nose and try to hold in my frustration. I feel Astra bristling beside me and give her a subtle nudge with my elbow to keep her from going Krakatoa on the guy. Though, I'd be lying if I said it wouldn't be satisfying.

"Agent Hartman, we're trying to solve a murder. The clues we have led us here," I tell him. "All I'm looking for is a little interagency cooperation."

"I'd be glad to cooperate. I'll give you all the manifests you want," he replies. "Just as soon as you go through the proper channels."

"Look, I understand you're getting off on this little power trip and that this fiefdom you've carved out for yourself here is what gives your life meaning," Astra finally snaps. "But we're trying to solve an actual murder here. On the scale of importance, it ranks about a billion rungs up from what you do—"

"Okay, we're done here. You two can see yourselves out," he cuts her off. "And don't come back into my—fiefdom—without the appropriate paperwork."

We watch as he turns and walks back through that door, slamming it hard enough behind him to rattle the framed pictures on the wall. I turn to Astra, and we walk out of the office frustrated and empty-handed.

"Well, that didn't go as well as I hoped it would," I said.

"That paper-pushing, pencil-necked, micropen—"

I laugh. "Yeah, maybe insulting him wasn't exactly the right way to go."

"He wasn't going to give us anything anyway."

"No. He wasn't," I admit. "You're not wrong."

"Then there was no harm done in making fun of the guy."

Going through the proper channels could take weeks. Bureaucratic red tape is one of the worst things in human history. It's not often that agencies refuse to cooperate with one another out of hand like that. The fact that he did, and did it so quickly, is putting dark thoughts in my head and I don't really like it.

"Was it a power trip?" I ask. "Or is he being paid to play these games?"

Astra blows out a long breath. "It's a tossup at this point."

"Yeah, that's kind of what I was afraid of."

CHAPTER EIGHTEEN

Bayview Motor Lodge; Woodcreek, WA

AFTER FINISHING UP AT THE PORT, WE GRABBED SOME TAKE-out and came back to the hotel to eat and keep working. We need a theory, and we need a profile. And right now, we have neither. Before we left the warehouse district in Little Kiev though, we jotted down the names of the companies who do business there. We counted fifteen warehouses tied to different companies and have been doing what we can to run them down on our own. I've tasked Rick with enough for the moment.

"Our computer sleuthing skills suck," Astra moans from her spot at the table.

I'm sitting cross-legged on the bed with my laptop open in front of me. I frown and nod.

"Sadly, I'm forced to agree," I say.

We've been at this for a couple of hours now and haven't gotten beyond the surface with any of these companies. On paper, they all look to be legit businesses.

"I don't know how they make it look so easy," I say. "People like Rick and Brody—even Mo—know how to dig beneath the surface in ways I don't think I'm ever going to understand."

Astra nods her agreement. "We need to learn to do a lot more than Google searches."

"This is why we have people like them," I say. "We're paid to kick in doors. They're paid to kick in virtual doors. We all have our specialties."

"Yeah, we'll go with the division of labor argument," Astra agrees. "It makes us seem less stupid."

"Exactly. I like that better."

I flop back onto my pillows and add the pieces of the puzzle to the already considerable pile on my mental table. I shift them around and try to put them together in some order that makes sense. But the more I try, the more incomprehensible it gets.

"Okay, we have a murdered girl—a witness in an upcoming trial that would be a problem for a lot of wealthy, violent people. We have a US Attorney and a Chief Science Officer involved some- how. Maybe. We have ties to the Ukrainian and Chinese mobs. And a Customs agent who might or might not be on the take and hiding evidence of illegal activity for the Ukrainian mob," I say to myself. "How do these things fit together? Do they even fit together? Or are we just chasing shadows here?"

Astra growls and sits back in her chair, her face a mask of irrita- tion. She takes a drink from her water bottle and looks at it for a long moment, then sets it back down before turning to me. She frowns.

"Okay, so let's see if we can cut through the noise and pare this down to basics again," she says. "Knowing what we know now, with all the information we've gathered. Let's ask the most fundamen- tal question you asked the other night—who stands to benefit the most from Madeline's death?"

"Knowing what we know now, I'd say the *Chlopciki* benefit the most," I say. "They not only get their revenge for Madeline killing their leader, but the case against them also goes away. You heard Craig. Without her, they have no case to prosecute."

I nod. "So, the *Chlopciki* broke into Whitehorn—"

"Or were let in," Astra jumps in.

"Or were let in," I agree. "They break in and murder Madeline. Then, Stein and Craig conspire to cover it up for—reasons yet to be determined. But they stonewall Sheriff Block, falsify the cause of death, and bury the truth. Literally."

"And it was all going fine until we rolled in and mucked it all up for them," Astra finishes it off.

It's a simple but still elegant theory. There are obviously a lot of holes that still need to be plugged and things that need to be explained. But as a framework, it seems like a relatively solid theory to me. We just need to figure out how to flesh out that theory and make it stick.

"There is still a lot of clutter," Astra says. "Like the deal down at the port—"

"Some things are extraneous. Things like what's going on down at the port may not be pertinent to this investigation," I say. "But things that are worth an investigation of their own."

She nods. "I'm really curious about what they're bringing into the port they don't want us to see. It's got to be drugs. That's the only thing I can see that would bring Ukrainians and Chinese mobsters together to do business. Drugs and weapons."

"I agree. And once we wrap up with Madeline's murder, I'm going to have Mo and Rick start doing some serious snooping around," I tell her. "I want to keep these guys on our radar."

"Sounds good to me."

I copy the list of businesses into an email and send it off to Mo, asking her to dig into them when she has time, stressing that it's a low priority at the moment. After that, I get up and stretch myself out. Sitting down so long has me cramping up and I'm starting to feel kind of claustrophobic sitting in the bungalow.

"I need a little air," I say.

Astra nods distractedly. "Yeah. I'm digging into the *Chlopciki* and the Odessa Mafia a bit deeper. Or at least, I'm trying to."

I laugh. "All right. Have fun," I tell her. "I'll be back shortly."

I walk out and stroll to the edge of the parking lot. The loose dirt and gravel crunch beneath my tennis shoes, seeming impossibly loud in the utter stillness of the evening. I stand at the edge of the trees that surround the motor lodge and breathe deeply, savoring the scent of the pine trees and the musky earth. Living in Seattle, surrounded by the odor of car exhaust and just general city life makes me miss the clean and pure scents of the forest. I've always loved the smell of nature.

As I watch the way the moon sparkles off the surface of Samish Bay, I turn our theory over in my mind. It makes a lot of sense and checks a lot of the boxes. I feel that small electric hit I get when things begin falling into place. What I don't feel is that sense of building momentum that tells me we're definitely on the right track. That tells me that maybe we're missing something. That our theory is incomplete. Somewhere out there is some small piece of the puzzle that will tie it all together. What that thing is though, I have no clue.

Of course, it's also possible that there isn't one small piece. There may be several small pieces that are missing from our puzzle. Many for all I know. There are just so many things that don't add up. So many disparate parts that aren't lining up. And maybe my vision of the whole picture is skewed. Maybe my judgment is off and I'm trying to overcomplicate things. Wouldn't be the first time.

Ever since everything went down with Mark, I haven't fully trusted my judgment. I fake it really well, though. I can come across as so confident that sometimes, I even believe it myself. For a little while anyway. That little voice that lives in the back of my mind always whispers to me. It always sows the seeds of doubt in me and makes me second-guess… well, everything. It's one reason I'm so gun-shy about things with Charles and with most things in my life.

What's killing me is that my work was the one place I never doubted myself. It was the one area of my life where I was sure of myself. Confident. Strong in my belief. Even when I turned out to be wrong, I went into any situation sure I was right. But ever since Mark, I've been anything but sure. I've been anything but confident. And that's what I hate the most. I hate him for what he did to me, of course. But I hate him more for what he's made me do to myself. For instilling that feeling of doubt.

As I stand there, staring out at the bay, I hear the sound of gravel crunching and assume that Astra decided she needed some air too. But when I turn around, I feel an electric shock of fear pass through me. Three men in black, shadowy figures moving against the darkness, are making their way toward my room. Toward Astra. She's alone and has no idea they're coming, and I know if I don't do something, she's going to die.

On instinct, I reach for my weapon and silently curse myself. It's sitting on the table in my room. My fear for Astra fuels me, galvanizes my nerves, and sets me in motion. I sprint for the room, screaming for Astra at the top of my lungs. The three shadows turn toward me and one of them raises his arm. I can't see it, but I know there is a gun in his hand. I throw myself to the side and a moment later, I hear the soft coughing sound of a pistol with a sound suppressor attached to it and see the muzzle flash of the shot.

I hit the ground, shoulder first, and grit my teeth when the jarring pain shoots down my arm. I'm on my feet in a heartbeat though, and see the door to my room fly open from the corner of my eye. Good. She's no longer unaware of the threat. But as I move, I lose sight of Astra as one of the shadows closes in on her. All I can do is hope she's all right. She's a fighter and knows how to take care of herself. There's nobody else I'd rather have in a fight. But that doesn't mean I don't worry about her still.

The first shadow closes in on me. It's a man dressed in black from head to toe, the balaclava over his head leaving only his eyes visible. He raises his gun again, but I manage to slip inside his guard and push his arm away with one hand while driving my knee upward into his groin. A loud "oomph" escapes him, and he tries to keep himself from doubling over from the pain, but the momentary delay gives me the opening I need.

I drive my fist into his face, then grab his wrist and twist it viciously. The man screams and drops the gun. I move quickly and kick it away. It skitters across the gravel and as I turn back to finish him off, I see the flash of the moonlight glinting on the edge of a blade. I spin but not fast enough and feel the knife slip across my ribs, then immediately feel the rush of warm blood spilling down my body. I grimace with the pain but push it away. If I give in to it, if I hesitate or flinch, I'm going to die.

I spin back around and grab the hand with the knife. He throws a punch with his other hand that catches me in the side of the head. The ringing in my ears is loud and I see stars bursting in my vision. The blow staggers and weakens me, and I almost fall to my knees, but I somehow manage to maintain my grip on his wrist. Using a move I learned in a self-defense class, I'm able to turn his wrist so the blade is facing him. I throw myself backward and carry him with me. As I fall, I hear the sound of gunfire. It's loud and makes the ringing in my ears sound even louder.

I feel weightless for a moment but then hit the ground with bone-jarring force. The man lands on top of me, driving the breath from my lungs. But he lies completely still and when I push him off me, I crawl to my hands and knees and see the hilt of his blade protruding from his chest. His eyes are wide open and unseeing as he stares into the darkness above.

The blood is still cascading down my side as I grab hold of it and turn, searching for Astra. She's standing alone in the glow of the light spilling from the open door to my room, her attackers gone.

The gun is hanging limply in her hand and she's looking down at her midsection, her face growing pale. The crimson stain on her shirt is growing and I feel my heart drop into my stomach. She raises her eyes to me. They're wide and filled with a fear unlike anything I've ever seen from her before.

The gun hits the ground with a solid thud, then Astra drops to her knees, her hand covering the wound in her belly, her face etched with pain.

"Astra!" I scream in absolute terror as I dash over to her.

CHAPTER NINETEEN

Woodcreek General Hospital; Woodcreek, WA

A S I STAND OUTSIDE ASTRA'S ROOM, LOOKING IN AT HER through the window, I have to fight back the waves of tears that are threatening to overwhelm me. She's sitting up in the bed, talking to one of the nurses. She's pale and drawn and it seems like her every movement sends a grimace of pain across her face.

"She's a lucky woman," Sheriff Block rumbles as he steps up beside me.

"She got shot," I snap. "You and I must have different definitions of the word lucky."

He shrugs his wide shoulders. "It was a clean through and through," he points out. "Went through her oblique and didn't hit any organs. I'd say that's pretty lucky."

"Yeah. You're right," I say softly. "Sorry, I'm just rattled."

"I'd be worried about you if you weren't," he replies. "You and your partner went through some stuff out there. It's only human to have some feelin' about it."

"Yeah, I suppose so."

I sniff loudly and look down at the ground beneath me, trying to keep it from shifting anymore. My wound was minor, the cut superficial. I didn't even need stitches. They patched me up and got me back on my feet in no time. If I hadn't moved the way I did, when I did, it would have been a different story. I would probably be as dead as the guy I left behind. My reflexes saved me. I suppose I'm pretty lucky too.

I raise my head and look at the sheriff. The hotel manager had called the sheriff when he heard the shooting, then the paramedics when he came out and saw the carnage. Thank God he did. I was paralyzed by the sight of Astra bleeding out in front of me. The only thought in my head was that I would be breaking the only promise I've ever made to Benjamin—to send her home safe every night.

"Do we have an ID on the dead guy yet?" I ask.

Block shakes his head. "The man is a ghost. Prints aren't in the system. He had no ID," he says. "About the only thing I can tell you is that he's Chinese. Got that from the morgue attendant just a couple of minutes ago."

I sigh. Chinese. As in the Triads. I shake my head, figuring that somebody got wind of Astra and me poking around the docks today and sent three Triad goons to take care of us. I'd assumed, according to our theory, that the *Chlopciki* were providing the Triads with drugs. But the fact that a hit squad showed up to take us out makes me wonder if the Ukrainians are working with the Chinese as partners. Or are the Triads just providing muscle for the Ukrainians to keep the product flowing?

"I'm going to need a photo of the dead guy," I say. "I'm also going to need somebody to do a full workup on Astra. I need her fingernails scraped—"

"Now, hold on just a minute," he stops me. "You don't come in here orderin' me around like I'm your lackey or somethin'."

I stop and take a beat, silently counting to five to get my frustration under control. When I feel composed enough, I raise my eyes to him again.

"You're right. I apologize, Sheriff," I tell him. "It's important though, that we gather as much evidence as we can while it's still fresh. My best friend and partner is lying in that room having barely escaped death, and I, for one, would like to find out who almost killed her."

Block takes his Smokey the Bear hat off and runs his hand through his close-cropped hair. The anger on his face melts away and is replaced by an expression of compassion. He looked away, as if ashamed.

"I'm sorry. You're right, o' course," he says. "I'm just not used to havin' somebody barkin' orders at me."

"That's fair. And again, I'm sorry."

He gives me an awkward smile and a nod. "I'll see about somebody down here to collect those samples."

"Thank you, Sheriff."

As he walks off, I turn back to the window and see the nurse finishing up with Astra. She leaves the room and I slip in behind her. I walk over to the bed and grab her wrist to avoid her hands and give it a squeeze.

"You scared the hell out of me," I say.

"Mission accomplished then," she replies, her voice raspy and weak. "That was my whole plan."

"Smartass."

"To the end."

"It almost was," I say.

"But it wasn't, so stop beating yourself up. This isn't your fault, Blake," she tells me. "And don't think I didn't get my licks in. I know

I scratched one of them. I might have gotten the second one too, but I can't say for sure."

"They both got away."

She nods. "Yeah, when I got to the backup weapon on my ankle and squeezed off a couple of shots, they took off running. They returned fire as they were fleeing and that's when I got hit."

I look away. Seeing Astra laid up in this bed, knowing how close I came to losing her, is hard. It takes me a couple of moments before I can turn back and when I do, she's looking back at me with a sober expression on her face.

"Listen to me. This isn't on you, so get that thought out of your head right now," she says sternly. "In fact, if you hadn't shouted a warning, they would have come down on me before I knew what was happening. I'd probably be dead right now if not for you."

I purse my lips and try to control the waves of emotion washing through me. It renders me unable to speak.

"Hey, look at me," she orders.

I raise my eyes to hers and she's looking at me with a serious expression on her face.

"You listening?" she asks.

"Yeah, I'm listening."

"You saved my life, Blake," she tells me. "Get that through your head. I'm alive right now because of you."

"I came so close to losing you," I say, my voice quavering.

"But you didn't," she responds. "And all things considered, I got really lucky."

"Yeah, Sheriff Block agrees with that. Maybe we should go buy lottery tickets."

She gives me a weak grin. "It was a clean through and through. Nothing major hit. They've already patched me up and I'll be back on my feet here in a couple of days—"

"I'm sending you back to Seattle."

"Like hell you are."

I nod. "I am. They're going to be coming in to scrape your nails and look for evidence," I tell her. "I'm going to need you to take that to Beks to run any DNA. We need IDs on these guys because the one I killed is a ghost in the system."

"We can have it couriered down," she argues. "I'm going to rest up and I'll be back on my feet again."

"This isn't negotiable. You're going to take some time off," I insist.

"Blake, I don't need to take time off. And I'm sure as hell not leaving you up here alone. Especially not with what just happened."

"I'm not going to argue with you. You're going home and you will take some time to heal up," I say. "That's an order."

I fold my arms over my chest and turn away, then begin pacing her room as I battle the tears that are welling in my eyes. I don't want to get all emotional in front of her but I'm having a tough time keeping myself in check. As I think about seeing her lying there, bleeding and fading in and out of consciousness, it lances my heart with a sharp spike of pain. It also makes me remember what she was saying the other day about wanting to marry Benjamin and starting a family. We came inches from possibly shattering those dreams tonight.

It's silly but seeing her get hurt makes me realize that in some small part of my brain, I thought Astra was indestructible. Sure, we've gotten our share of bumps and bruises doing this job but that's all they were—bumps and bruises. Knowing just how close I came to losing her, seeing her lying there and thinking she was bleeding out, is a stark reminder that she's not indestructible. That she really is just flesh and bone. How can I keep asking her to step into the field and risk everything? Sure, it's her job, but the cases we chase… they're high risk. The possibility that we could be killed is always hanging over our heads. I see that now.

And if Astra is serious about having children, how can I keep asking her to put herself in harm's way? How could I ever look that child in the eye and tell them that their mother died because of me?

Because of this job? How could I ever look at Benjamin in the eye again knowing the risks we take cost him the love of his life? Cost him his family and his shot at happiness? How could I ever look at myself in the mirror again if I lost my best friend because I push as hard and take the sort of stupid risks that I do?

In a lot of ways, it would be like losing Kit. Astra means almost as much to me as my own sister. Losing either one of them would be like losing a big part of myself. How could I go on knowing it was my fault that I lost either one of them? I'm pretty sure it would break something in me. Something that would be in worse shape than Humpty Dumpty and just as likely to never be put back together again.

For her part, I know that Astra is loyal. She'd never ask to be reassigned. She would never ask me to send her somewhere safer. She would absolutely stay with me to the bitter end and insist the entire time that it's an acceptable risk of the job we do. She loves being part of this team. Loves what we do. She loves me. But that love sometimes blinds her to the risks we take. Maybe it's my duty as both her boss and her best friend to do what's right for her. Maybe it's my job to protect her as best as I can—even if that means protecting her from herself.

Astra wants to be a federal agent. She wants to be the one kicking in doors and collaring bad guys. It's one of the reasons she gets out of bed in the morning. But she also now wants to be a wife. A mother. She's gotten that taste of happiness and the sort of life she wants. A peaceful life. And I know better than most that happiness is fleeting, and we have to grab that brass ring whenever we get the chance. Maybe it's time she grabs hers.

"You need to stop that, Blake."

Her voice snaps me back to the moment. "Stop what?"

"I see that big brain of yours working," she says. "I know you and because I do, I know you're looking for some big meaning to all this. Some big revelation. I know this has rattled you but don't let it rattle everything. It's all going to be fine. I'm going to be fine."

"Yeah, this time," I mutter. "But what about next time?"

"It's the risk we take to do what we do," she says. "And I love what we do. It's an acceptable risk."

A wry grin touches my lips as a tear slips from the corner of my eye. "I knew you were going to say that. And I doubt Benjamin— or the child you want to have—would agree with that sentiment."

She gives me a wavering grin. "Let me worry about that."

"I'm your best friend as well as your boss. It's kind of in my job description to worry about that for you," I reply. "And to do what's in your best interest when you won't."

Her smile slips entirely, and she looks at me with a grave look on her face. Astra tries to sit up a little straighter and grimaces from the effort. She takes a moment to gather herself and because she knows me as well as she does, I can see in her eyes that she thinks she knows exactly where my thoughts are going.

"Blake, this is a one-off. An aberration. It's not a big deal," she presses.

"You got shot!" I feel like I'm going insane. Why doesn't she care more about this?

"This is not even the first time I got shot this year, Blake. Remember? Just a while ago Wren Keaton got my shoulder in that Osweiler case. And remember back in Briar Glen, I got shot by those cultists?"

Oh, I remember all right. That was how I met Mark in the first place all those years ago. But that only adds to my distress. I don't need to be reminded of how many times I've put her in danger.

"That's different," I protest. "That's—"

"Don't do something stupid, Blake. Do not take away something I love because of some knee-jerk emotional overreaction."

All I can do is shut my mouth into a thin line.

The nurse sent by Sheriff Block comes in with the kit to process Astra for evidence. I give her a tight smile.

"Get this to Beks," I tell her. "Then call me with the results as soon as you can."

Before she can reply—and likely argue further—I turn and leave the room. Astra will never do what's in her own best interest. I know that. Just as I know she loves what we do. But now, she has not just the desire, but the chance, for a happy life and a beautiful family. Unfortunately, she can't have both. She's just too damn stubborn to see, let alone admit it.

So maybe, as her boss and her best friend, it's my responsibility to protect her. Even, as I said, from herself.

CHAPTER TWENTY

Mack's Tavern; Woodcreek, WA

"**S**O, AFTER TWELVE YEARS IN THE ARMY, CAME HOME, started working as a deputy. Ten years later, I was elected Sheriff," Block says. "I'm in my fourth term now. So, yeah, I've been around. Seen some things."

"I can only imagine," I reply.

"I'm sure you've seen some things in your line of work."

I nod, a grim smile touching my lips. "Yeah, the worst humanity has to offer."

After Astra was processed, she spent the night in the hospital. But the next morning, I put her in a car myself and sent her back to Seattle with the evidence, relying on the necessary "chain of custody" argument to finally get her to stop arguing. The rest of the day I spent bumping around, moving my hotel—choosing a place in a busier part of the city. This hotel didn't come up when I searched for lodgings before we came up or I would have booked us there rather than some hotel out on the edge of town. Maybe if we'd been staying there, Astra wouldn't have been shot.

I spent the balance of the day settling in and just trying to get my head right. Astra's shooting has left me more rattled than I care to admit, and I know I need to be focused to close out this investigation. And the stakes have suddenly gotten a lot higher.

Sheriff Block showed up at my new hotel about an hour after I checked in and said he'd have a deputy watching my back. I tried to argue but he shot me down and said since he drew the first shift, we might as well go get a drink and have a conversation. Since I had nothing else to do, I decided a little company might be nice, so we walked down to a local watering hole. He was greeted warmly when we walked in, though dark looks of suspicion were cast my way. He told me not to worry about it and to just ignore them. Yeah, easy for him to say.

He takes a sip of his bourbon and I study him. Block looks tired. There are deep shadows beneath his eyes and a haunted look in them. There's a hard set to his jaw and I watch the way he scans the crowd inside the bar. He's lived among these people for most of his life, knows most of them intimately. But he seems to be looking around for suspects. For threats. I have to wonder if that hypervigilance is a result of his job or his time overseas.

"You look like a man who might have seen enough," I say. "Thinking of hanging it up after this term, Sheriff?"

Block laughs softly to himself. "That some of your fancy profilin' voodoo?"

I smile. "Profiling isn't voodoo, Sheriff. It's just observing human behavior. Being able to analyze and understand it," I tell him. "It's picking up on the small details. A person's tells. That's really it. It's not magic. You do it every day."

"I don't know about that."

"You watch people. You get a feeling about what somebody

might do based on how you see them behaving, right?" I point out. "For instance, I've seen you look at that guy at the end of the bar a few times. He's loud. He's acting a little belligerently. There's some small part of you wondering if he's going to throw a punch. And you're sitting there, your muscles a little tense, ready to pounce if he does. Right?"

He looks at me for a moment, an expression of astonishment on his face. But then he takes a sip of his drink and smiles as he nods to himself.

"Impressive," he admits.

I shrug. "Like I said, it's just a matter of picking up on the small details most people miss. Nothing mysterious about it," I tell him. "You're also ducking my question."

"I'm not duckin' it. Just givin' it some thought."

"And?"

"Been in this town my whole life. Born here. Came back after my service. Gonna die here," he says. "And it's just not the same place it used to be."

"How so?"

Block shakes his head. "It's bigger. More prosperous. That's good stuff," he tells me. "But there's more crime. More death. And a whole lot more drugs. It's just not the same town I grew up in."

"Time changes everything," I say. "Progress brings changes. And not all those changes are good. But you have to figure out if the positive changes outweigh the negative."

"Jury's still out on that," he tells me. "I've seen more death in Woodcreek in the last five years than the rest of my life combined. Most of it because of drugs—either overdoses or drug-related murders."

"Do you blame Whitehorn?" I ask. "I know a lot of people in town blame them for a lot of the ills in town."

"I don't blame them much. I may not like 'em, but I can't blame them for what's been goin' on around here. Truth be told, I think more of the fault is with the Ukrainian mobsters who are infecting this town like a damn cancer," he replies. "I suspect half my deputies are on somebody's payroll, and there ain't a thing I can do about it because the union protects them. Everything these Ukrainians touch rots, then dies."

A moment of silence stretches out between us as Block looks down into his glass as if he's searching for the answers at the bottom of that amber-colored liquid. He's a man who obviously loves his town. A man who's always tried to do right by it. A man who's given his life in service to it and has done everything he can to protect it. Now he's having to sit back and watch as the fabric of his town erodes. He's having to watch as the drugs and violence are starting to rot the foundations of the town he loves. And I can see the toll it's taking on him.

"Anyway, enough about an old man's moanin' and gripin'," he shakes it off. "How'd you end up doin' what you do?"

A wry grin twists my lips. "The short story is that my parents were murdered when I was a kid," I tell him. "I was sent out to Seattle to live with my aunt. Got interested in psychology and eventually found my way to the Bureau. I guess on some level of my mind, I joined the FBI to avenge their deaths."

"And? Have you?"

I shrug. "I suppose so," I tell him. "Every time I put somebody away I kind of feel like I'm doing it for them."

"That's some deep psychological stuff," he says.

I grin. "Yeah, I'm a headcase. I learned to live with that a long time ago."

"You're good at what you do. And you strike me as a good person," he says. "For whatever it's worth, I'm sure your folks would be proud."

"Thank you, Sheriff."

He waves for another round and we both fall silent as we wait for the waitress to come by and drop off our drinks. She eventually does and I raise my glass to him.

"Thanks for inviting me out for drinks tonight," I tell him. "This is much better for me than sitting in my hotel room staring at the walls."

"Don't mention it," he replies. "I know we got off to a rough start and I've always found that bourbon makes a better olive branch than an actual olive branch. Tastier, anyway."

I laugh softly. "You are not wrong, my friend."

He looks at me with a sober expression for a long moment. "I've had friends shot before. I know how difficult it is."

"I keep telling myself that I know she's all right. I put her in the car and watched her drive off. Very much alive," I say. "But I still can't get the image of her lying on the ground covered in her own blood out of my mind."

"And you never will, Agent Wilder," he tells me. "When you see somebody you love—as much as you obviously love her—in pain like that, it stays with you. Forever. All you can do is find a way to make peace with it."

"I don't know if I can ever make peace with seeing my best friend nearly dying."

"Then you learn to live with it."

I nod. "I guess that's about the best I can hope for. I just—it's just…"

"Just what?"

"It's just that Astra has finally found a good man. The right man. She wants to start a family," I tell him. "I never expected that she would ever settle down or… it's just, Astra's always been a wild child. But now that she has everything she never even knew she wanted, watching her get shot reminds me how quickly it can all be taken away."

"And you feel guilty for that. For her gettin' shot," he intuits.

"Now who's a profiler?" I jab at him softly.

He shrugs with a sympathetic smile.

"Yeah. I do," I nod. "I know I push too hard sometimes. I know that doing the big game hunting we do entails extreme risk. But I push anyway. And I think it might have finally caught up to us."

He shakes his head. "This line o' work entails risk. She wouldn't be here if she didn't accept that," he tells me. "Hell, for that matter, there's risk crossing the street every day. Gettin' up each mornin' and livin' your life entails risk."

"I know. I just—yeah, you can't avoid that risk of crossing the street. You never know when that bus is going to come careening in out of nowhere. I get that," I reply. "But then there's avoidable risk. Such as riling up a Ukrainian mob and all but daring them to come after you. I just—I don't think I can let her do that anymore."

He frowns. "No offense intended, but ain't that her decision to make?"

"Astra is loyal to a fault. She would quite literally run into a burning building if I asked her," I say. "I value her loyalty, but it sometimes leads her to make decisions that aren't in her own best interest."

"And you know what's in her best interest, I assume."

"In this case, yes. As her friend and her boss, I have to look out for her. That's part of my job description. And it's because I'm just as loyal to her as she is to me."

"True friendship and loyalty are good things. You'll never hear me say otherwise. They also seem to be in real short supply these days," he starts. "And I know I don't know you well, but I think I already know you well enough to say you'd never put your friend in a bad spot."

"Not intentionally, no."

"Agent Russo strikes me as a real smart lady."

I nod. "She's one of the smartest people I know."

"And do you trust her?"

"With my life."

He gives me a sly grin. "Do you though?"

"Of course I do. The only person I trust more is my sister."

"Seems to me if she's not just the smartest person you know, and somebody you trust with your life, that you'd trust her to know what's best for her and to make her own decisions," he says. "I don't doubt Agent Russo's loyalty one bit. But I really doubt she'd actually run into a burning building just because you told her to."

A rueful smile touches my lips as I see the trap he's so neatly walked me into. Block is a lot cleverer than I expected. I underestimated him and feel the sharp sting of my embarrassment making my cheeks flush. He's right about Astra. But even that doesn't necessarily make me feel any better about her following me into dangerous situations. No, she wouldn't actually run into a fire on my say so. But I fear her loyalty to both the job and to me might lead her to running into a dangerous situation with me. And given what she wants, it's a risk I don't know I can countenance anymore.

"If Agent Russo is as smart as you believe and you trust her with your life," he continues, "trust her to tell you if the risks you're takin' are out of bounds. Because let's face it, in the business we're in, risk is the name of the game. And that's the last thing I'll say about it. I don't think you need a lecture. Or more of a lecture, anyway."

He grins and it cuts the tension that had been saturating the air between us. I hate that he has a valid point. But he does. I don't know what to think of it right now though. I'm still more than a little conflicted about it all.

"So, anyway," Block says. "Tell me more about this theory you two have been working on. I'm curious to see where this investigation of yours is leading you."

I blow out a long breath and shake my head. "In circles, mostly. But things seem to be slowly coming into focus. I think. I'll be honest, this case has been confounding."

I take a swallow of my bourbon then start by telling him what we've learned, what we don't know, and where we think this is all going. And when I'm done, Block whistles low.

"You two have been busy," he comments.

"We've covered a lot of ground," I confirm. "But we've still got a long way to go."

"Well," he says. "If it turns out that you're right and I don't stand for re-election again and this is my last ride, I'd like to be able to say I did some good on my way out the door."

"What do you mean?"

"It means that I want to help. In whatever way I can," he says. "Just tell me what you need and hopefully, when the fighting's over and all the dust settles, Woodcreek can be a town I'm proud to live in again."

"I appreciate that, Sheriff. More than you know."

Things are getting hairy though. The last thing I want is for Block to be putting his life on the line. As Astra and I found out, these guys are not messing around. No, I want to keep the sheriff as far from the blast radius as I can. I know I have to navigate a mine-field of Ukrainian mobsters, Chinese Triads, and kill squads to try to bring this case to a close and find justice for Madeline. And I don't want to be responsible for anybody else getting hurt.

No, it's better that I do this alone.

CHAPTER TWENTY-ONE

Whitehorn Foundation, Conference Room 12-A; Woodcreek, WA

"**S**O, YOU DIDN'T SEE ANYBODY ON THE WARD THAT NIGHT?" I ask. "Somebody who shouldn't be there, Nurse Franklin?"

The woman sits before me, her eyes red and puffy, the memory of Madeline's death obviously still hitting her hard. She shakes her head. According to her personnel file, Nurse Franklin is thirty-seven years old. But she's got a spritely, youthful appearance that makes her look much younger. She's a short, thin woman with rust-colored hair cut into a bob, green eyes, and smooth, pale skin. She's a little fidgety and nervous and can't seem to sit still.

"I didn't see anybody that night," she responds.

"And you clocked out at—"

"Ten-thirty," she tells me. "I was home in time to watch the news at eleven."

I nod. "Did Madeline mention anybody she was having trouble with?"

"No, everybody loved Maddy," she replies with a loud sniff. "The hospital, as you can see, is a grim place. But she was a bright light on this ward."

"All right, let's look at it the other way. Do you know if she was having a relationship with anybody?"

"A relationship?" Nurse Franklin frowns.

I nod. "Yes. Anybody she was having a romantic or sexual relationship with?"

"No. No, of course not. Relationships between patients are forbidden."

I give her a sly smile. "And you don't think patients find a way around that?"

She shrugs. "Maybe. I don't know."

"What about any of the staff?" I ask. "Do you know if Madeline might have been involved with any of the orderlies? Doctors?"

She shakes her head again. "No. That's even worse than patients fraternizing with each other," she says. "It's simply not allowed."

Nurse Franklin is sincere in her words. She's a straight arrow; I can see she's a woman who believes in following the rules. She's a woman who has a strict schedule and follows it to the letter. There's a lot to be said about having a routine and adhering to it faithfully. But if you're not careful, you can become a slave to that routine.

She also has a naïve worldview. She seems to think that just because she follows the rules that everybody else does too. She doesn't seem to conceive of the fact that other people out there might not have the same reverence or respect for the rules that she does. That everybody isn't as rigid and strict about following them. It's a weakness and a blind spot for her. Not that she recognizes that.

I frown and sit back in my chair. "What about friends?" I ask, as the thought occurs to me. "Was there anybody she spoke to regularly? Somebody she might have confided in that wasn't Dr. Langenkamp?"

Franklin laughs. "She never confided in Langenkamp. Nobody does. They all tell her what she wants to hear just to make their sessions end," she says. "But nobody likes her. That extends to most of the staff too."

"No? Why's that?"

"She's just not a pleasant person," Franklin shrugs. "As far as friends go, she was very close with Lucy Vargas."

I jot the name down on my notepad. "Lucy Vargas," I say. "Okay great. Anybody else?"

Franklin shakes her head. "No, for the most part, Maddy kept to herself. But she and Lucy were always huddled together in the day room. As I said, they were very close."

"Great," I say. "Thank you, Nurse Franklin. I appreciate your help."

She nods and gets to her feet then leaves the room. I look through the files until I find Lucy Vargas and flip it open. She's twenty-three years old and was admitted eight months ago after a severe bout of depression led her to attempt suicide. Twice. Her parents, fearing for her safety, sent her here for treatment. I can see they've tried a number of different mood stabilizers, and that while most of them have had a positive effect, that uptick in her mood has only lasted a short time. So far, they've not been able to find a permanent solution.

That Lucy was a close friend of Madeline's is news to me. It's not much, but it's something. All I can hope is that she proves more useful than any of the others in this facility have been so far.

⁓

"Good morning, Lucy."

"Mornin'," she mutters.

"Coffee?"

"Sure. Whatever," she says, her voice low.

Astra and I ended up bringing in our own coffee maker. We got tired of schlepping down the hill to the coffee house every day and we sure as hell weren't about to use the disgusting one in our makeshift office, so it made sense. I'm currently on my second pot. I get up and fix both of us a cup then set hers down in front of her and retake my seat. Lucy cups it in both hands as if drawing warmth from it rather than being interested in actually drinking it. But it does seem to leech some of the tension out of her.

Lucy is a pretty girl. Her complexion is rich and tawny, her eyes the color of warm chocolate, and dark, wavy hair spills down past her shoulders. She's about five-four with a narrow waist and delicate features. She sits with her head down, unable to look me in the eye. She's drawn in on herself and looks like she'd rather be anywhere but here. More than that, she has a look of sadness about her. Her full lips are drawn down and she looks like she's on the verge of sobbing.

"So, I was told you and Madeline are good friends," I say.

She nods then raises the cup to her lips and takes a small sip of the rich, dark brew. She still won't look at me. I know she's depressed, but getting her to speak is like pulling teeth. But I have no choice. If I'm going to get any information out of this poor, damaged girl, I'm going to need to find a way to connect with her. The only way to get her to open up is to forge a bond with her. Which means I need to do something Dr. Stein, Dr. Langenkamp, and their entire staff haven't been able to do in the past eight months.

I think the only way to forge that bond is by playing to her relationship with Madeline. If Lucy sees me as an ally, as a friend of Madeline's and somebody who wants the best for her, that might be enough to crack through this hard exterior of hers. It might be enough to get her to open up to me. Maybe.

"You and Maddy," I start. "You talked a lot?"

"Yeah. I guess."

"She seemed like a really nice person."

"She was," Lucy confirms. "But then somebody killed her."

"And that's why I'm here. I want to find out who hurt your friend, Lucy," I say. "I want to put away the person who did this to her."

She frowns but raises her head slightly. Lucy isn't quite meeting my eyes just yet but hearing me tell her that I want to help Madeline at least got her listening. It's not much but it's something.

"What happened to Madeline was wrong, Lucy. Very, very wrong," I say. "And I want to bring her some peace. Bring you and all her loved ones some peace by finding the person who did this and punishing them. But I can only do that with your help. Can you help me?"

This time, she finally raises her head and looks me in the eye. I can see the pain she's feeling over the loss of her friend and her desire for whoever killed her to be punished. Right now, she seems entirely present and engaged.

"Nobody will ever be able to punish him," she says.

"Why do you say that?"

"It was the ghost of her boyfriend, that bastard Pasha, who killed her," she replies. "His spirit snuck into her room and killed her."

Oh great. The ghost did it defense again. If I shoot her argument down, I risk shutting her down entirely. I need to keep her talking, but the last thing I want to do is lend credence to this outlandish idea some people in this facility are having. Astra and I found the nest of the person who more than likely killed her. It was no ghost. Not some avenging spirit. It was somebody living in an unfinished room in an unfinished wing of the hospital. We reported it to Dr. Stein immediately and he assured us he would be increasing security patrols.

If I tell her Madeline's death has a more earthly explanation, I'm afraid Lucy is going to draw inward again and shut me out completely. So, how do I get her to talk without feeding into this delusion? I decide to table that for now and circle back to it later if I need to. The odds are good that she doesn't actually know anything about the murder itself, so it's a dead-end line of questioning anyway.

"Okay, Lucy, do you know if Maddy was having trouble with anybody?" I ask. "Was anybody giving her a hard time?"

She shakes her head. "Pasha. Only Pasha," she said. "He would follow her everywhere. The day room, the cafeteria. She even said she saw him in the bathroom once. He just stood there and watched her. She was terrified."

I tap my pen on my folder and try to think of a way to steer her away from Pasha since that's going nowhere. But then I think about things girlfriends tell each other. And only each other. Before I can ask, though, Lucy jumps in.

"We were going to get a place together. Maddy and I," Lucy tells me. "When we got out of here, we were going to get an apartment somewhere far away from here. LA or New York maybe. It was going to be great."

"I'm sorry, Lucy. I'm sure that would have been wonderful for you," I say, genuine sympathy in my voice. "And I'm really sorry that's not going to happen now."

"Yeah. Me too," she mutters. "I would have really liked that."

My heart breaks all over again for both girls. To be so young, with so many dreams, and to have them ripped from you is such a tragedy. It makes me think again of the too-close brush Astra and I had with death.

"Lucy, can you tell me if Maddy was... involved with anybody?" I ask. "Did she have a boyfriend here? Somebody she liked?"

Lucy looks away quickly. Too quickly. She gnaws on her bottom lip and wraps her arms around herself protectively. It tells me she knows who got her pregnant. She knows who Madeline was involved with.

"Lucy, it's really important to know who she was involved with," I tell her. "We know she was pregnant and there is a chance that the man she was—seeing—might have hurt her."

Lucy shakes her head vigorously. "No. Johnny would never hurt her—"

She bites off her words quickly and clamps her hands over her mouth like a child who knows they said too much.

"Johnny? Who's Johnny, Lucy?"

"I can't say."

"It's really important, Lucy. This could help us find the person who hurt her," I press. "You want that, don't you? You want us to get and punish the person who hurt your best friend, don't you?"

"But I promised her I'd never say. I swore to her," she tells me.

"And you're a really good friend for holding onto her secret, Lucy. But there's no reason to hold onto it anymore," I point out sympathetically. "Maddy's gone. And she would want you to do whatever you can to help us. To bring her justice."

"I—I can't. I promised."

"Lucy, I get it. I know you promised. And like I said, you're a good friend for keeping that promise. But she would want you to tell me. To bring her peace and let her rest," I say. I'm trying really hard not to scare her off, but I need more information from her. This is about all I've got.

"I—I don't know."

"Who's Johnny, Lucy? Please," I push. "It's really important."

She sniffs loudly as a tear rolls down her cheek. I can see her weighing the pros and cons of telling me what I want to know. Trying to decide whether it's better to keep her word and hold onto the secret of a dead woman, or perhaps put her soul to rest by helping catch her killer. She frowns and when she looks at me again, I can see she's come to a decision.

"Jonathan Beckett," she finally admits. "She had something going on with him."

I have to think about it for a minute before the name comes back to me. Of course. Jonathan Beckett. The orderly who'd been assigned to escort us.

CHAPTER TWENTY-TWO

Whitehorn Foundation, Conference Room 12-A; Woodcreek, WA

H E SITS AT THE TABLE, AVOIDING MY EYES. HE FLEXES HIS hands over and over again, making the muscles in his forearms ripple, giving a strange, rolling effect to the tattoos on them. I'm struck again by the sheer size of the man and how strange it is that he's got such a baby face. It's hard for me to imagine, likely because he sees me as an adversary, but I suppose in the right setting, he could seem… gentle. Maybe that's what Madeline saw in him.

Though he's doing his best to mask it, I can see that he's nervous. He chews on his thumbnail, taps his foot on the ground, and sighs.

"Are you all right, Jonathan?"

He nods. "Fine."

"Why do you seem so nervous?"

He shrugs. "Don't know."

"It's all right, Jonathan. I just need to ask you some questions," I say. "Same as I've been asking everybody else."

"Yeah, okay."

"There's nothing to be nervous about."

He nods. "Okay."

His foot tapping speeds up as does his gnawing on his fingernails. The guy looks like he's practically ready to stroke out. There's some small part of me that feels bad for him. But then I remind myself that no matter how kind his eyes are or how much of a gentle giant he may seem like, it's entirely possible he murdered Madeline. He may be the one who wrapped his hands around her neck and squeezed the life out of her. He's certainly large and strong enough to have accomplished it.

"Do you know who killed Maddy Donaldson?" I ask.

He shakes his head. "I don't. I wish I did but I don't."

I give him a small grin. "And here I half-expected you to tell me you thought it was the ghost of her dead boyfriend. You wouldn't be the first to say it."

He rolled his eyes and shook his head. "I'm not an idiot, Agent Wilder. I know it was a delusion caused by her illness. I hoped in time, with her meds, that she'd be able to let that go."

I nod. "Good answer," I say. "So, tell me about your relationship with Maddy then."

He shrugs again. "She was a patient here. I'm an orderly," he says. "There's nothing more to it than that."

"You're certain?"

He swallows hard and nods. "Yeah," he says. "I'm an employee. She's a patient. We're not allowed to mess with the patients."

I take a drink of my coffee, eyeing him over the rim of the cup. After he finishes speaking, he goes right back to gnawing on his nails again, the steady *tap-tap-tap* of his foot on the floor echoing around the room.

"You wouldn't be the first employee to strike up a relationship with a patient," I offer.

"Didn't happen."

"What if I told you I know for a fact it did?"

"I'd say you were lying. Or misinformed."

"Did you kill her, Jonathan?"

He finally looks at me, eyes wide, an expression of near outrage on his face.

"What? No, I did not kill her," he snaps.

"You sure?"

"Yes. I'm sure," he says, his voice colored with anger.

I take another drink of my coffee and let him simmer on all of that for a couple of moments. He shifts in his seat and that tapping gets faster and louder. Jonathan is growing more agitated. I just need to push him a little harder to get him talking. He'll either kill me or give me the information I want.

"Did you know she was pregnant, Jonathan?"

His eyes widen slightly but he's quick to cover it. Jonathan runs a hand over his face, giving himself a beat to gather his wits about him. He shakes his head.

"I—I didn't know she was pregnant."

"Do you know who the father was?"

He shakes his head again. "N—no. I don't."

"Are you sure?"

"What kind of question is that? Of course I'm sure."

I lean back in my chair and let out a long breath. A five-year-old could see that he's lying and that he's hiding something. Jonathan is a lousy liar, which, I guess, is probably a good thing. Honesty is a good quality to have. A rare quality in people.

"What if I told you that I know you were the father?"

"I wasn't. I don't know what you're talking about."

"Did you know that Dr. Stein terminated the pregnancy?"

His eyes shimmer with tears, and he shakes his head. He looks stricken and he's trembling but is trying to keep himself composed. Jonathan seems ready to go, so I decide it's time to crank up the pressure. This is the part where I miss Astra a lot. With both of us hitting him from either side, peppering him with questions and statements non-stop, it's so much easier to trip up and confuse a suspect and get them to say something they don't intend to say. Doing it solo doesn't quite bring the same level of ferocity. It might not be enough to make him stumble over his own tongue.

"I know you were the father of Madeline's child, Jonathan."

He shakes his head as the tears start to roll down his face. "No. No. I wasn't."

"Yes. You were," I insist, my voice growing louder. "Don't lie to me, Jonathan."

"I'm not lying."

"Yes, you are lying, and you need to stop!" I shout.

I punctuate my words by slapping my palm on the table, the sharp crack of it making him flinch. It was strange to see a man who could have broken me into two pieces without breaking a sweat sobbing and blubbering like a child and I had to wonder if maybe he was telling me the truth. Jonathan isn't the brightest crayon in the box and he's not especially cagey. From what I've learned of him, he doesn't say much but when he does speak, it's usually blunt and true. Like I said, he's not a very good liar.

"Did you kill her because she got pregnant, Jonathan?" I growl. "Or because the pregnancy was terminated?"

"I didn't kill her!"

"I don't believe you!" I scream.

He recoils like I just slapped him across the face and sits back in his chair. The anger that had been coloring his features fades and is replaced by an expression of absolute grief. He looks down at his hands for a long moment, his body trembling with quiet sobs. I give Jonathan a few moments to gather himself and when he does, he raises his eyes to mine.

"Why would I kill her, Agent Wilder? I was in love with her."

I open my mouth to fire back, but the words die on my lips. That was not what I'd been anticipating. I run a hand through my hair and give myself a minute to recover.

"You were in love with her?" I ask.

He nods. "We were in love. When she got released and the whole court thing was done, we were going to leave. We were going to leave together."

"I thought she was going to get a place with Lucy."

"Lucy was going to come stay with us once we got settled," he explains. "But it was going to be our place. We were going to get married."

I study him closely and can tell that he's being truthful. I see no deception in his eyes. The look on his face is one of sheer grief and I don't think it's an expression that can be faked.

"So, you two were involved in an intimate relationship?"

He nods. "Yeah. We were," he confirms. "But please, if you don't have to tell Dr. Stein... I really need this job. Please."

"I'll do my best to keep you out of it, Jonathan," I tell him. "But you really didn't know she was pregnant?"

He shakes his head, the grief on his face growing thicker. Jonathan looks up at me and seems like a man who'd just had his legs kicked out from under him. He's suddenly lost. Adrift. And has no idea where the shore is.

"A—are you sure? You sure she was pregnant?"

I nod. "I'm sorry, but yes I am. And the pregnancy was terminated."

He shakes his head. "I was going to be a dad," he whispers, his tone mournful. But then he looks up at me again, his eyes growing harder. "She never would have aborted our baby. She was Catholic and didn't believe in that."

I don't bother pointing out the hypocrisy of that statement. If she were really that devoutly Catholic, she never would have been having premarital sex in the first place. But then, there are a lot of practicing Catholics I know who have more premarital sex than Wilt Chamberlain. So, people can apparently pick and choose which teachings are sins and which are merely flexible guidelines.

I clear my throat. "Surely, her parents—"

"They're Catholic too. Devout. They never would have agreed to it. Never in a million years," he says. "If the pregnancy was terminated, it's because she was forced into it."

His words hang in the air between us for a long moment and I can see the grief twisting and contorting his features. I think he's had enough. More to the point, I believe that he was in love with her and had nothing to do with her death. The pain I see in him is just too raw and too real. Like I said, I know he's not that talented of an actor. I'm comfortable striking Jonathan off the suspect list.

"Thank you for talking to me, Jonathan."

"Please find who did this," he pleads. "Please find them, Agent Wilder."

"I'm doing everything I can."

That is true. I just fear it won't be enough.

⁓

Dr. Stein sits across from me, one leg folded over the other, his hands folded in his lap, and an expression of extreme annoyance on his face. I hadn't planned on confronting Stein with anything until I had something concrete, I could bludgeon him with. I would have preferred to have something to throw in his face other than speculation and innuendo.

But that's not the hand I was dealt, and I need to play with what I have rather than whine about the things I don't have. Jonathan gave me an interesting way in, though. I want to hit Stein with it just to see how he'd react. He's a man who's usually very tightly controlled. It'll be interesting to see how he handles what I'm going to throw at him. It's about all I have right now, so hopefully it's enough to rattle him a bit.

"Will this be quick? I'm a very busy man," he snaps irritably. "I do have an entire hospital to run, Agent Wilder."

"It will take as long as it takes. I appreciate your patience."

He sighs dramatically as I deliberately and pointedly open up his personnel file so he can see, then take my sweet time poring over all the information I already have committed to memory just to annoy him.

"Dr. Stein, did you know one of your orderlies was engaged in a sexual relationship with one of your patients?" I ask.

"I most certainly did not. That's prohibited here."

"So is smoking, but I did notice a couple of your nurses on the unfinished wing copping a couple of cigarettes," I counter.

"What do you want with me, Agent Wilder?"

"I'd like your cooperation," I tell him. "A woman was murdered on hospital grounds, Dr. Stein, and you walk around like you couldn't care less."

"I assure you that isn't true—"

"You sure act like it," I spit. "You have done nothing to help this investigation."

"Nor have I hampered you in any way. I've given you access. I haven't saddled you with any burdensome restrictions," he says. "I have given you everything you required."

"Except answers," I growl. "And you play word games with me. You speak in riddles and tell me nothing. So, yeah. You have been hindering my investigation."

"I won't quibble with you, Agent Wilder," he sighs. "Now, if you would kindly ask your questions so I can go about my day. I'm a very busy man."

"Fine. Straight to the point," I say. "I want to know why you covered up the circumstances of Madeline's death. I want to know why you ruled it a suicide rather than the murder it was."

"It was an unfortunate mistake," he replies. "Call it negligence if you wish. Call it whatever you need to for your little reports. But it was an honest mistake. I don't have the facilities here that your ME does—"

"You have a morgue here?" I ask.

"Yes, of course—"

"You have an x-ray machine? CT machine?" I ask. "Tools like scalpels, forceps? You have lights and electricity?"

"Yes, of course."

"Then you have the facilities the ME does," I reply. "The only thing you needed was a competent medical doctor."

He glowers at me, making no effort to hide the sheer disdain he has for me. I guess we won't be exchanging Christmas cards. Boo-hoo.

"I want to know why you terminated Madeline's pregnancy," I say.

"It was at the request of her parents."

"Oh? Her parents requested it, did they?"

"I do believe that's what I said."

I flash back to what Jonathan said about her parents being Catholic and their views on terminating a pregnancy.

"So, you didn't just take it upon yourself to do it, fearing the impact it would have on your hospital's reputation? Or on the federal funding you receive?"

"Don't be absurd."

"Okay, great. Then I'm going to need Madeline's medical file… which you are required to keep for up to seven years," I remind him.

"I'm afraid I can't do that."

"Yes, you can. I have a warrant that says—"

"Your warrant covers her therapy records and papers," he clarifies smugly. "Not her medical records. There is a difference. And because of doctor-patient confidentiality, I cannot give you what you want. By law. If you want her records, you'll need to obtain a warrant."

Anger courses through me and my veins feel like they're filled with liquid fire. It's taking everything in me to keep from reaching across the table and throttling him. I control myself though. I'll get my warrant and I'll be back. And when I do, I'm going to stick it to him in the worst way possible.

"Is there anything else?" Stein asks. "Or may I go?"

I'm frustrated, but manage to keep my cool. "You're dismissed. For now," I tell him. "But believe me when I say that I will be coming back, and I intend to expose all your dirty little secrets. All of them."

"Well, good luck to you then."

CHAPTER TWENTY-THREE

Office of James Craig, US Attorney, Western District of Washington; Seattle, WA

I DIDN'T WANT TO MAKE THE TRIP BACK DOWN TO SEATTLE, BUT I didn't feel this conversation should be had over the phone. The long drive made me grumpy, and it's obviously written all over my face because the receptionist flinches when I come through the door. It's like she's bracing herself for me to smack her. It's a little dramatic, but after what I did to her last time, I suppose I can't blame her too much.

"Good afternoon," I say, trying to sound as pleasant as I can.

She blinks and looks at me like I've just confused her. But without a word, she gets up and briskly walks over to the keypad and punches in the code. There's a harsh buzz and she pulls the door open for me.

"Thank you," I say as I walk into the inner offices.

I walk through the bullpen, feeling all the eyes on me as I pass through. I ignore them all as I make my way down to Craig's office and rap sharply on the door.

"I told you I'm not to be disturbed," comes his voice, muffled through the door.

I rap again, a little harder this time.

Through the door, I can hear him muttering darkly, though the door is a little too thick for me to make out what he's saying clearly. A moment later though, the door opens, and a young blonde woman walks out, carrying a stack of folders while doing her best to carry an air of dignity and importance. It would have been believable if not for her slightly mussed hair and the smear of lipstick on her chin.

I step into his office and watch as he catches himself, just barely keeping from rolling his eyes when he sees me. I close the door behind me and give him a grin.

"Was she taking dictation?" I ask suggestively.

His face darkens and he gives me a frown. "We are prepping for a trial."

"Yeah, looked like you guys were pretty hot and heavy with the trial prep," I say.

"What do you want, Wilder?"

I arch an eyebrow at him and purse my lips, letting him see my own displeasure with his discourteousness. He sighs and this time doesn't bother trying to hide his eye roll. He leans back in his chair and puts on a smile that looks more like a pained grimace.

"What can I do for you, Agent Wilder?"

He hasn't invited me to take a seat yet, so I drop down into one of the wingbacks in front of his desk anyway. I cross my legs and fold my hands in my lap, looking at him evenly.

"I need a warrant," I tell him. "I need to get Madeline Donaldson's medical records. Stein isn't cooperating with me."

"And what do you need her records for?"

"I'm building a case, Mr. Craig. I believe there is evidence in those records that will help me provide a motive for her murder."

"And what is your theory?"

"It's still a work in progress," I tell him.

"Then what will those records provide you?"

"Information. Just like with any investigation," I say.

"So, it's a fishing expedition."

I sigh. "Dr. Stein said Madeline's parents signed the forms that authorized him to terminate her pregnancy," I tell him. "I have it on good authority that they're devout Catholics and would never have signed off on it."

"And who is this good authority?"

"The man who got Madeline pregnant."

"And who might that be?" he asks.

"I'm keeping that to myself for now."

He shakes his head. "You don't have enough for a warrant, Agent Wilder."

I stare at him for a moment, feeling my outrage growing. It's bad enough that Stein is jerking with me, but now Craig, who is supposed to be on my side, is doing the same thing.

"We've gotten warrants with less, Mr. Craig."

"Maybe you're used to dealing with people willing to cut corners, but that's not how I do business, Agent Wilder," he says. "You want a warrant? I need some actual evidence. I'm sorry but your intuition or gut instinct, while maybe good for some things, I'm afraid won't hold up in a court of law."

"Are you even kidding me, Mr. Craig?"

"I'm afraid not. I need evidence before I can request a warrant from a federal judge, Agent Wilder," he says. "As I told you, I don't play fast and loose with the rules here."

"You also only seem to do your job when it suits you," I snap. "I might not be here if not for you signing off on a case you didn't even review."

He frowns and looks down. "That was regrettable. It was a poor decision," he says. "And I hope we can agree it was a mistake and leave it at that."

"You're asking me for a favor right now? Seriously?" I snap. "After you just turned down a legitimate request for a warrant?"

"You don't have evidence, Agent Wilder. Think about it," he says. "If we get a warrant, that means we have to bring up charges. And bringing up charges just hoping we'll have evidence to prove them later will more than likely be challenged by the defense. They'll argue the lack of probable cause invalidates the warrant under the Fourth Amendment. And if that happens, all the work you've done, all the work you're still doing, will get tossed out of Court. If you really think about it, I'm doing you a favor."

"Yeah, it sure feels that way."

"What do you want me to do here, Agent Wilder?"

"Help me catch a murderer," I growl. "That's what I want."

"And I sincerely want to help you. But I also have to adhere to the law. And I hope I don't have to remind you that you do too," he says.

"No, you don't have to remind me," I grumble. "I'm perfectly aware of my responsibilities under the law."

"If you're so hot to get her records, go to her parents," he says. "They allowed you to exhume her. Surely, they'll waive her confidentiality."

I arch my eyebrow at him. "You know damn well they can't waive her confidentially under HIPAA rules."

We both fall silent and stare at each other for a long moment. He's got a small, smug grin tugging at the corners of his mouth and it's all I can do to keep myself from going across the table and slapping it off his face. I really, really want to, though.

"Tell me something, Agent Wilder, is Dr. Stein a suspect?"

He's watching me closely, searching my eyes for the answer. I'm better at masking my thoughts and emotions than he is though, and so I give him nothing. I'm not about to tip my hand to him or to anybody else at this point. With so much uncertainty and so many suspects still in play—Stein and Craig both among them—it would be foolish for me to show my cards.

"I have a list of suspects," I tell him.

"So, Stein is one of them, then."

"By that same token, you are as well, Mr. Craig," I point out. "You signed off on Madeline as a suicide, which could look like a coverup. From a certain perspective. You also very well may have a mole in your office and you're preventing me from checking into any of your employees. You have, in fact, hampered my investigation, counselor. It sends up red flags for me."

"You can't be serious," he says.

I shrug. "It's like I told you, I'm still developing my theory. And right now, there are still a lot of moving parts."

"I don't like where you're going with this."

"You, of all people, should know that until I can cross your name off the suspect list, you remain a suspect," I tell him.

"So, because I made an error, that's enough to land me on your suspect list?"

"Yes," I say bluntly. "I mean, it's a pretty big error, counselor. And some might deem it to be highly suspicious."

He sighs and runs a hand over his face. "This is ridiculous."

"I don't cut corners, Mr. Craig," I say, throwing his words back in his face.

He grins wryly. It quickly slips away though and that sour look returns. We stare at each other across the desk for a long moment, the air between us crackling with tension.

"So, you're really not going to help me out here?"

He shakes his head. "No probable cause. Any evidence gained is fruit of the poisonous tree," he tells me. "It would be pointless."

"Fine. I guess we're done here," I say as I get to my feet.

I walk toward the door but pause and turn around. He's watching me closely, an almost predatory look on his face.

"You know. I thought we were supposed to be on the same team here, Mr. Craig," I tell him. "But you make me feel like we're not. In fact, it feels like you're throwing up roadblocks that I have to overcome at every turn."

"I'm sorry you feel that way, Agent Wilder."

"Yeah, I'm sure you are."

I walk out of his office and slam the door behind me, then storm back through the bullpen and out to the elevators. Craig is behaving like a lawyer for the defense rather than like a prosecutor looking to help me build a case. And it's frustrating the hell out of me.

I don't necessarily believe Craig was directly involved with Madeline's murder. But by acting like an advocate for the defense, he's making it harder for me to hold onto that belief.

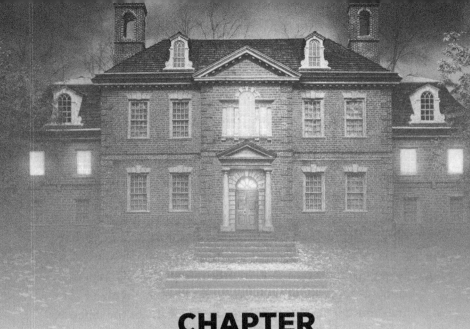

CHAPTER TWENTY-FOUR

The Aurora Hotel; Woodcreek, WA

NOT EVEN THE THREE-HOUR DRIVE WAS ABLE TO DIFFUSE all the anger and frustration coursing through me. I lean against the wall next to the window and pull the curtain aside. Out on the street, I see a sheriff's car go by. I've noticed that since I checked in here, Sheriff Block made good on his word and has his deputies heavily patrolling the area. My only concern is that according to him, a number of his deputies may possibly be in somebody's pocket, so I have some concern about how well they're going to keep an eye on things out on the street. I wouldn't want them to "miss" another kill team sent to take me out.

The Aurora sits just off Hamilton, Woodcreek's main artery. This street is also lined with shops, and like the main drag, has a lot of foot traffic. In theory, the presence of so many civilians—and potential witnesses—should discourage a hit squad. But both the

Ukrainians and the Triads—my two leading contenders for the employer of the team sent to kill Astra and me—aren't exactly known for their subtlety. I don't think I'm going to get a lot of sleep here. Just to make myself feel better though, I've thrown all the locks, have jammed a chair beneath the door handle, and am leaving my window propped open slightly, allowing me a quick exit out the fire escape. It's not much, but it's all I can do.

I step back from the window and take a long swallow of water from my bottle then set it down, my mind spinning a thousand miles a minute. Folding my arms over my chest, I start to pace my room. It's not the Four Seasons but it's a lot nicer than the Bayview, I'll give it that. The room is actually cleaned regularly, so that's a plus. The walls are all a soft cream color that matches the patterned bedspread. The furniture definitely came from IKEA but it's not all nicked and chipped like at the Bayview. It doesn't scream elegant, but it's comfortable and isn't quite nearly as rustic. Nor does it give off that serial killer chic vibe, which is a plus.

As I pace, I try to work through the theories in my head. The problem is that all my working theories feel like a tangled, jumbled string of Christmas lights in my head. It seems like I can't seem to unknot the stupid thing. The more I try, the more tangled up it all gets. I've got names, facts, dates, and various other data points—but no idea how to put it all together. No idea how one fact fits with another. The only thing I have right now is one dead girl and a whole slew of questions.

The only viable suspects I have right now are Stein, Craig, and of course, Jonathan Beckett. But they're all problematic as suspects, to say the least. While they all had feasible reasons for killing Madeline, none of them actually have what I'd think of as a solid motive. Stein's reason would be to cover up her pregnancy and the forced termination. He would want to hide the appearance of impropriety at his hospital. But that's a very weak motive since

Madeline's pregnancy likely wouldn't be a major scandal that could impact his funding.

Craig… ever since I learned Jonathan is the father, I have no viable reason that he would want Madeline dead. But he is behaving like a man with something to hide. From closing the case as a suicide to what I believe is him obstructing my investigation, he is acting like a suspect. But I have absolutely no motive to ascribe to him. To me, it almost seems like he's protecting Stein. He signed off on the doctor's botched postmortem exam and is denying me records that might prove important to my case. It raises red flags, but I still have no real motive. My biggest question when it comes to Craig is, why is he protecting Stein?

Of the three, Jonathan has the strongest motive to kill her. He sounded almost desperate when he realized there's a possibility he could lose his job over this. The prospect of losing his source of income, of possibly losing everything, if it were ever found out that he was sleeping with a patient, is a strong motive for murder. That's tempered by the fact that I believed him when he said he was in love with her. I heard the sincerity in his voice when he said he'd never do anything to hurt Madeline.

The problem is that I'm having trouble trusting myself and trusting my judgment. Am I just falling for a sob story? Wanting to believe something that simply isn't true because on some deep level, I want to believe in love? That I wanted two people to have something I don't have? Something I may never have? I feel like I've lost some small bit of perspective when it comes to Jonathan. But even still, I can't make myself believe that he killed her. He just doesn't ring those bells with me.

I pivot from thinking about those three to the Ukrainian mob and the Triads. How do they fit into all of this? Do they fit into all of this? They have the strongest motive by far, and if I were placing a bet, my money would be on one of them. After all, she was going to testify against them, which would obviously put a big crimp in their operations. It would give them more than ample reason to want her dead. But I've found nothing that connects them to Madeline. Not the slightest hint they were somehow involved with her murder.

But that's when the idea hits me. It makes me think that maybe the idea running through my head suddenly isn't so outlandish at all. As I try to flesh the idea out in my head, things start to feel right. I start to feel the pieces falling into place and that unmistakable feeling of momentum that I've been waiting for finally kicks in. I think I may very well be onto something here. I won't say I'm one hundred percent sold on it, but this feels like the right path to be taking through this warped, twisted forest in my head.

Snatching up my phone, I dial up the CDAU and start pacing, feeling the excitement bubbling up in my belly. Rick picks up after the first ring and I put it on speaker then set it down on the table so I don't have to carry it.

"We must be sharing a brain," he answers. "I was just about to call you."

"Put me on speaker," I tell him.

"I love it when she's so forceful and demanding," Rick cracks.

"Yeah, he usually has to pay extra for that," I hear Astra chime in.

"What?" Rick gasps, sounding offended. "You've been charging me extra?"

I hear the three of them laughing, which brings a smile to my face. I don't have to be there to know there is an obscene gesture or two being shot back and forth. The laughter ebbs after a couple of moments.

"Astra, what are you doing in the office? I recall specifically telling you to get some rest and spend time with Benjamin," I say.

"Benjamin told me to go back to work," she replies, sniffing with indignation. "Said I was too grumpy to hang out with."

As I hear Rick burst into laughter, I can't keep the smile off my face. A moment later, Rick yelps in pain and says something about a stapler. I don't want to know.

"Anyway," Astra continues. "I cleared it with Rosie. She said I could do desk duty."

"Probably because she knew you'd be as big of a pain in the butt as Benjamin and wanted to avoid you pitching a fit," I say.

"Hey—"

"Just take it easy in there," I cut her off with a small laugh. "Seriously, go easy."

"I think the most strenuous thing I've done today is carry a piece of paper to Mo."

"Yeah, and she needed help with that," Rick cracks, and again yelps in pain. "She's strangely accurate when throwing office supplies."

"Don't worry about me. I'm fine," Astra says.

"You got shot. By definition, that means you are not fine," I counter.

"Yeah well, this whole being benched thing sucks."

"Then stay out of the way of bullets," I say.

"I'm so going to kick your butt when you get back here," she sighs. "Speaking of which, when you get back, you and me, we're going to have a long, serious talk, Blake."

The playful tone in her voice is gone, and in my head, I'm envisioning her telling me that she's leaving. That she came too close to losing everything that matters to her and that she thinks it's time to pull the pin. I don't disagree. Maybe it would be for the best. That doesn't mean it doesn't still feel like a kick in the gut though.

"Yeah, we'll do that. Promise," I say. "In the meantime, the reason I called—"

"Wait, wait," Rick says. "Let us go first."

There's an urgency in his voice that tells me whatever he's got is important. I feel a quiver of anticipation and nod to myself.

"All right. Go," I say.

"So, we've been digging into the financials of both Stein and Craig," he starts.

"Mostly Craig," Mo interrupts. "We haven't gotten too deep into Stein just yet."

"Why is that?" I ask.

"Because it took both of us to cut through this byzantine web of shell companies and offshore accounts that belong to US Attorney James Craig," Rick explains.

"Doing business under various assumed names and business entities, of course," Mo adds. "There was a lot to untangle. It was rough."

"But we got it done," Rick says.

"All right, so he's got a lot of shell companies. It's definitely suspicious, but what does it mean?" I ask.

"It means he's funneling money to an offshore account in Jersey. And a lot of it," Mo says. "Money he's not paying taxes on and whose origin is dubious at best. The amount he's running through these shell companies far outpaces what he makes as a US Attorney."

I cock my head, confused. "He's going through all these shell companies and this whole rigamarole just to have his money end up in New Jersey?"

"No, not New Jersey," Mo corrects me. "Jersey is one of the Channel Islands between England and France. It's been a notorious tax haven for years. In fact, it's widely regarded as one of the most aggressive tax havens in the world."

"Huh," I say. "I've actually never heard of Jersey."

"It's an insignificant chunk of land," Astra throws in. "Unless you happen to be the one percent of the one percent and don't want to pay your taxes on that wealth."

"All right, so where is Craig's misbegotten wealth coming from?" I ask.

"Payments are routed to him through another byzantine set of offshore accounts and shell companies," Mo tells me. "These people are working really hard to hide where the money is coming from and where it's going."

I nod as I absorb all the information. The fact that Craig is on the take is a nice piece of evidence. But evidence of what though, I'm not sure. We can probably build a case against him for tax fraud. Which I'm sure he can weasel out of with a slap on the wrist and a fine. Yeah, he'd lose his job as a US Attorney but a scumbag like Craig will probably land on his feet in some white-shoe law firm, which will net him far more prestige and money than he could dream of.

I feel my stomach churning with excitement as the pieces start to fall into place. The picture that's shaping up isn't going in the direction I expected it to go, but that sometimes happens. The important thing is that there are pieces clicking together and, in my gut, I can feel that they're right. They're leading me exactly where I need to go.

"That's not even the best part," Rick adds.

"It gets better?"

"Oh yes," Rick confirms. "It gets better."

"Don't do that whole storytelling thing again," Astra groans. "I'm here in person now and I will kick your butt."

"If you do that, you'll rip your stitches, bleed all over the place, and Rosie most assuredly will send you home," Rick counters.

"I hate you so much right now," Astra says.

They chuckle in the background together and though I smile, I can't help but silently urge them to stop laughing and get to the point. I feel like we're starting to gain momentum here. The wheels on the train are slowly starting to move and I want to keep that going.

"So, out with it," I finally urge him to go on. "Let's hear the best part."

"All right, all right, keep your shorts on," Rick says. "The best part of this is the big-time plot twist."

"And that plot twist is?"

"On all the papers filed for Craig's shell companies," he says, "one of the officers on record is named Evgeni Federov."

"Evgeni Federov," I repeat, and feel that surge of excitement growing in me. "A Ukrainian."

"Give the girl a kewpie doll," Rick says. "That's right, he's a Ukrainian investment banker."

"Supposedly," Mo adds.

"Supposedly?" I ask.

"Yeah, the guy is a ghost," Mo says. "We have all his papers but about five years ago, he just dropped off planet Earth. No employment records, tax filings, rental agreements—nothing."

"What was his last known address?" I ask.

"Brighton Beach," Mo says. "And before you ask, yes he was hooked up with the Odessa Mafia. Brokered a lot of business deals for them. Apparently made them a ton of money. Legit money. There was no case to be made against him."

"So, big earner for the Odessa Mafia who hasn't been seen or heard from in five years," I muse. "I suppose it's probably safe to think he crossed them some way and assume he's a corpse."

"Probably so," Mo says. "But that still gives you a connection between Craig and the Ukrainians."

"Yeah, that's a good thing. It's one piece of the puzzle you guys just snapped into place. That's really good work, guys," I say.

"It was just Mo and me," Rick shouts in the background. "Astra just sat around moaning and groaning about getting shot."

"That's not totally untrue," Astra admits.

"Should we start applying for warrants to move on Craig?" Mo asks.

"No, not yet," I reply. "He's crafty. We need a bulletproof case before we start applying for warrants. We do not want to tip him off that we're really looking at him."

"We're only going to get one shot at him. The last thing we want to do is miss," Astra says soberly. "We need a kill shot if we're going after him."

"Agreed. Okay, this is all really good stuff. But now I need you guys can dig deep into Stein. Give him the same treatment," I tell them. "I need you guys to find a connection between Stein and the Ukrainians. Or between Stein and Craig. If it exists, we need to find it. We need to put those two guys together with the Ukrainians for my theory to hold water."

"We're on it," Mo and Rick both sound off.

"I have some news for you too," Astra says.

"It's not going to be as cool as ours," Rick shouts in the background.

"You're all equally special to me, children," I say, grinning to myself. "What do you have, Astra?"

"I talked to Beks this morning," she says. "DNA results from the attack came back."

She lets her statement hang in the air between us for a long moment. If I were sitting, I'd be on the edge of my seat but since I'm pacing, I just start pacing faster, waiting for her to go on. She doesn't for a long moment though and I blow out a chuckle.

"You're doing it now," I say. "That whole storyteller's pause you're always climbing on Rick's butt about."

"I just wanted to see how it felt," she replies. "It was kind of fun."

"Wonderful," I laugh softly. "Now, out with it."

"You're no fun."

"Not usually."

"All right, I had two different samples under my nails," she starts.

"Two? You were a busy girl."

"I don't mess around."

"Clearly not."

"Anyway, one of the samples didn't turn up anything. Guy wasn't in the system," she says. "The second, though, came back to a guy named Hai Deng."

"Hai Deng?"

"Yep. Twenty-nine years old. Has a rap sheet longer than—shut up, Rick," she calls. "Sorry. "He's been busted for rape, assault, grand theft auto, and a couple of weapons charges in his illustrious career."

"Triad affiliated?"

"You're good," she says. "He's a low-level enforcer. A goon trying to make his bones."

"So, we've definitely got Ukrainian connections to the US Attorney. Triad hit teams trying to take us out. And I'm going to guess some connection between them all and our Chief Science Officer who might have facilitated the murder of a key witness," I say.

"Right now, it's all circumstantial. Lots of maybes and might haves. We have no way of putting them all together," she says. "I mean, maybe there isn't any sort of link, Blake. All these different parts, tantalizing as it is to think, might not actually fit together. We may be looking at just a series of coincidental connections."

I fall silent as I pace my room, letting my mind try to unravel this complex knot of information

"I don't believe in coincidences. There has to be something we're missing," I say. "We need to find that piece. And maybe this Hai Deng might be able to give that to us."

"Yeah well, he's unfortunately in the wind," Astra says. "Unless you can pull him out of a hat, that might be a dead end."

I frown and turn it over in my mind for a long moment. "I can't pull him out of a hat," I say. "But I know somebody who might be able to."

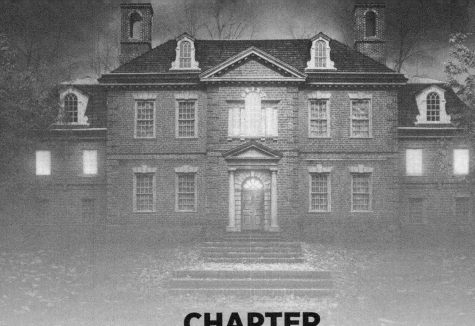

CHAPTER
TWENTY-FIVE

The Aurora Hotel; Woodcreek, WA

I PACE THE ROOM, THINKING ABOUT EVERYTHING GOING ON. There are a lot of moving parts and not a lot of solid conclusions I can draw. We've got the connection between Craig and the Ukrainians now. He's obviously doing something shady. But for all I know, it could be simple corruption—declining to bring cases against the *Chlopciki* associates. Or it might include tipping the Ukrainians off to the whereabouts of a certain witness set to testify against them and deal a big blow to their organization.

I know we need to move carefully, though. I can't afford to move against Craig until I have some concrete proof. The network of shell companies and offshore accounts is a good place to start, but until we can find who's sending him all that money and conclusively link Craig to a criminal enterprise that involves the Ukrainians, it's not enough. Not by half. And when you move against somebody with as much pull and as many connections as James Craig, you had best have all your ducks in a row. I don't intend to take the shot until we can be sure we're going to put him down permanently.

Astra is right, though. All we have are these disparate parts with no way of knowing how—or if—they fit together. When you look at them all out of context, the picture it paints is very suggestive. We're talking political corruption, a conspiracy to commit a murder to protect a criminal enterprise, and even more. But it's my job to put it all into context, and right now, I have zero clue what that might be. The entire picture is opaque, and I can't see it clearly. There's just too much noise and juicy tidbits that make it easy, not to mention all too tempting, to head down the wrong path.

Hai Deng is the one person who might be able to help break that opacity. Perhaps. Somebody hired him and his two buddies to come kill me and Astra. There is no question about that. It wasn't just some random attack. What confuses the issue is that he's Triad affiliated. It lends credence to the idea that the Ukrainians have teamed up with the Chinese, but it doesn't conclusively prove it. Which means I need to find him, question him, and figure out who sent him. Deng could be the thread that, when pulled, could unravel the whole tapestry and show me exactly what's going on here.

But finding him is the problem. Criminals have a really nasty habit of being able to disappear and avoid being found when they want to hide. They're never around when you need them. It's a good thing for me I have a friend who's plugged into the criminal underworld and has a penchant for finding those people who don't want to be found.

I grab my phone and send him a videochat request as I sit down at the small table in my room and wait for the call to be connected. He picks it up a moment later and I'm greeted by the sight of a half-naked man sipping a glass of wine as he sits in the bathtub. As I stare at him for a moment, the most absurd thought passes through my head—even in the tub his hair is perfectly coiffed, not a single strand out of place.

"Jesus, Fish, you're in the bathtub," I exclaim.

"As always, Agent Wilder, your keen observation skills prove why your star is on the rise within the Bureau," he replies with a grin.

"Why did you answer my call?"

"I always answer your calls. You know that."

"Fine, let me rephrase that," I stammer. "Why did you answer my call while you're sitting in the tub? I don't need to see that."

He laughs and like his speaking voice, it's a rich, cultured sound. "To be fair, you can't see anything below my chest. Anything else you're seeing must be a product of your imagination, which I find most interesting."

My face flares with heat and a nervous laugh passes my lips. "Oh my God, I hate you so much right now."

He chuckles again and takes a sip of his wine. Fish is an old friend and is one of the oddest, quirkiest people I know. He's also been a very reliable informant over the years. I'm fortunate to have one of the leading figures in Seattle's criminal underworld on speed dial—or at least he was before he made a play to go legit. He postures like he's a legitimate businessman and a pillar of the city's economic community. And to some extent, he is starting to become that. However, I know for a fact that he's still got his fingers in some illicit pies.

But we have an arrangement and have had it for years. He feeds me intel and directs me to bad guys we might not be aware of, and I look the other way to some of the shadier things he does. Of course, the criminals he directs me to are usually his rivals so from that perspective, I am helping him build and grow his criminal empire. I'm helping him remain on top of Seattle's dark underbelly. But he also knows there is a line with me, and he's always taken care to avoid crossing it. Or at least, not telling me when he does.

I know some would frown on our arrangement. They'd say

I'm selling my soul to the devil just to make a few collars. But on the whole, the information Fish provides me more than balances out his illegal gambling halls and the illicit liquor he brings in. He has divested himself from the portion of his portfolio that deals in anything violent. He's moved away from trafficking drugs, guns, and women. If he hadn't, I wouldn't have gone into business with him.

What most people don't realize is that Fish is actually a good guy who loves the city. And as he goes legit, he is giving back to Seattle, a city that gave him everything. From his humble beginning as an immigrant fishmonger on the docks, Fish rose to the pinnacle of power and amassed a fortune so vast it's obscene. And now that he's in his fifties, he's looking at his legacy and has realized he wants to leave something positive behind. He wants to make a lasting mark that more or less erases his violent, criminal past, and casts him in a better light.

Some people would say he can't rewrite his history. He was a thug and a criminal and that's all he'll ever be. And I think they're absolutely entitled to that point of view. After all, when he was younger, Fish did a lot of very bad things and hurt a lot of people—though, to be fair, the only people he truly hurt were other criminals. He absolutely carved a bloody swath through the criminal underworld on his rise to becoming the undisputed king of Seattle.

But I believe in second chances. I believe if you're sincere and you make a good faith effort to reform your life and do good things, then there's no reason you can't rewrite your history. There's no reason you can't change your image and leave a better legacy.

"How are you doing, Agent Wilder?" he asks. "I heard you and Agent Russo were attacked."

"How did you hear about that?"

He arches an eyebrow and gives me a look that says the answer to that is the most obvious thing ever. I grin and give him a shrug. It probably is.

"Right," I say. "You know all and see all."

"Not everything," he replies. "Just what interests me. And you very much interest me. You always have."

A lot of people would likely see that as sexually suggestive. But I know Fish and know it's not. He has never been inappropriate with me. Hasn't ever hit on me and never tried to steer things in that direction. He's never been anything but a gentleman. When Fish says I interest him, that's exactly what he means—I interest him as a person.

"How is Agent Russo, by the way?" he asks.

"She's all right. She got very lucky," I say. "But she's going to need to take it easy for a little while."

"I would imagine. Being shot is a traumatic thing and it takes the body a little while to recover," he says. "I do hope she will give herself the time to heal. I know she can sometimes be rather… excitable."

I laugh. "That's one word for it," I tell him. "But I'm doing my best to keep her on a short leash and make her take it easy."

"That's wise," he nods. "So, what is it I can do for you, Agent Wilder?"

"I need your help with something."

"Please, name it. If it's within my power, I'll do whatever I can for you," he says. "You know that."

"Well, we were able to ID one of our attackers—the other two are ghosts," I say. "But the man we were able to identify is named Hai Deng. He's connected to the Triads. And he is, as of right now, in the wind. I was hoping you could work your magic and track him down."

"Of course, I can. If he can be found, rest assure that I will find him," he says.

"Thank you, Fish."

"It's always a pleasure, Blake."

I clear my throat and laugh. "I'll uh—let you get back to your bath."

He smiles. "You really should take more baths. They're just so rejuvenating," he says. "I will send you some special bath salts that are relaxing and restorative. They will open your pores and sinuses. It will help calm and soothe you. Baths are good for the body, mind, and soul."

"I have no doubt they are," I nod. "I'll give it a shot. God knows I need something soothing and calming in my life."

"As do we all."

"Thank you, Fish. I appreciate you."

"And I appreciate you as well," he says. "Have a good night, my friend."

"You too."

I disconnect the call and set my phone down then look over at the bathroom. It may not be as luxurious as Fish's tub but a hot bath sounds pretty good right about now.

CHAPTER TWENTY-SIX

Jade Leopard Imports & Exports; Woodcreek, WA

I T TOOK TWO DAYS, BUT I FINALLY GOT THE CALL FROM FISH TO come to a warehouse he owns that sits in one of Woodcreek's smaller ports on the other side of the city from the Ukrainians. I don't know why it surprised me to learn he has a warehouse here. I mean, it makes sense. Fish has a lot of goods he wants to bring in with minimal observation and Woodcreek is apparently the place to do just that. I would not be surprised to learn somebody was smuggling nukes through here. Though I hope that Customs isn't that compromised.

On the other hand, I should be impressed that it only took Fish two days to find that particular needle in the haystack. I mean, if I were trying to track him down, it would likely take me weeks and there was no guarantee of success. I like to think I'm fairly well-connected in my own right, but my network is nothing like Fish's. I'm going to have to remember to send him something nice.

I get out of my car and walk to the warehouse door. It's closing in on eight and dark as pitch down here. It's well after hours, so the place is virtually abandoned, as are the rest of the docks. A fog bank is starting to roll in off the bay and somewhere out there, a horn blows a long, plaintive note. It's all very creepy and sends a cold finger of ice up my spine.

I knock on the door then take a step back and wait. A few moments later it opens, and I find myself face to face with a thirty-something man with dark hair and dark, almond-shaped eyes. He's about five-seven and lean. His face is smooth and though he doesn't have a threatening look about him, there's an understated air of violence about him. He reminds me of that martial arts actor Daniel Wu, and strikes me as somebody who knows how to take care of himself in a scrap.

"You Wilder?" he asks.

I nod. "And you are?"

"Liang," he says. "Come in."

I step through the door, and he closes it behind us. The interior is dim, murky, and eerily quiet. All around us are tall shelving units—twenty or twenty-five feet high—loaded with crates and boxes. The interior of the warehouse has a strange aroma that reminds me of incense.

"Follow me," he says.

I do as he says, and he leads me through the labyrinth of shelves, our footsteps echoing hollowly off the concrete floor. Eventually, we emerge into a small square clearing set between rows of crates and the shelving units that tower over us. A single fluorescent light hangs over the clearing, illuminating a rectangular section as bright as a spotlight. And in the middle of that rectangular section of light sits a man tied to a chair.

The man is Chinese. He's probably about five-eight and trim,, with dark hair and eyes. He's definitely the same build as our attackers out at the Bayview. I stop a few feet in front of the bound man, crossing my arms over my chest, and glower at him. Liang stands behind him, his arms folded over his chest as well, and is then joined by a man who looks so similar to him, I can't help but think they're related.

The man in the chair turns his head, trying to get a glimpse of his abductors, then turns back to me. He's doing his best to look hard. To look unconcerned. But I can see the fear in his eyes. He licks his lips nervously and clears his throat, doing his best to master his emotions and the expression on his face.

"You're Hai Deng," I say. "You and a couple of your buddies tried to murder me and my best friend."

"I got no idea what you're talking about," he replies.

"You sure about that?" I ask.

"Go to hell," he spits.

Liang moves so quickly and gracefully, he's a blur of motion. Hai grunts heavily as a fist is driven into his gut and he draws in a sharp, wheezing breath. Liang steps back, folding his hands in front of him and staring hard at Hai. The bound man gasps and retches, trying to get his air back, but the bonds holding him to the seat keep him from doubling over.

"You all right, Hai?" I ask.

He grunts and snorts, then tries to speak, but all that comes out of his mouth is a hoarse croak. I give him a minute to get himself sorted out. And when he seems able to breathe again, I give him a grin.

"Let's try this again," I say. "Who hired you to kill us?"

"I didn't try to kill you. You're high or somethin', lady. I never seen you in my life."

"Huh. So, if that's true, how did your DNA end up under the fingernails of my partner?" I ask. "She got both you and your buddy, by the way. I just killed the one who came after me."

He spits on the ground and gives me an angry look. "Go to hell."

"Yeah, you said that already."

Liang flashes in again and this time, the sharp crack of his fist meeting Hai's face echoes around the warehouse. Blood flows freely from his nose and the split in his lip. Hai winces in pain as Liang steps back again, standing as still as a statue. Ordinarily, this isn't how I'd interrogate somebody. But I'm not going to lie and say I don't derive some small bit of satisfaction from seeing the man who shot Astra getting what he deserves.

"Let's try this again, Mr. Deng," I say. "And before we go on, let me assure you that Liang here seems to be in excellent shape and can probably keep this up all night long."

"I can," Liang confirms.

"Excellent," I nod, then turn back to Deng. "Now, who hired you to take us out?"

He remains silent and looks away from me. Liang delivers a long flurry of punches, rocking Deng, who slumps limply against his bonds. Blood spills from his nose and mouth, one eye is swollen shut and the other is red and puffy. He's gasping and looks utterly exhausted, so I give him a minute before I resume my questioning.

"Was it the Ukrainians?" I demand. "Are the Triads providing muscle for the Ukrainians now? Is that what's going on here?"

He spits a big glob of blood onto the floor and continues to ignore me. I fold my arms over my chest again and start to pace, trying to figure out how to crack him. He seems as immovable as a stone, but I know everybody's got a breaking point. I just need to figure out what his is.

"Tell me about Madeline Donaldson," I say.

He finally turns to me and cocks his head. "Who?"

"The girl you guys killed," I say. "Was it the Ukrainians who told you to kill her?"

"I don't know what you're talking about."

I watch him closely as he answers and can see his reaction is genuine. He really doesn't know. He wasn't involved with Madeline's death, so I pivot back to my original questions.

"Who hired you to kill me?" I ask.

"You can beat on me all day and I'm still not going to tell you."

As if acting on cue, Liang steps forward and delivers another shot to the face, rocking Deng's head backward. He groans but sits up again, just sitting there staring at me as he bleeds. Pain isn't his pressure point. I get the idea that Liang is enjoying himself though, and I don't entirely hate seeing him get what he deserves.

"Liang," I start. "What did Fish say we should do with him when we're done here?"

Deng's eyes widen slightly, and he swallows hard. Fish's name continues to strike fear into the hearts of criminals everywhere. It's a nice ace card to have in my back pocket.

"Fish sent you?" Deng asks.

"No, Fish delivered you to us at my request," I correct him.

"Fish said we can do whatever we want with him," Liang answers. "Or we can turn him over to the Triads and they will take care of him for us."

Deng shudders and I can see he truly believed that because I'm a federal agent that he would simply walk away from this. Maybe he thought he'd do a little time, but that's a badge of honor to scumbags like this. I need to make him see that I can and will cross the line when necessary. My badge doesn't automatically protect him. I need to shake his belief that his attempt to kill us won't carry serious consequences. And not just for him. I need to raise the stakes in a very real way.

"Does Deng have family?" I ask.

"Wife. Two children," Liang answers. "Mother and father both still alive. Two brothers, a sister, and a grandmother."

"That's a lot of family," I note, staring directly into Deng's eyes. "That's a lot of people to lose in one fell swoop, isn't it?"

Deng licks his lips. "You won't do nothin'. You're a fed."

"Does it look like we're in a Bureau building?" I ask.

"You can't do nothin' to me or my family," he says. "It's against the law."

"So is trying to murder federal agents. And yet, here we are," I shrug. "Liang, if we needed Deng's entire family wiped out of existence, is that something the Triads could handle for me?"

"All it would take is for Fish to ask," Liang replies. "And I'm sure he would be more than happy to. He does not like trash who have no honor like this piece of filth."

"You can't," Deng gasps. "You can't do this. You're—"

"Do you see me wearing a badge right now?" I shout, my voice echoing around the cavernous warehouse. "You shot my best friend. You tried to kill me. I take that personally, Deng. I may be a fed but I'm a human being first. And believe me, that desire for vengeance runs through the veins of every human being alive."

He looks at me with his one good eye, his face twisted in an expression of fear. His lips are quivering, and I see a shudder run through his body. I feel like I've got him backed against the edge of the cliff. I just need to give him one more shove to send him toppling over the edge.

"You tried to take my family from me," I hiss. "I can think of nothing more fitting than taking your family from you."

"Balance," Liang says.

I loom over Deng, staring down at him as I muster as much rage as I can, letting him see it in my face. He recoils and looks away, unable to meet my eyes.

"Tell me what I want to know or I swear I will ask Fish to have your family wiped off the face of the Earth. Do you hear me?" I scream at him.

Deng flinches like I just smacked him, and I can see him searching my face, trying to decide whether I'm bluffing or not. There is fear in his eyes as he contemplates the idea of Fish taking his entire family from him. I can only imagine the horrible things going through his mind right now. All I can hope as he contemplates what Fish will do to his family are the most horrible things his mind can conjure. I need him to believe that I have no limits and that I really will order his entire family killed.

Deng sighs and slumps against his bonds again. He finally raises his gaze to me, and I see the look of defeat in his eyes. That's when I know that I've got him.

"You have to protect me," Deng says. "And my family. You have to tell Fish to leave my family alone."

"I don't have to do anything," I say coldly. "Tell me what I want to know, and I'll consider it."

He swallows hard then licks his lips nervously, wincing when his tongue hits the split that's raw and bleeding. Deng finally nods to himself, his decision made.

"I don't know anything about any Ukrainians," he says. "It was one of the sheriff's deputies who hired us to take you out."

His words hit me hard. Of all the things I was expecting to hear that wouldn't have even been on my list. A sheriff's deputy? Is Block somehow involved in all of this? Is he compromised as well?

"What about Block?" I ask, a worm of worry writhing around in my belly.

Deng shakes his head. "Nah. The sheriff don't know nothin'. He's clueless."

"Then who hired you?"

"His name is Mullins. Scott Mullins," Deng says. "Now please, tell Fish to leave my family alone."

I pull my phone out of my pocket and set it up to record. When it's ready, I look at Deng, pinning him to his seat with my eyes.

"I want you to repeat everything you just said for the camera," I tell him.

"Will you swear to tell Fish?"

"Do what I say, or I swear I'll tell Fish to annihilate your entire family," I growl, my voice colder than the Arctic.

"Fine," Deng says miserably.

I hold the camera, careful to keep him in frame as he tells me the whole story, including how much they were paid. Ten thousand bucks to split between the three of them for murdering two federal agents seems criminally low to me, but whatever. When he's finished, I save the recording and slip my phone back into my pocket then give Liang a nod.

"I think I've got what I need here," I say.

"What should we do with this piece of filth?"

I look at Deng, fixing him with my most menacing glare. "You need to leave the state of Washington. You've lost your privileges to be in this state," I tell him. "If I even catch wind of you being back here, I'll tell Fish to pull the trigger and wipe out your family. Am I understood?"

Deng's shoulders slump and he looks like he wants to argue, but in the end, he simply hangs his head and nods.

"I'm not playing with you, Deng," I press. "You set foot in Washington again, your entire family will pay the price."

"Fine," he replies weakly.

"You owe me a hundred bucks."

I look at the man standing in the shadows behind Deng. He hadn't said a word or done a thing the entire time we were handling Deng. I'd almost forgotten he was there, to be honest. But Liang is laughing softly and shaking his head.

"I'll see you out," Liang says to me.

I follow him out of the warehouse and when we're standing in the moonlight again, I turn to him with a small grin on my lips.

"And why do you owe him a hundred bucks?" I ask.

"We made a bet. He said you wouldn't take Deng's life," he says. "I believed that after he tried to kill you and your friend, that you would have your vengeance."

I laugh softly. "I was tempted. Believe me, I was," I tell him.

"But that's not who I am. It has nothing to do with being a fed. It's just not in me to kill somebody in cold blood like that."

"I should have known better," Liang says. "Fish says you're a good person like that and have a good heart. But I believe we all have a monster inside of us. We're all capable of terrible things. I was simply betting on the idea that you would let that monster out of its cage."

"Sorry," I shrug.

"Don't be. It's a good lesson," he tells me. "I can now see why Fish says that he likes you as much as he does."

"Why's that?"

"Your humanity," he tells me. "Fish says you're a good influence on him. You remind him to maintain his own humanity. He credits you with many of the changes he is making in his life and in his business."

"As much as I'd like to take credit, Fish is a good person as well. Those changes he's making are all coming from within him," I say.

"I agree. But if he needs to credit you to justify it to himself, let's not take that idea away from him," Liang says with a smile.

"He'll never hear different from me," I say. "Thank you for everything, Liang. I appreciate your help tonight."

"It was my pleasure," he nods. "Be safe, Agent Wilder."

"You too," I say then head to my car.

I drive back to my hotel, replaying it all in my head over and over again. Far from answering things for me, what Deng said has only opened up a thousand different questions for me. This situation is growing more confusing as more players step onto the stage. And yet despite that, I still feel that sense of momentum building. I feel like we're picking up steam. I see no reason for it since I've gotten no answers to anything and only have more questions to show for my efforts to this point. But that sense of motion remains.

I just hope that sense of momentum isn't actually me hurtling toward a cliff that I can't see right now.

CHAPTER
TWENTY-SEVEN

Woodcreek Sheriff's Station; Woodcreek, WA

BLOCK SEEMS TO PALE, THEN AGE TEN YEARS AS HE WATCHES the video I play for him. He runs a hand over his face and shakes his head.

"Play it again," he whispers. "Please."

He's already watched it twice but if he wants to see it again, so be it. I have to imagine getting confirmation that one of his deputies is on the take has to be difficult for him. I mean, he suspects it already, but to find out that he's right has to be tough. I feel bad for him.

"What happened to him?" Block asks. "Why is he so beat up?"

I clear my throat. "Must have walked into a door."

"Right. A door."

"What can you tell me about Mullins?"

"He's a good kid. Good cop," he says. "At least, I thought he was. He's the last person I would've thought would be mixed up in something like this."

I spent the morning filling Block in on where I'm at with this investigation. I wanted him to have the right context, know all the players, and know what I'm thinking before I played the video of Deng for him. I dare say it would hit differently if you didn't have all the facts than it does if you know what's actually going on.

"I can't believe he did this," Block mutters. "I can't believe he'd be mixed up in trying to kill you and your partner."

"Money makes people do crazy things," I say.

"You do realize we can't use this video in any prosecution, don't you?" he asks. "A defense lawyer will have a field day with it. Say it was a coerced confession. And to be honest, I can't say I wouldn't say the same thing."

"I do understand that. But I can tell you with certainty that he was telling the truth," I tell him. "And I can also tell you that Deng is one of the shooters from the attack that night. DNA doesn't lie."

"If the DNA was conclusive, why didn't you just bring him in?" Block asks. "Let the system do its work?"

"Because the system wouldn't have gotten him to confess, let alone give up a name," I say. "Jail for these guys is a badge of honor. It would be building his cred. He never would have given Mullins up if we'd put him on trial."

"I can't say I approve of your methods, Agent Wilder."

"I don't either," I reply. "But believe me that this is the exception and not the rule. I don't normally condone this sort of... interrogation method."

He sighs and shakes his head. I can feel the disapproval radiating off him and feel a stab of guilt for having disappointed him. It's crazy, I know. But I think more than anything, it's a case of me disappointing myself. I let my emotions over Astra cloud my judgment and lead me down a path I would normally avoid. But it is what it is.

"I'll be harder on myself than you can ever be, Sheriff," I say.

"And I'll have to find a way to deal with what I've done. That time, though, is not right now. Right now, we need to find out who gave Mullins the order to greenlight us because I don't believe for a second that he's the mastermind behind this entire episode. There is something bigger in play here."

Block pauses for a minute and seems like he wants to argue further. He wants to make sure I understand his displeasure with what I've done. But he bites it back, perhaps realizing what I said about being harder on myself than he could ever be is true. No need to keep beating on that dead horse.

"All right, so what's your play then?" he asks.

"Well, since we can't present Deng's confession, we need to squeeze one out of Mullins," I tell him. "We need to leverage, then flip him. We need to get him to roll on whoever's on the next rung of the food chain."

"And how are we going to do that?"

"I thought you might want to take a ride out to his place with me."

"Not if you're planning on beating the pulp out of him. I won't be party to anything like that, Agent Wilder."

"I'm not planning on doing anything like that," I say honestly. "I am going to present him with this video though. And I'm going to squeeze him as hard as I can to get the name of the next man up. I thought with you being there, he might be less likely to lie."

Block frowns and looks down at his desk. He taps his finger on his blotter for a moment, considering. It's not necessary for him to come. I just thought I'd extend the offer since it's one of his deputies and I have no desire to step on his toes.

"All right. Let's go talk to him," Block finally says.

⁓

"Sheriff. What are you doin' here?" Mullins asks.

Mullins gets to his feet, wiping his greasy hands off on a rag.

It's his day off and we found him in his garage working on his motorcycle. He gives me a nod.

"Scotty, this is Agent Blake Wilder of the FBI," Block introduces us. "Agent Wilder, Scotty Mullins."

"Nice to meet you, Deputy Mullins."

"Likewise," he says. "I'd shake your hand but…"

He holds his hands up, showing me all the grease. I give him a smile and simply nod in return. Mullins stands about six-three and wears his white-blonde hair in the same flat-top cut the Sheriff does. His skin is tanned, obviously from spending a lot of time outdoors, and he's got blue eyes. He's lean but well-proportioned and strong—the tank top he's wearing showcases arms that are muscular and well-defined.

"So, what brings you and the FBI out here today, Sheriff?" Mullins asks.

I catch the nervous tremble in his voice when he speaks. It's subtle and he quickly covers it, but I heard it all the same. That waver in his voice matches that faint spark of fear I see briefly flash through his eyes.

"Might be best if we speak inside, Scotty," Block says.

Mullins looks from Block to me then back again. He clears his throat, and I can practically see him drawing in on himself. It's like he sees the walls closing in on him and is looking for a way out.

"Nah. It's a mess inside. Maid's week off," he says, his laughter forced and wooden. "Out here's fine."

"Suit yourself," Block says.

"What's going on, Sheriff?" he asks, trying his best to ignore me completely.

"We got a problem, Scotty."

"Yeah? What's that?"

Block, obviously picking up on his deputy trying to ignore me and freeze me out, looks at me pointedly.

"Agent Wilder? You want to tell him why we're here?" Block asks.

I turn to Mullins. "We're here because of Hai Deng."

"Who?" he asks, trying to sound surprised.

"Hai Deng," I repeat. "The man you hired to kill me and my partner."

He laughs nervously. "I have no idea what you're talking about," he says. "Sheriff, what's this all about?"

"Just listen to her, son," Block tells him.

"You hired Hai Deng, a member of the Chinese Triads, to kill me and my partner," I tell him. "Don't insult my intelligence by denying it."

"I guess I'm going to have to insult your intelligence then because I have no idea what you're talking about."

I sigh and pull the phone out of my pocket, cue up the video, and hit play. He stands there frozen for a long moment as he watches the video play. He licks his lips nervously and gets a wild look in his eye as if he's going to bolt. Block apparently picks up on it as well and steps forward, putting one of his big, meaty hands on Mullins' shoulder.

"You can't use that video. Look at the guy," he points. "He's beat to hell. That ain't going to be admissible in court."

"Maybe not. But Mr. Deng will be able to give his testimony live and in person," I say. "And I guarantee you he'll be fully healed up by then."

"The game's up, kid," Block tells him. "It's time to come clean."

Mullins shakes his head. "I'm serious, Sheriff. I don't know—"

Block frowns and looks down for a moment. I can see how painful this is for him and I feel that stab of guilt again. He finally raises his head and looks Mullins in the eye.

"Let's not do this. I always thought you were a stand-up guy," Block says. "It's time for you to take responsibility for what you done. So, answer Agent Wilder's questions. Be honest, son. Be the stand-up guy I know you can be."

He looks at my phone, at the frozen image of Hai Deng on the screen. That nervousness flashes through his eyes again and he shifts on his feet.

"Cooperate with me and I'll talk to the US Attorney about leniency for you," I say. "You're a small fish, Mullins. I want the next man up. Who ordered you to hire Deng and his buddies to take us out?"

Mullins takes a step back and looks at Block, then at me. An expression of absolute betrayal is etched into his features. His eyes narrow and he looks at the both of us with a light of pure hatred gleaming in his eyes.

"How many times do I have to tell you that I don't know what you're talking about?" he demands, his voice rising.

"Deputy Mullins, I've already had my team look into your financials and those of Hai Deng," I tell him. "I know you took out ten thousand dollars. Deng has a corresponding deposit a day later."

Block looks at me and chuckles. "I see now why you say he can't be the mastermind."

Mullins rounds on him, an expression of rage coloring his features. "You shut up, old man. You don't know anything."

"I know enough that I wouldn't leave a trail that obvious," Block says.

"Deputy Mullins, your financial records, combined with Mr. Deng's testimony, will be enough to put you away for a very, very long time," I tell him. "I want to know who instructed you to hire a crew to take us out. You can either cooperate or you can take the full weight of trying to murder two federal agents. You know what that means?"

"Enlighten me," he replies, sounding as if he's bored with this conversation.

"It means that's the needle, Deputy Mullins. Trying to murder federal agents carries stiff penalties," I tell him bluntly. "Now, do you really want your little girl growing up without her father? Cooperate with us and you may still have a chance to watch her grow up."

A stricken expression crossing his face, Mullins puts his hands on top of his head and turns away from us. He's muttering softly to himself as he starts to pace his garage. I lower my hand, leaving it hovering over the butt of my weapon just in case he gets squirrely. He paces for a couple of minutes, and I exchange a glance with Block who also has his hand near his weapon. He shrugs, telling me with his eyes to give Mullins a minute to process what's going on. I imagine his mind has to be spinning a thousand miles a minute.

"Why'd you do it, Scotty?" Block asks. "Why'd you get into bed with these animals?"

Mullins stops pacing then turns to Block, an expression of sadness on his face. He shakes his head and runs his hands through his close-cropped hair.

"Nina had some expensive medical bills," Mullins said. "You remember when she—"

Block nods. "Yeah, I remember."

Mullins' eyes shimmer with tears as he recalls whatever landed his little girl in the hospital, the memory of it every bit of it obviously just as raw and painful today as it was when it happened. He sniffs loudly.

"He knew all about Nina," he says. "He told me he'd take care of everything. That he'd give me a monthly salary if I did jobs for him when he asked me. At first it was nothin'. Just small things here and there that didn't hurt anything."

"That's how it starts," Block says.

Mullins loses his battle with his tears, and when the first one spills down his cheek, that opens the floodgates. The man sobs like a child as he feels his entire world crashing down around him.

"I need to know who gives you your orders, Deputy Mullins," I press.

"It's time to get ahead of this, son," Block encourages him.

Mullins wipes his eyes and looks at us. He runs a hand over his face and tries to compose himself. Tries to salvage some shred of his dignity.

"If I tell you, can you promise me that I won't do any time?" he asks.

I shake my head. "I can't promise you that. You're an accomplice to the attempted murders of two federal agents," I say. "But if you fully cooperate, I can promise that I will talk to the prosecutors about giving you some consideration. It might mean you'll do less time than if you take the full weight of the charges on your own."

"It's the best deal you're going to get, Scotty. You need to take it."

Mullins looks around and I can see the struggle in his mind. He's weighing his options in his mind and the look on his face tells me he realizes he doesn't have any. Mullins turns to me, finally meeting my eyes.

"All right," he says, his voice wavering. "I'll cooperate."

CHAPTER TWENTY-EIGHT

Hannigan's Park; Woodcreek, WA

"IT'S FIVE AFTER," BLOCK SAYS. "WHAT IF HE DOESN'T show?"

"He'll show. Just relax."

Block and I are sitting in the back of an undercover surveillance van I had sent up from the Seattle Field Office. The tech is sitting at the console, adjusting the controls to get the best picture and sound possible. And on the video monitors, we're seeing Mullins' point of view through the pinhole camera he's wearing.

After we dropped the hammer on him yesterday and gained his cooperation, we got him to schedule a face-to-face meeting with his boss. After that, we spent an entire day going over what we needed him to say, rehearsing his lines over and over again until they sounded natural. More or less. Mullins is never going to win an Oscar, but I'm hoping he can get through what we need him to do.

"He's late," Mullins grumbles, his voice quavering with nerves.

I key open the comm. "Relax, Mullins," I say. "Take a couple of deep breaths and settle yourself down. He'll be here."

"What if he doesn't show?"

"He'll show," I tell him. "He's got way too much to lose."

The world outside the van is fading into shadow as the sun slips toward the horizon. The park we're at is small and sits on the shore of Samish Bay and is filled with soaring pines and thick screens of bushes. It's private and off the beaten path, which makes it ideal for this kind of a meeting. Not many people are barbecuing with the November cold setting in.

"We've got a car," the tech, a guy I've worked with a few times before named Julio, announces.

I look at the monitor he's pointing to and see the Range Rover pull into the parking lot. He sits there with the lights on and motor running for a couple of moments. It's as if he's sitting behind the wheel debating whether to get out of the car or not.

"That's a one hundred-thousand-dollar car sitting there," Block notes.

"Obscene, isn't it?"

He nods. "I've been drivin' my F-150 for the last fifteen years. Still runs like a champ," he says. "And I paid less'n twenty grand for it."

"I drive a Prius," Julio notes. "Drove off the lot for sixteen grand and it will run forever."

Block mutters to himself. It's so low I can't make out anything other than the words, "hippie" and "granola." I laugh as Julio frowns and turns back to the monitors. The lights on the Range Rover go out. He's made his decision. I key open the comm again.

"Okay, it's game time, Mullins. Take a deep breath, relax, and be ready," I tell him. "He's here and he's on his way to you."

On the screen, he gets out of his car and pulls his dark overcoat around him a little tighter as a breeze rolls in off the bay. He wraps his scarf around his neck then heads off into the park to the appointed meeting spot.

"Ten seconds," I tell Mullins.

"I see him," he mutters.

On the screen, we watch as US Attorney James Craig approaches Mullins with an expression of irritation on his face. Mullins takes a step back.

"You have got a set of stones on you," Craig hisses. "Not only are you not supposed to contact me, but when you break that rule, you do it to extort me?"

"I—I'm not tryin' to extort you, Mr. Craig," Mullins stammers. "And I'm sorry I had to break the rule about contactin' you. But we got problems."

"Yes, we do. You extorting me is a very big problem."

"That fed—Wilder or whatever—she knows," Mullins says. "She came by my place and started questioning me about the hit you ordered."

"The hit you bungled, you mean," Craig snaps.

Sitting next to me, Block sits up. "That sounds like a confession to me."

"Not quite," I reply. "It's open to interpretation. We need a little more."

"It's not my fault Deng screwed up," Mullins says. "We've used them how many times now? And he's come through every single time."

"Until this time."

"Yeah," Mullins says quietly. "Until this time."

"So, the feds obviously have Deng and he's talking," Craig mutters. "And now they're circling you."

"Now you can see why I need to get out of town," Mullins says. "So, I'm not tryin' to extort you, Mr. Craig. I just need to get away from the feds."

"I fail to see how that's my problem. You know what will happen to you if you suddenly develop a conscience. I don't believe I need to remind you of that," Craig says.

"No, you don't need to remind me. But I'm beggin' you. Please, help me," Mullins says. "They're goin' to fry me if they catch me. Not just for the screwed-up hit but for the girl up at Whitehorn that got murdered. They think I had something to do with that too."

Craig looks at him for a long moment, an expression of confusion on his face. "The girl up at Whitehorn?" he asks. "I have no idea what you're talking about."

Mullins shrugs. "Makes no difference to me. All I know is I didn't kill her."

"I didn't kill her either," Craig objects. "I have absolutely no idea what you're going on about. I have no idea who this girl is."

I turn to Block. "It's the damnedest thing. I believe him," I say. "Maybe we were wrong from the jump."

"I don't know. Maybe," Block says. "To use your words, I need more before I buy it."

"Why would he lie to Mullins about it?" I point out. "He has no reason to. If anything, I'd think he would want to tell Mullins just to increase his own personal body count. It's street cred, which makes other people fear him. It's a win-win from his point of view."

"Maybe. I guess we'll need to ask him," Block says.

"I suppose we will."

"I need the money, Mr. Craig," Mullins says. "Did you bring it?"

On the monitor, Craig taps his breast pocket. "It's in here," he says. "But before I give it to you, I need to know what you told the feds. Every word of it."

"I didn't tell them anything. I told them to go to hell," Mullins replies.

"So, not a word then?" Craig presses. "Not a single word? To anybody? Not to Wilder? Your neighbor? Not even your dog?"

Mullins shakes his head. "No, man. Nobody. I haven't said a

word," he says. "I just need the money to get out of town. Please, man."

A sick feeling grips me and my stomach lurches as I see exactly where this is going. Craig's body language is just too calm. Too peaceful. He's just been told the feds are poking around his business and he has all the reaction of a stone. He doesn't seem to care. Even worse, he seems to accept Mullins' answer without so much as a single question. The questions Craig has asked make me think he's trying to gauge how much I know. It tells me this is going to end badly unless I can stop it.

"Good," Craig says. "Very good."

Knowing what's coming next, I reach for the door handle and throw it open. I jump out and start to sprint toward Mullins as three shots ring out. The cracks of the shots echo through the trees around me and roll out across the bay. As I run, I pull my weapon and hear the heavy footsteps of Sheriff Block right behind me.

The shots are still ringing in my ears and just ahead of me, I see Mullins fall to his knees, looking up at Craig. The US Attorney lowers his gun, the barrel scant inches from Mullins' face. The shot is sharp and startling, making me flinch. I see Mullins' head snap back but then, still on his knees, he slumps forward then falls on his face into the pool of his own blood.

"James Craig, drop your weapon!" I shout as I keep running.

Craig turns to us, and I see his eyes widen when he sees a pair of deputies closing in on him from the left, two more from the right, and Block and I coming straight at him. I can see him glance at his weapon and know he's thinking about trying to shoot his way out of this.

"Don't do it, Craig!" I bark as I raise my weapon. "Drop your weapon."

He hesitates, still holding his gun down at his side. He's shocked to see us standing there, weapons all trained on him. Then he looks down at his weapon again, that desire to go down in a blaze of glory flashing across his face again.

"Drop the gun, Craig. Do it now," I order. "I will shoot!"

I'm ten feet from him, my gun pointed at his face, and the urge to pull the trigger growing stronger by the moment. This is the man who ordered Astra and me to be killed, and there's some small part of me that wants him dead. No, scratch that. A large part of me wants to pull this trigger. Block steps up beside me and gives me a meaningful look. A look that says it's not worth it. To let the system do its job.

The air is crackling with tension as Craig looks at us, knowing his entire life has just been effectively blown up. He never saw this coming, can't believe Mullins betrayed him, and knows that life as he's always known it is effectively over.

"Last chance," I demand. "Drop the gun."

Craig looks at me then down at his gun one more time. I almost think he's going to do it and go down firing. But then he drops the gun at his feet instead and gets down on his knees, placing his hands behind his head. As I approach him with a pair of cuffs, he closes his eyes, his face draining of color.

CHAPTER TWENTY-NINE

Woodcreek Sheriff's Station Interrogation Room; Woodcreek, WA

"YOU KNOW YOU'RE DONE, DON'T YOU, MR. CRAIG?" I ask.

He just sits there staring off into space, not speaking, not moving, and hell, I don't even think he's breathing. I sit back in my chair and look around the small interrogation room. Acoustic tile lines the gray and dingy walls. The tables and chairs are all nicked and scarred, and the linoleum on the floor is peeling. The observation window has been tagged by what looks like generations of degenerates, and the overhead fluorescent bulb flickers incessantly. I've been in some crappy interrogation facilities but this one has to rank near the top. I just have to hope the audio and visual equipment Block is using doesn't fail.

"Mr. Craig, I need you to acknowledge that you have been read your rights," I say.

It's like he's catatonic or something, so I snap my fingers in front of his face.

"I need you to acknowledge that you have been read your rights," I repeat, louder this time.

When he still doesn't answer, I slap the table as hard as I can. He flinches, startled. He finally focuses on me but looks like he's still somewhere far away.

"Mr. Craig, I need you to acknowledge—"

"Yes, fine. You've read me my rights. I understand."

"Great. So, you know you can have a lawyer present."

"I am a lawyer."

"Are you waiving your right to counsel?"

"Yes. I don't need one. I forget more about the law every day than most anybody will ever know," he spits.

"If arrogance and delusions of grandeur were illegal, I'd be charging you with those as well," I say. "As it is, we have you on video murdering Scott Mullins. And that's after you admitted to setting up a hit on two federal agents. Seems pretty safe to say that you are done."

"Looks can be deceiving," he fires back. I'm not convinced, though.

Craig is trying to get his swagger back. Trying to take control of the situation and dominate the room. It's his usual MO. But I can see in his eyes that he knows he's waist-deep in a pile of crap— and he's sinking.

"The first thing I'm going to do is move to have that video thrown out," he says.

"Good luck with that. You weren't coerced. You offered your testimony of your own free will," I say. "But really, go ahead and try to get it kicked."

"I'm very well-connected—"

"Do you really think anybody's going to put their reputation on the line for you?"

"I do."

"Well, I guess we don't have anything to talk about then," I tell him. "We'll just go ahead and charge you with the full boatload. Oh, and you ordering the hit on me and Astra? That's federal time, Mr. Craig. And since Deputy Mullins was acting as our agent, that too is a federal charge. I certainly hope those connections you say you've got have a lot of pull or you're never going to see the light of day again."

I stare at him for a long moment, letting my words sink in. He frowns and says nothing, so I shrug and get to my feet. I'm at the door when he stops me.

"Wait," he says.

I turn around. "Yes?"

"Sit down."

"Let's get something straight here, Mr. Craig. You don't order me around," I say. "I don't have to listen to you. I'll be perfectly happy with charging you with what I have and let you roll the dice in court. Oh, and by the way, I'm still building a case to charge you with Madeline Donaldson's murder as well."

"Yeah, Mullins mentioned that. Oh, but you were listening, and you knew that already," he says. "My answer is the same though—I have no idea what you're talking about. I did not murder Madeline."

"I have no doubt. You're not a man who likes to get your hands dirty. Frankly, I'm surprised you had the stones to shoot Mullins yourself," I say.

"Mock me all you want. But I'm telling you that I didn't murder Madeline, nor did I order her murder," he snaps.

"If you say so."

"I do say so," he replies. "What's my motive? Why would I want the girl dead?"

"Because she was going to testify against your employers—the Ukrainians. I'm sure they ordered you to kill her to keep that from happening," I tell him. "Oh, and before you try denying your connection to the *Chlopciki* and by extension, the Odessa Mafia, you should know that we have your financials. My team has unraveled your network of shell companies and offshore accounts. We know you're taking money from them and because her testimony would be so damaging to your bosses, they ordered her killed."

Craig slumps back in his seat and stares at me. The look on his face tells me he did not see that coming. As Rick would say, it's a plot twist. And one he wasn't ready for. But he clears his throat and tries to look confident.

"That's a nice theory," he says. "The only problem with it is, it's entirely wrong."

"Oh? Well then enlighten me."

"The case was never going to trial. I was going to strike her as a witness. Her mental illness made her an unreliable witness," he says smugly. "And without her testimony, there is no case. If there is no case, there is no trial. Problem solved. So, as you can see, I had no reason to kill Madeline. No motive."

I try to hide my surprise. That was a plot twist I wasn't ready for. If what he's saying is true, he does take motive off the table. And as I look into his eyes, I can only conclude that it's true. I can hear the truth of it in his voice and see it in his eyes. This would normally be the point where I start second-guessing and doubting myself. But I'm not. There's not even a hint of doubt in my mind that what he's saying is true.

"Then what is it you were doing for the Ukrainians?" I ask.

He shakes his head. "Uh-uh. You don't get that until I get a deal."

"You know how this works, Mr. Craig. Any deal you get is contingent upon the actionable information and/or names you provide us," I say. "And since we're going to be needing a new US Attorney to come in, it will be that person who has the final say. However, as I told you, if you give me something good, I'll tell the new USA that you're a cooperating witness. Might help your case."

"I want full immunity and witness relocation."

"Wow, would you like the moon and the stars too?"

"Sure, if you can manage it."

"You've got real stones, Craig. I'll give you that."

"It's why I'm the best at what I do."

"If you say so," I respond. "Tell me what you were doing with the Ukrainians."

"Where's my deal?"

"I need you to take a leap of faith with me, Mr. Craig," I say. "I mean, you know you're never getting out of prison, right? The fact that we have you on tape killing somebody and the attempt on our lives guarantees you are looking at life without parole."

"Then what is my incentive to help you, Agent?"

"Because maybe, just maybe, I can make your time a little easier," I tell him. "Maybe I can help you avoid going to a Super Max prison and going somewhere a little nicer."

"WITSEC. Full immunity," he says.

"And as I told you, I'll take it up with the prosecutor," I say. "But I need something to go to them with. I need some good faith proof of your cooperation."

He sighs and shakes his head. "Like I told you, I was going to strike Madeline as a witness and let the case crumble, so there is no motive," he says. "But my business with the *Chlopciki* had nothing to do with her."

"Then what is your business with them?" I ask. "Take a leap of faith with me, Mr. Craig. Give me something."

He sighs heavily and scrubs his face with his hands. "Oh, what the hell. I worked with the *Chlopciki* to keep their members out of jail. I actively tanked some cases, declined to prosecute others," he says.

"And Dr. Stein?"

"He manufactures variants of popular street drugs like oxy and fentanyl among others," he says. "He sells them to the *Chlopciki* who, in turn not only distribute nationwide, but supply the Triads exclusively. A lot of the drugs manufactured here at Whitehorn flood the streets of Seattle. We are all making money hand over fist with this arrangement."

"And do you have proof of this?"

"Do you think I go into business with somebody without stockpiling CYA information?" he asks. "I've got all the goods on everybody."

"That's good. It'll help your case."

"That better buy me a one-way ticket to witness protection-ville because the second I spill that tea, I'm a walking dead man. The Ukrainians don't take well to traitors," he says. "And that's what they'll see me as—a traitor."

"I will do what I can for you, Mr. Craig. You have my word."

"I'm going to need more than that if you clowns want me to testify," he says.

I sit back in my seat. Some questions are being answered and portions of this case are being closed out. Just not the portions I expected. And it still doesn't answer the most pressing question and the reason I'm here.

Who in the hell killed Madeline Donaldson?

CHAPTER THIRTY

The Aurora Hotel; Woodcreek, WA

"YEAH, THAT'S RIGHT. THEY'RE RUNNING A LARGE-SCALE drug cooking and distribution network out of Whitehorn," I say.

"And you think we can trust Craig's word on this?"

I pace the floor of my room, my arms folded over my chest. I called Rosie to update and coordinate with her on our next steps. I'm an assertive woman but taking down this ring is too much for me to handle on my own. It's going to require massive interagency cooperation and probably dozens, if not hundreds, of federal agents to participate in the raid. And that's going to take a little bit of time to organize.

"I do," I say. "I know it's strange to say given the circumstances, but I think we can take his word for it. The evidence he's shown me so far checks out and backs up what he's saying. But he won't give us all the goods until he has a deal."

"Well, the USAG of the Eastern District of Washington will be taking over on an interim basis so it's her call to make," Rosie says, her voice sounding tinny through the speaker on my phone.

"Fair enough. It's a deal with the devil but if it helps us take down a national drug network, I think it's worth it," I say.

"I tend to agree with you. But we'll have to see how it all shakes out," she says. "Nothing like stumbling onto a multi-billion dollar drug network by mistake, right? This is going to look really good for you, Blake."

I laugh softly. "Which will, in turn, look really good for you."

"Of course, it will. And that's really all that matters," she says. "But where are we at with the actual case I gave you? You know, the one the Director himself wanted you to look into?"

"That's a good question," I say. "I'm still working on it. This case has not been what I expected. Not even close. I feel like I'm back at square one. I'm frustrated as hell, Rosie."

"I get it. But if there's anybody who can figure this out, it's you, kid."

"I'm not so sure about that right now."

"You need to stop second-guessing yourself, Blake. You need to learn to trust yourself again," she says. "As well as the people around you."

"I do—"

"No, you don't. Ever since that doctor of yours ended up how he did, you've been different. I've never seen you doubt yourself the way you have been lately," she tells me. "You need to find a way through that."

"Easier said than done."

"Maybe. But it's not an impossible task. What happened then wasn't something anyone could have seen coming," she says. "You can't be faulted for that."

"I should have known. Should have been able to see him for what he was."

"Because you've become psychic all of a sudden?" she replies, her tone dripping with sarcasm. "We're human, Blake. We get things wrong sometimes. And as appalling as it is for you to even consider, that includes you. We're not going to get things one hundred percent right one hundred percent of the time. Holding yourself to that impossible standard is absolutely insane."

She's right. I know she is. But that doesn't make it any easier for me. It's not something I can just flip a "get over it" switch and be all right again. But I know I need to try.

"Thanks, Rosie," I say.

"Anytime, kid," she says. "Now, figure out who killed that girl. Please. I don't want to have to take back all the nice things I've said about you to the Director."

I laugh softly. "I'm on it, boss."

"Good girl. Go get him."

I disconnect the call and start pacing around my room again. I try to clear my mind and see things from a different perspective. There's so much noise in my head right now that it's hard to think straight. But if I'm going to catch Madeline's killer, I know I'm going to have to find a way to do just that: clear my mind and focus. More than that though, I need to get back to basics. I need to answer the most fundamental questions.

I've spent so much time and energy chasing down these leads that ultimately led to an entirely different case that I've drifted away from the main questions. I've looked into what feels like a hundred different people already. And in terms of answering the question of who killed Madeline, none of them have panned out. There is one person, though, I haven't looked into at all. One person I haven't paid the least bit of attention to.

Pasha Sobol.

Yeah, he's the dead boyfriend, but I don't know the first thing about him. And since I'm starting from square one, it seems fitting that I look into him. That I profile him and see if I can build out from there. If I can get to know Pasha, learn his ins and outs, it might yield some clues. It might even lead me to the person who killed Madeline.

That was why I called Rick and asked him to do a deep dive on him before I called Rosie. Waiting for him to call me back has me on pins and needles. Going back to the beginning like this feels right. It's a decision I'm strangely enough not second-guessing. We'll see what comes of it though.

About an hour later—most of it I spent pacing—my phone rings. I snatch it up, see it's Rick and feel my heart stutter. I connect the call and put it on speaker.

"Tell me something good," I say.

"I wish I could."

I feel my heart sink and I frown. I'd expected that he'd be able to dig up something on the guy. Something that would give me a direction to run in. Something that would give me the barest hint I could use to begin figuring out who murdered Madeline.

"Tell me," I groan. "What did you find?"

"I found a big, fat, federal roadblock."

I cock my head. "What do you mean?"

"What I mean is that Pasha Sobol has a file with the US Marshals."

"You're kidding me."

"Not even a little bit."

I step over to the window and look out at the street below. The foot traffic is light, as is the vehicular traffic, leaving most of the street empty and in shadow as night begins to descend over the town. Thankfully, there are no Ukrainian or Chinese mobsters out on the street coming to kill me. It's only then I realize I'm half-expecting it to happen. They took a run at me once, why wouldn't they do it again? Especially now that I've put them in federal crosshairs.

"A file with the Marshals Service," I say.

"Yes ma'am."

"You know what that means don't you?"

"That I can't crack their files to see what's what?" he asks.

"It means that Pasha Sobol isn't a real person. It's his WITSEC identity," I say.

"So, wait, they put this fool into WITSEC, give him a new identity and all, and he starts a criminal enterprise up there?" Rick asks. "Guess he didn't make much of the second chance he was given."

"Guess not," I say. "But I'd like to know who this guy really is."

"Got any friends in the Marshals Service?"

"None who'd give me his file."

"Some friends."

"Right?" I say with a laugh. "All right, keep digging in and tell me what you can find. If anything."

"Will do. Oh, and I thought you'd like to know that my programs on the video feed and keycard logs finally came back," he says. "You were right. They were both tampered with. It was subtle and really delicately done, but they left behind some artifacts. It's inevitable. But whoever altered the records was really good and finding those artifacts was almost as much luck as it was my awesome program."

I laugh softly. "Any way you can track down who altered the records?"

"I don't think so. I'm trying to analyze the program they used to wipe the logs and that might give me a lead," he says. "But don't count on it. Plan on finding another way to make your case."

"Thank you for lowering my expectations."

"That is what I do."

"All right, good. Good work, Rick. And thank you."

"You got it, boss."

I disconnect the call and pause for a moment, letting my brain work. It's intriguing as hell to know that Pasha has a file with the

Marshals. Who was he? What did he do that necessitated a new name and a new life? Those are questions I need the answers to because I feel like answering them will lead me to Madeline's killer. Or at least get me a lot closer than I am right now. I take a deep breath and hold it for a five-count then let it out and remind myself to take this one step at a time. And I know what the first step has to be.

I pick up my phone and dial the number. He picks up the call on the second ring.

"Brody," I say. "I need your skills."

CHAPTER THIRTY-ONE

The Aurora Hotel; Woodcreek, WA

"**S**ORRY TO DROP ALL THAT ON YOU THE OTHER NIGHT. I know it's a lot," I say. "But I'm feeling kind of desperate out here."

"Are you kidding? It's the most excitement I've had in a while," Brody replies.

"Pax not meeting your thrill quota?"

"Not even close. Outside of the odd bitter, cheating spouse showing up at the office with a baseball bat, we haven't had a good life-threatening case in a while. And ever since he got together with May, he seems to be avoiding them," Brody says. "On the plus side, he's getting really good at being the brooding billionaire. He's one secret identity and skin-tight rubber suit from actually becoming Bruce Wayne."

I laugh softly as I pace my room with Brody's voice issuing

from the speaker on my phone. Brody is Paxton's tech genius—his version of Rick. But there are certain tasks I farm out to Brody simply because Rick has a stricter moral compass. The fact that Brody doesn't freak out when I ask him to hack the US Marshals database and in fact, sees it as a fun and exciting challenge, is a quality I need from time to time. Rick's skill is undeniable, and I'd put him at 1B to Brody's 1A. The difference is, I can't ask Rick to cross those lines while he's an official employee of the Bureau. Brody being a civilian, however, gives me just the amount of plausible deniability I need when doing things that would definitely get me in big trouble.

Is it a risk? Sure. Same as calling up Fish to provide information. But hey, what are friends for?

"I'm pretty sure that's his life goal," I say.

"He's well on his way then."

"And how are you? How are things with Marcy?"

"She's pretty amazing," he says. "Some days I still have to pinch myself. I don't know how I got so lucky."

"Yeah, I'm still wondering myself."

"Ouch," he groans. "If you prick me, do I not bleed?"

I chuckle. "I'm kidding. You two are great together," I tell him. "And I especially enjoy the way she keeps you in line."

"Not half as much as I do," he replies.

"Yeah, I don't need the steamy details. Save it for your memoirs."

Brody laughs. "I'll do that," he says. "Anyway, sorry it's taken me so long to get back to you. Turns out the Marshals upgraded the security to their system in a big way. Of course, that only made it all the more satisfying to break into their system."

"Taken you so long? I called you last night," I reply with a chuckle.

"Thirteen hours and thirty-two minutes ago, to be exact. This was a long, complicated hack," he specifies. "Definitely won't get me into the Hackers Hall of Fame."

"I'm pretty sure your place is already cemented."

"You say the sweetest things," he says. "Anyway, back to your mysterious boyfriend here. All I can say is you know how to pick 'em."

"It's a gift."

"Yeah well, you might want to consider returning it then," he says. "This guy Pasha Sobol. You were right about it being an assumed identity."

"I figured."

"This guy worked as an investment banker for the Odessa Mafia back in Brighton Beach about five years ago. He was making them tens of millions of dollars—legit money," Brody goes. "But then he had one investment go bad and cost his employers a tidy quarter of a billion dollars."

I whistle low. "That's a pretty penny. I'm assuming his bosses weren't too thrilled with him about that."

"Not even close. Didn't matter that on the whole, they were still up a couple hundred million, even with the loss. All they could see was that big red mark in their ledger," he goes on. "They were apparently going to kill him. Our boy Pasha got wind of it and went running to the US Attorney and turned state's evidence. On Pasha's evidence, the authorities raided a bunch of Odessa spots and rounded up a lot of people. Not without violent incident, of course."

"I remember that," I say. "The papers called it Bloody Sunday."

"Bingo. After that, he testified against the heads of a few Odessa factions, which of course ignited internecine warfare as people fought to step into the power void. Lots of people died in that whole mess," Brody says. "But our boy Pasha was swept away and was given a new name and a second chance at a brand-new life. Turns out he couldn't shake the old ways because it wasn't long before Pasha had ingratiated himself with the heads of the Seattle branch of the Odessa Mafia. They forgave him for cutting the heads of the snakes back east after he used his skills to make them a quick hundred million."

"Apparently money, and not time, is what heals all wounds," I remark.

"Hey, I might be willing to forgive anybody for anything if they made me a quick hundred mil," Brody replies.

"You act like you're poor," I say with a laugh. "I know how much money you come from, Mr. Singer. If anybody should be crying poor, it's me. All I have is my meager civil servant's wage."

"Well, it's a shame you didn't know this guy before his girlfriend put two in his chest and one in his head."

"It really is a shame," I say with a laugh.

"Anyway, with the consent of the heads of Odessa West, Pasha set up his own little criminal empire in good ol' Woodcreek. Organized and ran the *Chlopciki*, who are their own entity but are vassals of Odessa, and very nearly built Little Kiev single-handedly," Brody explains. "Under Pasha's watch, drugs, guns, and sex trafficking victims flow through Woodcreek in staggering numbers. He's paid up with the right people and has terrified others into submission."

"Wait, the Marshals know all of this? And they haven't done anything about it?"

"They know some of it. I don't believe they know all the specifics. Some of this I've gleaned from other reliable sources," he says. "But I can say for a fact the Marshals knew he was running a drug empire out of Little Kiev and looked the other way. I guess they thought they'd be able to yank his leash when the time was right and get him to help them neuter Odessa out west the way he did back east."

"Jesus," I mutter.

I process everything he's already told me and put it together with what I know. The story is familiar to me. I turn it over in my mind for a minute and that's when it hits me. The investment banker from Brighton Beach who went missing. It makes sense now.

"Brody, Pasha's former name—his old identity," I say. "It wouldn't be Evgeni Federov, would it?"

There's a long pause on the line before he speaks. "Wow," he comments, sounding deflated. "Way to take the fun out of the big reveal, Captain Buzzkill."

"I'm sorry. Rick's been trying to teach me about storycraft but I just get too excited when I feel like I'm onto something," I explain with a laugh.

"Rick is a luddite who has absolutely nothing useful to teach you," Brody says. "Except for not interrupting as a storyteller is ramping up to the big finish. That's a lesson you should learn from him PDQ. For obvious reasons."

"Noted," I say.

Rick and Brody have a friendly rivalry that's been going since the first day they met. There is nothing quite like watching two nerds verbally battle it out. But to me, that's what family does. I like to think of Pax's people as my people, and my people as his people, and we're all just one big, oftentimes dysfunctional family. And I love it.

"Sorry, Brody. Didn't mean to spoil the ending."

"That's all right because wait, there's more," Brody announces excitedly. "There's still plot twists yet to come."

"Not sure I can deal with many more plot twists."

"Oh, trust me, you're going to want to hear this one. This one's a zinger."

"Okay, lay it on me."

"Well, as it turns out, Evgeni has a twin brother named Ilya," he starts. "And, hold onto your panties here: Ilya entered the country one week after Evgeni's untimely demise."

The moment he says the words, I feel my stomach start to churn. Of course. That has to be it. That has to be why Madeline had been seeing Pasha's—aka Evgeni's—ghost everywhere. She wasn't crazy. Ilya was gaslighting her. Making her think she was going insane. He was waging psychological warfare against her.

"Brody, I don't know how to thank you for this. You have just solved a murder," I say.

"This is what I do, my friend."

"Thank you."

"You're welcome," he replies. "Oh hey, we're doing Thanksgiving at my place. You're more than welcome."

"I appreciate that, and I may stop by later, if that's all right," I say. "I have some plans earlier, that's all."

"Door's always open for you, Blake. *Mi casa es su casa*," she says. "I know Marcy would love to see you."

"And I'd love to see her too. Give her my best for now," I say. "And thank you again, Brody. You are an absolute lifesaver."

We disconnect and I set the phone down as a smile creeps across my face. That was it. That was the missing piece. And now that I have it, everything is falling into place, and I can see the whole picture in front of me. That feeling of momentum is off the charts and it's time to bring this whole sordid story to a close.

CHAPTER THIRTY-TWO

Office of Dr. Franz Stein, Whitehorn Foundation; Woodcreek, WA

"**S**O, YOU HAVE COMPLETELY LOST YOUR MIND," STEIN says. "That's what you're telling me?"

I sit back in my chair and fold one leg over the other, my eyes boring into his. We stare at each other in silence for a long moment. He squirms in his seat. He's not a man used to being questioned, let alone on the hot seat, so I take a moment to just savor his discomfort.

"I have to admit, the whole evil twin thing I did not see coming," I tell him. "But it makes absolute sense. That was the supposed ghost Madeline was seeing around the halls of your fine institution, Dr. Stein. The ghost you allowed to walk these grounds. You were helping to gaslight her. You allowed him to kill her. My question is, why?"

"I have no idea what you're talking about, Agent Wilder. You're making no sense whatsoever," Stein replies.

"Dr. Stein, we're past all of your denials and explanations," I tell him. "We have you cold on your massive drug manufacturing and distro operation. You're going away for a long time. That part isn't in question. The only question is, do you want to go away for even longer when I slap you with an accessory to murder charge?"

Sheriff Block is standing at the back of the room next to the door, a large, silent, and intimidating presence. Stein cuts his eyes to Block then turns them back to me quickly, licking his lips nervously. He sits up a little straighter and tries to compose himself.

"Agent Wilder, I'm not sure what you think you know, but I can assure you that you are mistaken," he huffs. "I have no idea what you're talking about."

"Do your employers at Whitehorn know what you're doing here?" I ask. "Do they know you're manufacturing knock-off street narcotics then using the Ukrainians to distribute them nationwide?"

He shakes his head and tries to put a sympathetic smile on his face. "It sounds to me like you might benefit from a stay here," he says. "A little therapy and treatment perhaps."

"Smug little bastard, isn't he?" Block finally speaks up, his voice a low, deep rumble.

I nod. "He most definitely is."

Stein's eyes drift to Block then back to me and he clears his throat. "I'm sorry, but this is all getting tedious. If there's nothing else, you can show yourselves out."

"We're just getting started, Dr. Stein," I tell him. "Now, you can either cooperate with us or you can take the entire weight. I will charge you with Madeline's murder in addition to all the various charges we'll be hitting you with for your operation here."

"Agent Wilder—"

"US Attorney James Craig—sorry, former US Attorney James Craig—has been arrested. He's confessed to his role in your scheme already," I interrupt. "My team has also analyzed the video and key-card data and has found evidence that it was you who tampered with them the night of Madeline's murder. You wiped the evidence of anybody coming or going. And by anybody, I mean Ilya Federov."

The last bit is a bluff. Rick told me he tried but he'll never be able to definitively prove who wiped the data. But Stein doesn't know that. It's another stone I'm adding to his funeral cairn, hoping the sheer weight of it forces him to bend, then break.

"Craig's already flipped on you. As has my deputy, Scott Mullins," Block says. "We got everything we need to bury you."

Stein's face darkens and he looks down at his hands. For the first time since I met him, I see uncertainty and even a trace of fear cross his face. He looks like a man who knows the walls are closing in on him and has that rat-caught-in-a-trap look about him.

"This facility is going to be shuttered and you are going away," I tell him.

"For a long, long time," Block adds.

"Now, you can either help us and lead us to Madeline's murderer, or I'm going to hit you with first-degree murder charges on top of it all," I say. "And because Madeline was a federal witness, that means federal weight, Doctor. Not state. That means you're very likely going to take the needle for her death. Is protecting Ilya Federov really worth that?"

Stein finally cracks and buries his face in his hands. He sits like that, hiding his face for a long moment and I let him take the time he needs to get his head on straight. I've got nowhere else to be right now. I turn and look at Block, giving him a smile, which he returns. He can see the skies above Woodcreek are starting to clear and that once we get rid of Stein and Craig, then dismantle the *Chlopciki*, things will be different on the other side. Maybe it can even be a town he's proud to keep serving. At least for another term.

"I have a team from Seattle on their way here, Doctor. They'll be here within the hour. And they're coming with warrants," I say, deciding to turn the screws a little harder. "They are going to tear your foundation apart, brick by brick. They'll find your drug lab down in the basement. They'll find out what you've been giving these patients and what sort of twisted experiments you've been putting them through. You can either help us and maybe help mitigate your own case. Or you can do nothing and bear the full brunt of it all on your own."

"What will happen to my patients?" he mutters through his hands. "I am helping them."

"They're not your patients anymore. As for helping them? Yeah, I don't know about that," I tell him. "All I know is that I've got you cold. You can help us and maybe help yourself in the process. Or you can sit there and do nothing and probably catch a hot shot when you're found guilty. At this point, I don't care. I know who murdered Madeline. I just want to catch him. And I will, with or without your help."

Stein sighs heavily and drops his hands down onto his desk in front of him. He looks at me for a long moment. His expression tells me he's struggling with the decision, which is surprising. Most people looking down the barrel of a needle will do anything to save themselves. He finally slumps back in his seat, and I can see by the look of defeat in his eyes that he's finally going to do the smart thing.

"Ilya showed up here shortly after Ms. Donaldson was admitted. He told me he wanted to terrorize, then kill her for murdering his brother. He wanted vengeance and he wanted to torture her," Stein says quietly. "He also said he's going to take over the *Chlopciki*. He was going to pick up where his brother left off and grow it into an even bigger organization. He's got plans to eventually replace the Odessa Mafia on the west coast. For starters."

"And when he showed up with these grand proclamations, what did you do?" I ask.

"I... I dummied up employment records that say he's been here for years. Gave him a new name to work under," Stein says. "Let him stay on the grounds so he could terrorize Madeline."

My mind flashes to the nest Astra and I found in the unfinished room. "He's staying in the wing that's being renovated, isn't he?"

"He is," he confirms with a nod. "I'm only telling you all of this because I never wanted Ms. Donaldson to die. I tried to talk him out of it up to the last day. He wouldn't hear of it though. He said only blood can pay for blood. I liked her."

"Yeah, whatever you need to tell yourself," I say. "Is Ilya here right now?"

Stein nods. "Yes. He's struck up a relationship with one of my patients. He's staying here to be closer to her as he organizes himself to take over the *Chlopciki*."

My eyes widen and I stare at him with disgust in my eyes. "You're letting him sleep with one of your patients? Are you even kidding me right now?"

"What am I supposed to do? These people are vicious. Brutal," Stein counters. "They will kill me if I deny them. What do you want from me?"

"How about you learn how to be a man rather than a sniveling little rat and stand up?" Block says. "That seems like a fine place to start."

"Easy for you to say. I'm not a Neanderthal. Violence doesn't become me," Stein says.

"Yeah, you carry those hoity-toity ideals all the way to prison, Dr. Stein. See how far they get you there," I say. "Now, where is Ilya Federov?"

He shrugs. "Probably sleeping. He likes to sleep late."

I get to my feet and give Block a nod. He opens the door and lets one of his deputies—one he's vetted and trusts completely—into the office. The deputy is tall and brawny. He looks athletic and agile, and I can see the light of intelligence in his eyes. I'm sure the man is as sharp physically as he is mentally.

"This is Deputy Hampstead. He's goin' to stay here to make sure you don't get up to any mischief," Block says then turns to Hampstead. "No calls. Nobody in or out of here. Keep your eyes on this weasel and don't let him out of your sight for an instant. He needs to go to the bathroom, you hold it for him. Am I clear, Deputy?"

"Yes sir. Crystal."

"Get comfy, Dr. Stein. It's going to be a very long day," I say, then turn to Block. "Ready to go ghost hunting?"

His chuckle is deep and sounds like thunder rolling in off the bay. "After you."

CHAPTER THIRTY-THREE

Whitehorn Mental Health & Research Foundation; Woodcreek, WA

"**Y**OU READY FOR THIS, SHERIFF?" I ASK.

He gives me a mischievous grin. "To be honest, this is kind of exciting," he says. "I haven't felt this alive in a long time."

"Just be sure to watch yourself. This guy is dangerous, and he's already murdered at least one person. With his bare hands, no less," I say. "So, just be careful. The last thing I want is to have to give your wife the death notification because you were a yutz who underestimated a brutal murderer."

"Don't worry, I'd make one of my deputies do it."

"Not funny."

"If it weren't for gallows humor, I wouldn't have a sense of humor at all."

I laugh softly. "I can relate to that."

I've come to not only respect Sheriff Block, but like him a great deal. He's a good man who wants to do right. He loves his town and only wants the best for it. Yeah, his demeanor can be a little gruff and rough around the edges at times, but the same can be said of me. If I judged the guy for it, I'd be a flaming hypocrite. And I want nothing more than to send him home to his wife and children whole and in one piece.

We stand outside the door to the third floor of the south wing, and I feel my stomach clench. I swallow hard and steel myself. I slide my weapon out of my holster and Block does the same. I look at it and laugh softly.

"A revolver? Who in the hell uses a revolver anymore?"

"Old guys," he shrugs. "Like us old guys, revolvers are more reliable and are always ready for some action."

I roll my eyes. "That was corny."

He shrugs. "Maybe. Don't mean it ain't true though."

"Fair enough," I admit with a laugh. "Okay, here we go."

I open the door and we both slip through. I head for the room where we'd seen Ilya's nest before, pushing my way through the sheets of plastic hanging from the ceiling. I motion for Block to go to the right while I move to the left, just in case Ilya's not actually asleep and is prowling around in here. I'd rather have a little space from Block so Ilya can't take us both out in one fell swoop. It'll give both of us a chance to react if he comes.

I push a curtain of plastic aside and find myself staring into a pair of icy blue eyes. Ilya Federov stands about six-three, has hair so blonde it's almost white, and looks like he was chiseled out of a block of marble. He's got a strong jawline, a patrician nose, and high, sharp cheekbones I'm sure women and modeling agencies would die—or kill—for.

It all happens so fast, I don't even have time to scream. He swings a thick pipe at me and when it slams into my wrist, the hard jolt of the impact reverberates all the way into my shoulder. My fingers suddenly go numb and my gun hits the floor with a metallic thud. Ilya moves quickly and kicks it away and sends it skittering across the concrete floor.

"Block!" I scream.

My words are cut short though when Ilya drives his fist into my stomach. The air is forced out of my lungs with a loud "oomph", but I manage to keep myself from doubling over. Instead, I close the distance with him and feint with a left hook. He bites and hesitates just long enough for me to drive my knee into his groin with all the strength I can muster. He turns green before my very eyes but manages to keep his feet.

We both hear the heavy footsteps of Block charging toward us. He sounds like a freaking rampaging bull. I strike quickly and drive my fist into Ilya's face, sending him staggering backward as a fount of blood erupts from his nose. He wades back in though and this time, I see the glint of the dim ambient light on the edge of a blade he produced from somewhere like magic. He swings the blade in a murderous arc that narrowly misses me, but as I reach for his wrist to disarm him, he spins and drives the point of the blade into my shoulder.

I cry out as I feel the blood spilling down my chest, but stagger back quickly. Block is almost on us, so Ilya turns to flee. Without thinking about what I'm doing, I pull the blade out of my shoulder and hurl it at the fleeing Ukrainian. He disappears in a swirl of plastic sheeting, but I hear him grunt and know I hit him. I just can't see where or how bad it is. Block arrives and stops but I wave him off.

"I'm fine! Go. Get him," I shout.

Block nods and is on the run again in the blink of an eye. For such a large man, he moves quickly and gracefully. I clamp my hand to my shoulder and wince. The blood is flowing freely from the wound, but I don't think it's too serious, so I go in search of my gun. It takes me a few minutes to find where Ilya kicked it to. I snatch it up and dart after them. We have Madeline's killer and there's no way in hell I'm going to let him slip through my fingers.

I find a trail of blood spots, most of them smeared on the concrete thanks to a size fourteen boot print, but it's good enough for me to follow. They went down the stairwell, so I give chase. Every step I take jars the wound in my shoulder, sending lightning bolts of pain through my body. But I finally make it to the ground floor and burst through the door and step out onto the pristine green grounds of the hospital.

I swivel this way and that, looking for Block and Ilya, but see nothing. There's a path that leads to the forest behind the Foundation, and I figure they had to have disappeared into that, so I grit my teeth and take off after them. I step through a concrete archway in the wall and find myself surrounded by soaring pines. The day is overcast, the clouds blotting out the sun, which makes the interior of the forest even darker.

"Block!" I shout, my voice echoing through the woods.

"Here!" he screams back.

He sounds far away but I know the wide trunks and thick canopy of the trees distort the sound. At least I know he's in there. I start to run in the approximate direction I thought his voice came from and search the ground in front of me. There. I see bright crimson droplets on the leaves and grass that litter the forest floor. It has to be Ilya's, so I keep moving, slower though, so I can track the blood I'm finding. They don't have much of a lead on me and I know I need to move carefully and keep aware of my surroundings. But I know I need to get to Block quickly, afraid that Ilya will get the drop on him.

The silence in the forest is so thick, it has a physical pressure to it. The fact that I can't hear anything starts to worry me. I don't want to think the worst. I don't want to think that Ilya got to Block, but not being able to hear anything—no sound of somebody crashing through the undergrowth, branches breaking, or heavy footsteps on the forest floor—has me worried. But then I remember that Block said he is an avid hunter. Perhaps he's moving silently, trying to quietly stalk his prey: Ilya.

I take another step on what must be an old deer path when I hear a shout of surprise. It's quickly followed by a bellow of pain, and it makes my heart jump. I plunge into the forest headlong, heedlessly sprinting past the wide, ancient trunks of the trees, crashing through the bushes that litter the path.

The drop-off is so sudden I don't have time to react. For a second, I feel utterly weightless; that lighter-than-air feeling flutters through my stomach as I plunge over the lip of the small bowl in the forest floor. I hit the ground with a jarring impact that makes my teeth click together hard. My momentum carries me forward and I pitch forward into a roll down the embankment. A white-hot spike of pain pierces my ankle as I tumble down the slope and strike a rock hidden in the dirt, drawing a cry of pain out of me.

As I'm sliding to a stop, half in and half out of a shallow creek at the bottom of the bowl, I see Ilya standing over a prone and unmoving Sheriff Block, the blade of his knife coated in blood. He turns to me with a malicious grin stretching across his lips. He turns to me and I can see a pronounced limp in his step. Ilya reaches behind him, and it looks like he rubs his butt then shows me his hand. It's slick and red and he laughs like a lunatic.

"You stabbed me," he says, his voice thick with a Russian accent. "In the ass."

He laughs like it's the funniest thing that's ever happened to him, and though the idea that my wild throw had sunk the blade into his rear end makes me want to laugh too, I can't seem to muster the mirth. I only wish my aim had been true and I'd buried that blade in his back. To my right, I see my gun half-buried under a pile of leaves. I dropped it when I fell down the embankment. It's relatively close, but it might as well be miles away. I don't know that I can get it before Ilya gets to me and carves me up like a Thanksgiving turkey.

"That obsequious little man, Dr. Stein, told me all about you,

Agent Wilder. He was not impressed with you. I looked you up online. I wanted to know my adversary better," he says. "What I learned is that Stein doesn't understand people like us. Fighters. Warriors. He's a coward. He does not know what it is to fight for his life," he says. "But you do. I do. And after everything I read, I'm very impressed with you."

"Yeah, gee, thanks," I shoot back. "Your approval is all I ever wanted."

Ilya's distracted with his speechifying, which is good for me. I try to use that to subtly move toward my gun. It's not easy to move with my ankle throbbing as wildly as it is, sending sharp shocks of pain through my entire body. I don't think it's busted, but it's not going to feel good again for a little while. I'm going to need to appoint somebody to kick in doors for me.

"We could be allies, Agent Wilder," he goes on. "Just think about it. I could make you obscenely wealthy. You would have anything you ever wanted with a snap of your fingers. You would have more money than you could ever possibly imagine."

"I don't know," I reply, trying to disguise my scooting to the right. "I can imagine a whole lot of money."

"And it can be yours," he says. "Work with me. Work with Stein. Let us help you become incredibly rich and fulfill every fantasy and desire you could ever possibly have."

Ilya takes a step toward me and all I can focus on is the edge of that knife. On the crimson drops falling from it. I cut a glance at Block and when I see him move his head, I let out a silent breath of relief. He's alive. How long he stays that way, though, depends on how quickly I can do away with Ilya and get us out of here. Of course, given the way my ankle feels right now, doing away with Ilya is anything but certain.

"What do you say, Agent Wilder? Do you want to be rich beyond measure?"

"Who doesn't?"

"Then say you'll work with me. Tell me you want to be my ally."

"Yeah. Sure. I've always wanted to travel the world," I shrug. "Make me rich, Ilya."

He stops moving and stares at me for a long moment. His eyes are hard and send a flood of ice through my veins. A frown pulls the corners of his mouth down as he looks at me, obviously realizing I'm only trying to stall him.

"This is a shame, Agent Wilder," he says. "You could have had anything and everything you ever wanted."

"What makes you think I don't already have that?"

"So be it."

With a wild, savage cry, Ilya rushes at me, the point of his blade high above his head. If he strikes home with that, I'll be pinned to the forest floor as securely as a bug on a pinboard in a biology class. Gritting my teeth and trying to shut out the searing agony, I roll to my right just as Ilya falls on me. The point of his knife slams into the ground I'd been lying on a split second ago with a hard thud and a muttered curse from him.

He rips the knife free just as I roll back over, the familiar weight of my Glock in my hand. I see his eyes widen in surprise as I pull the trigger. Once. Twice. Three times. I watch his body jerk and twitch as my bullets tear through him. For a moment, he seems like a statue frozen in time. He's kneeling beside me, his eyes wide and filled with a maniacal light, the knife raised above his head, poised to strike. But I watch as the crimson stains on his shirt grow. Watch the blood spattering onto the ground beneath him. First a trickle, then a flood. He's dying and he knows it.

Ilya has one final burst of energy in him though, but I anticipate it, and when I see his body tense, I fire one final shot. His head snaps back violently and his momentum topples him backward. He hits the ground with a wet, meaty thud. I watch him for a long moment, my heart racing, my breathing ragged, waiting for him to make one final play. But he doesn't. He remains still. Dead.

And like that, it's over.

"Wilder," comes the hoarse, raspy croak.

Block's voice snaps me back to the present and I turn to see the big sheriff with his head turned, looking at me. A thin rivulet of blood trickles from his mouth but his eyes are still wide. Vibrant. He's fighting for his life. Agony has me in a tight fist that is squeezing the breath from me, but I manage to roll onto my belly. I try to stand but the pain is excruciating, so I'm forced to crawl on my stomach over to Block.

I see a stab wound in his belly and immediately put pressure on it. The feel of his blood, warm and viscous, spilling over my fingers twists my stomach and makes my eyes well with tears. I shake my head.

"You're not going to die," I tell him.

He draws my attention and taps the radio clipped to his shoulder. "Cavalry's comin'."

His voice is a raspy whisper that seems like it's fading. His eyes flutter and start to close so I give him a sharp slap across the face.

"Wake up, Sheriff. You are not going out like this. Not today," I tell him. "The cavalry's coming so you had better hang on. Do you hear me?"

He nods. "I hear you. I hear you."

The sound of voices shouting our names echoes through the forest. They seem to be growing louder, as does the sound of heavy footfalls crashing through the undergrowth. The relief I feel is instant but is tempered by the man clinging to life in front of me. I have to smack him again to keep him awake.

"Stay awake, Sheriff. You are going to live," I demand, as if my words alone can will it to happen. "I will totally kill you if you don't."

His laugh breaks off into a series of wet, raspy coughs. More blood spills from the corner of his mouth and I can see him growing pale. My hope that help will get to us in time is beginning to fade. But then I hear a shouting voice so loud, it sounds like he's standing right next to me. I turn to see people coming over the lip of the bowl we're in like an army swarming over the walls of a castle they're invading.

"We're going to be all right," I tell Block. "We're going to be fine."

He nods. "I think it's time I give this job to somebody younger."

It's such an absurd thing to say that I can't help but laugh. It's not funny but I laugh like a loon as the medics and other agents reach us. We're going to be all right. We're going to be fine.

CHAPTER
THIRTY-FOUR

*Residence of Astra Russo & Benjamin Harper, Capitol Hill District;
Seattle, WA*

"IN THE ASS?" BENJAMIN ASKS. "YOU ARE KIDDING ME."

I shake my head and laugh. "It was an accident. A one in a million shot. I probably couldn't do it again if I tried."

That sends Benjamin and Charles into a fit of laughter. Most of what went on at Whitehorn didn't make it into the press. The powers that be thought it best to keep most of the details from the public. Which is fine. But Astra, Benjamin, and Charles all wanted the details. So, after swearing them to secrecy, I filled them in on what happened out there. It's a story that kept them on the edge of their seats and highly amused, apparently.

It's Thanksgiving, a couple of weeks after the events out at Whitehorn. Since then, a joint task force made of all the alphabet agencies crashed down on Woodcreek. The hospital was raided, as were the docks in Little Kiev. At last count, more than two hundred people had been arrested, the power of the *Chlopciki* broken, and thousands of pounds of drugs and arms seized. And best of all, Ilya is dead and justice for Madeline had finally been served.

Sheriff Block's injuries were serious and will keep him from being the town's sheriff any longer, but he's alive and will eventually recover. For the most part. The important thing is that he may no longer be a lawman, but he'll live a long, normal life. Dr. Stein and James Craig are cooperating, but they'll never taste freedom again. They're both going to prison for the rest of their miserable, rotten lives.

As for me, my ankle wasn't broken, as I'd thought. It is pretty dinged up though and I'm in a walking boot for a while. The injury to my shoulder was more worrisome and is going to take a lot of rehab. And even then, they say I might never gain full function again. So, for the moment, I too am on the bench—a fact that Astra is taking no small amount of joy in reminding me of. Daily. More like hourly, actually.

All of us stuffed to the gills after an amazing feast, the boys settle in on the couches to watch the Turkey Day football games. Astra motions for me to join her in the kitchen, so I hobble out there with her. We both lean against the counter, glasses of wine in hand. There's a certain tension in the air that makes me worry though. It just feels like she has something important to say. And part of me is worried that I already know what it is.

"Thanks for having us over today. It's been amazing," I say.

"I'm glad you came. And I'm glad you brought Charles. He really is a great guy."

I nod. "I thought it was time. I'm trying something new."

"Yeah? What's that?"

"Being a little more open and trusting myself."

"Now, that's a good thing," Astra says. "That's a really good thing."

We both pause as we take a sip of our wine, letting the moment play out. She looks at me, a serious expression on her face. Here we go.

"So? How are you doing?" she asks. "Really doing, I mean."

"I—I'm good. I'm really good," I tell her. "Other than not being able to walk like a normal human being, anyway. How are you doing?"

She nods. "I'm good too. The wound is healing up nice and I'll be back on active duty here in the next few days," she says and flashes me a mischievous grin. "You won't, but I will."

I laugh softly. "Yeah, rub it in."

"Oh, count on it," she says, then pointedly adds, "And you can count on it for a long, long time to come, Wilder."

I purse my lips as I look at her. "That so?"

She nods. "Listen, I know why you benched me. I get it. I was hurt, blah, blah, blah," she starts. "But I also know you benched me because you're worried about me. Worried about me getting hurt and worried about what it will mean for my future—for that whole conversation we had about marriage and children."

I shrug. "Yeah, if I'm being honest, I can't say that didn't enter into my mind."

"Well, you need to get it out of your mind, Blake. I'm a big girl and I accepted the risk this job entails when I took my oath. Same as you. Benjamin knows what we do is dangerous, but he supports me. And I know he'll love me no matter what comes. If it means we can't have kids down the line, so be it. He wants me to be happy, and this job, what we do, it makes me happy," she says. "Which is why I need you to trust me. I need you to believe that I'll tell you if things are too hot and I need to step back. I need you to believe I'm not going to be stupid and reckless. I don't want to die, Blake. I'm not an idiot. And I need you to trust that."

"I do."

"Do you though?"

I think back to my conversation at the bar with Sheriff Block. For not really knowing her, he had a lot of insight into Astra. Things he instinctively knew that I should have known. But what I realized is that it's not that I don't trust Astra. It's more that I don't trust myself. But that is something I'm working on changing. That's one thing I'm taking away from everything that happened up at Whitehorn—a renewed trust in myself.

"I plan on doing this job for many years to come, Blake," she says. "This job is part of me. But there will likely be a day when I'm ready to hang it up. I need you to trust me to know when that day comes. Trust that I'll tell you instead of trying to make that decision for me."

I give her a long look and a nod. "I will," I say softly. "I will."

Astra steps forward and pulls me into a tight embrace. It makes the pain in my shoulder flare, and I wince but push through it and ignore it as best as I can. We embrace for several long moments. It's silly, but both of us tear up. The emotions coursing through me are overwhelming, but I give into them and let them carry me away.

Astra is my family. She feels like home. And it's a feeling I don't ever want to lose or let go of. Ever.

EPILOGUE

Wilder Residence, The Emerald Pines Luxury Apartments;
Downtown Seattle

"ARE YOU IN THE TUB?"

I laugh and nod. "I am."

"Look at you being all luxurious," Kit says, her smile wide. "Good for you."

"A friend sent me some bath salts that are just amazing. I haven't felt this relaxed in a while," I tell her.

It's the day after Thanksgiving and I decided to push off all my paperwork for another day. Charles is working so I decided that I'm going to take this day for me. Today is all about me. And I'm starting it with a decadent bath like Fish had suggested—and it's glorious. I had just climbed in when Kit Facetimed me, and since I wasn't going to miss an opportunity to talk to my sister, I answered the call, which made me feel a bit hypocritical after giving Fish such a hard time about doing the same thing.

"Is that a glass of wine I see?" Kit asks.

I nod. "Yep. It sure is. And it's lovely."

"At two in the afternoon?"

"It's five somewhere," I offer. "What about you? Where are you today?"

"Somewhere it's not five," she replies. "Sorry I wasn't able to call yesterday. I was thinking about you though."

"I thought about you too. I'm hoping we can get together for Thanksgiving one day soon."

"That makes two of us."

"What about Christmas? Can you come? Or maybe New Year's?"

"I'd love to. Let me see what I can do," she says. "I can't promise anything though."

"I understand. It would just be really nice to wake up on Christmas morning to find you here. It'd be the best present ever."

"If it's safe, relatively speaking, I'll do everything I can to be there."

"Thank you, Kit."

We chat for about an hour, getting caught up on each other's lives and doings. I tell her about Charles, and she seems excited for me. Kit has nobody serious, of course, but she tells me in great detail about her paramours and the string of broken hearts she's left in her wake. On the one hand, my sister is living an exciting, 007 kind of lifestyle. New places every day. New faces. Excitement and danger everywhere she looks. It's like something out of a book or a movie.

On the other hand, it sucks that her nomadic kind of life is a necessity. It sucks that if she stops moving and settles in one place too long, it could be the death of her. Or me. Or both of us. I hate that she has to stay away for fear of both of us catching a bullet.

But that's our life as it is right now. My hope is that it will change. Sooner, rather than later.

"All right, I should go," Kit says.

"I hate that you have to."

"Me too."

"Think about Christmas. Maybe we can meet somewhere totally off the grid," I tell her. "Somewhere we can just be alone."

She nods. "I'll look into it. I'd love it."

"So would I."

"All right. Love you, Blake."

"Love you back," I say. "Talk soon."

The line goes dark as she disconnects the call, leaving me to wonder where she is and what she's doing. She could be anywhere from Shanghai to right next door and I'd never know. My sister has become an elite-level spy. And I wish to God she wasn't. I wish she was just my normal kid sister again. But I'm holding onto the hope that one day, we can have that again.

As I settle back into the tub, adding a little bit more hot water and Fish's salts, I groan in delight. But then my phone rings, shattering my calm. I pick it up and see the call is coming from a blocked number. Ordinarily, I wouldn't answer it but part of me thinks it could be Kit calling me back to tell me something she forgot so I answer.

"Hey," I say.

"You will know no peace. We will not stop coming until you and your sister are both dead," the voice says. "If I were you, I wouldn't let myself get too comfortable because things are in motion that you cannot stop. Nor will you see us coming."

I roll my eyes. It's all very dramatic, but these threats are nothing new to me. They don't strike fear into me the way the caller is hoping. It irritates me more than anything. I listen hard though, trying to pick up any trace of an accent. My natural inclination is to assume this is somebody from what remains of the Thirteen. But after the case in Woodcreek, it very well could be the Russian mafia. The Ukrainian mafia. Maybe even the Chinese Triads. It seems as if my list of enemies and people who want to murder me is growing with every passing day.

"So, why bother calling to warn me?" I ask. "If you don't think I'll see you coming, why on Earth would you warn me? I mean, doesn't that defeat the purpose? If you guys are relying on the element of surprise, I'd say you just blew it because now I'll be looking for you guys."

"You think you're smart—"

"No, I know I am," I cut him off. "And you should know that I don't fear you people. You think you're intimidating me but you're not. All you're doing is making me more determined than ever to find you and put an end to you. Do you hear me? You think you're coming for me but I'm the one coming for you."

There's a whispered laugh on the other end of the line. "We'll see you soon, Blake. We'll see you very soon."

"I'll be waiting. Do you hear me? I'll be ready for you," I reply and disconnect the call.

I can only hope that when push comes to shove and they do come for me, I'll really feel as confident as I do now. But until that moment, all I can do is wait.

Wait and prepare.

AUTHOR'S NOTE

Thank you for reading *Night at the Asylum*, book 9 of Blake Wilder FBI Mystery Thrillers. I hope you're enjoying this season two of Blake's adventures just as much, if not more than season one. My intention is to give you a thrilling adventure and an entertaining escape with each and every book.

Being a new indie writer is tough. However, your support has helped tremendously. I don't have a large budget, huge following, or any of the cutting edge marketing techniques. So, all I kindly ask is that if you enjoyed this book, please take a moment of your time and leave me a review and maybe recommend the book to a fellow book lover or two. This way I can continue to write all day and night and bring you more books in the Blake Wilder FBI Mystery Thriller Series. Also, don't forget to check out my Pax Arrington Mystery Series and Olivia Knight FBI Mystery Thriller Series. By the way, if you find any typos or want to reach out to me, feel free to email me at mailto:egray@ellegraybooks.com

Last but not the least, Happy holidays and stay warm!
Your writer friend,
Elle Gray

ALSO BY
ELLE GRAY

ALSO BY
ELLE GRAY| K.S. GRAY

Made in United States
Orlando, FL
24 December 2024

56499204R00153